A DANGEROUS TRAP LOVE DANIELLE'S STORY FINESSED

BY:

NIKKI NICOLE

Acknowledgments

Hi, how are you? I'm Nikki Nicole the Pen Goddess. Each time I complete a book I love to write acknowledgements. I love to give a reflection on how I felt about the book. I've been writing for three years now and this is my 19th book. I appreciate each one of you for taking this journey with me. I'm forever grateful for you believing in me and giving me your continuous support.

Book 19 Murder She Wrote! I snapped off y'all! I know y'all been waiting on this. I'm sorry for the wait. I had to get my re-releases back up. Here we are six months later. 87,000 words of straight heat. This book is everything. I think this is the most controversial book I've ever wrote. A lot of women can relate to Danielle's story.

I want to thank my supporters that I haven't met or had a conversation with. I appreciate y'all too. Please email me or contact me on social media. I want to acknowledge you and give you a S/O also.

I dedicate this book to my Queens in the Trap **Nikki Nicole's Readers Trap**. I swear y'all are the best. Y'all go so hard in the paint for me it's insane. Every day we lit. I appreciate y'all more than y'all will ever know. The Trap is going the fuck up on a Friday. I can't wait for y'all to read it.

It's time for my S/O **Yoashamia, Samantha, Tatina, Asha, Shanden (PinkDiva), Padrica, Liza, Aingsley, Trecie, Quack, Toni, Amisha, Tamika, Troy, Pat, Crystal C, Missy, Angela, Latoya, Helene, Tiffany, Lamaka, Reneshia, Misty, Toy, Toi, Shelby, Chanta, Jessica, Snowie, Jessica, Marla Jo, Shay, Anthony, Keyana, Veronica, Shonda J, Shonda G, Sommer, Cathy, Karen, Bria, Kelis, Lisa, Tina, Talisha, Naquisha, Iris, Nicole, Koi, Drea, Rickena, Saderia, Chanae, Shanise, Nacresha, Jalisa, Tamika H, Kendra, Meechie, Avis, Lynette, Pamela, Antoinette, Crystal W, Ivee, Kenyada, Dineshia, Chenee, Jovonda, Jennifer J, Cha, Andrea, Shannon J, Latasha F, Denise, Andrea P, Shelby, Kimberly, Yutanzia, Seanise, Jennifer, Shatavia, LaTonya, Dimitra, Kellissa, Jawanda, Renea, Tomeika, Viola, Barbie, Dominique, Erica, Shanequa, Dallas, Verona, Catherine, Natasha K, Carmela, Paris B, Shanika, Kalia, Felisha, Lakisha, Carletta, Kemeko, Veronica, Tokka, Simone J,**

If I named everybody, I will be here all day. Put your name here________ if I missed you. The list goes on. S/O to every member in my reading group, I love y'all to the moon and back. These ladies right here are a hot mess. I love them to death. They go so hard about these books it doesn't make any sense. Sometimes, I feel like I should run and hide.

If you're looking for us meet us in **Nikki Nicole's Readers Trap** on Facebook, we are live and indirect all day.

S/O to My Pen Bae's **Ash ley, Chyna L, Chiquita, T. Miles,** I love them to the moon and back head over to Amazon and grab a book by them also.

Check my out my new favorite Authors **Dedra B, Nique Luarks** baby these women can write their asses off. You heard it from me. I love their work! Look them up and go read their catalogs!

To my new readers I have six complete series, and four completed standalones available. Here's my catalog if you don't have it.

Bitch I Play for Keeps 1-3

Chosen by A Yung Rich Nigga 1-2

You Don't Miss A Good Thing, Until It's Gone (Standalone)

Journee & Juelz 1-3

Giselle & Dro (Standalone)

Our Love Is the Hoodest 1-2

Cuffed by a Trap God 1-3

I Just Wanna Cuff You (Standalone)

Crimson & Carius 1-2

A Dangerous Trap Love (Standalone)

Join my readers group **Nikki Nicole's Readers Trap** on **Facebook**

Follow me on Facebook Nikki Taylor

Follow me on Twitter @WatchNikkiwrite

Like my Facebook Page AuthoressNikkiNicole

Instagram @WatchNikkiwrite

GoodReads @authoressnikkinicole

Visit me on the web authoressnikkinicole.com

email me authoressnikkinicole@gmail.com

Join my email contact list for exclusive sneak peaks. http://eepurl.com/czCbKL

Here's a few playlists I listened to while writing the book.

https://music.apple.com/us/album/victory-lap/1316706552

https://music.apple.com/us/playlist/rip-king-nip/pl.u-r2yB1pqIPzrN3xv

https://music.apple.com/us/album/cry/931180022?i=931180030

Published by Pushing Pen Presents

www.authoressnikkinicole.com

Table of Contents

HE'S
A
GOOD MAN.

IT'S TWO SIDES TO EVERY STORY! MINE, HIS AND THE TRUTH.

PROLOGUE

Danielle

Crimson's wedding was so fuckin' beautiful. I don't know who cried more me or her? I'm glad I'm able to celebrate this moment with her. Her life's complete now, she has both of her parents by her side. A loving husband, two beautiful children and one demon spawn. I'm so happy for her. She deserves it and so much more. I'm tired. I didn't get any sleep last night. Crimson's bachelorette party was last night. It was so lit! Journee, Nikki, Malone, Alexis, Layla and Leah came through last night. We had a motherfuckin' ball. Everybody got fucked up accept Crimson. I took so many shots last night. I lost count.

I don't know why Crimson didn't get fucked up, and it was held at her house. I forgot she's still breastfeeding baby Carius. It's always a celebration when we link up. I couldn't enjoy myself like I wanted to. Rashad kept texting my phone. We were arguing through text all night.

Nikki had to grab my phone and cut it off. Ever since the bitch he was fuckin' with Mya caught us. I fell back from him. I can't fuck with that. She knew too much about me.

Granted she came to the clinic with him when he brought Cariuna and his son. She's been watching us for a long time. I asked him prior to her catching us was he still fuckin' her. He didn't lie to me. He said he was fuckin' her from time to time. I couldn't really get mad because I'm still married. I'm still fuckin' my husband whenever I want too.

Griff cut his bachelor party short and came home to his wife. Of course, the party was over. Rashad came with Griff. Something told me to leave an hour ago, but I didn't. We were still getting fucked up and kicking it. I didn't stay too far from Nikki and Skeet. We rode together we had a driver. I tried to avoid eye contact with Rashad. As soon as I walked past him to leave. He snatched me up and pushed me inside of the pantry. Nikki was giving me the side eye. I wouldn't dare tell her that I'm cheating on my husband. She's married too.

Rashad's mad because Baine's coming to the wedding as my date. He's still my husband of course I would invite him. Before we were even fuckin' around Baine was coming. It would look suspect if he didn't come.

Crimson and Griff both invited him. Rashad is being selfish as fuck. We argued in the pantry for about ten minutes before Nikki came back to get me. He finally let me leave after he made his threats. He called my phone all night threatening to pull up. I cut my phone off. Thank God Baine was asleep. The whole vibe between us at the wedding was awkward. I'm sure everybody could feel it. The moment he saw Baine come back to join me for some pictures. He was tripping.

Even when we walked down the aisle, he was talking shit. I ignored him. I'm ready to leave. I need to get Baine out of here fast before he does something stupid. I feel like some shit is about to pop off. Rashad and I haven't saw eye to eye since the Mya situation. Judging by their brief encounter they didn't have anything going on. Whatever they had going on she should've never been addressed in my clinic that's between them. Me and Rashad gave our toast and speeches to the bride and groom. We watched Crimson and Griff take their first dance. I went back to my seat and sat in Baine's lap.

His arms were rested around my waist. His face was nuzzled between the crook of my neck. Even though Baine is sitting behind me.

I can still feel Rashad watching me from afar. The DJ was lit too. Baine brought Crimson and Griff a case of Ace of Spades. We had our own personal bottle. He filled our glasses to the brim. Baine bit down on my neck and whispered in my ear.

"I can't wait to get you home and out of that dress," he slurred. A soft moan escaped my lips. Baine hands were underneath my dress. His beard is rubbing up against the side of my neck. His hands were massaging my nub. I just wanted him to rub this nut out of me. "You think I'm bullshitting. I'm dead ass serious. I want to show you exactly why I fuckin' married you. I got thirty reasons why Danielle, and the pussy between your legs isn't the first one. I love you Mrs. Mahone."

"I love you too Mr. Mahone." Baine grabbed my hair. My head rested on his chest. He leaned in and gave me a kiss. After our lip lock exchange. All eyes were on us. Baine looked at me and smiled. I shook my head and buried my face in his chest. His hands roamed through my hair. He whispered in my ear.

"You have nothing to be ashamed of." I nodded my head in agreement. The DJ played. **Gotta Be by Jagged Edge.** "Let's dance Mrs. Mahone."

Baine grabbed my hand and led me to the dance floor. He wrapped his arms around my waist, and I wrapped my arms around his neck.

Don't want to make a scene

I really don't care if people stare at us

Sometimes I think I'm dreaming

I pinch myself Just to see if I'm awake or not

Baine and I were enjoying our moment just the two of us. Somebody tapped Baine on his shoulder. He looked over his shoulder to see who it was. I noticed Baine flexed his back muscles. I rubbed his back to calm him. I don't know if somebody bumped him or what, but I didn't want them to fuck up Crimson's wedding. Baine's a hot head and shit can get ugly in a matter of minutes.

"CAN I CUT IN," he asked? I recognized his voice from anywhere. Why is he doing this? Please don't do this. My heart dropped instantly. I swear Rashad isn't playing fair. When Mya pulled up on him. I let him check her, but this isn't the fuckin' same. I'm married. Baine looked over his shoulder at me. He turned around and looked at Rashad. I stood beside Baine. Rashad's eyes are shooting daggers at me.

Baine rubbed the bridge of his nose. He looked at me and snarled his face up. I swallowed hard. I'm sure he could hear how my breathing sped up. It feels like I need to shit. I'm about to shit on myself and ruin this dress if Rashad exposes us. I got hot instantly. I used my hands to fan myself. If there's a God please don't let this happen to me right now. Please GOD forgive me for all my sins.

"NIGGA you're funny. You want to cut in and dance with my FUCKIN' wife? You're disrespectful as fuck. What would make you think I would FUCKIN' allow that to happen pussy ass nigga?" He asked. I know Baine's pissed. He flexed his back muscles again. His fists are balled up. It's about to go down. Rashad looked at me and smiled. Why is he doing this?

"You heard what the fuck I said. Pussy ass nigga I'm not bullshitting. I'm trying to cut in." Rashad argued. Baine stepped in Rashad's personal space. Baine and Rashad both started arguing. Baine pushed Rashad. Rashad pushed him back. I looked around to see who's watching. All eyes were focused on us and what's unfolding right here.

"Rashad, please don't do this shit here and ruin Crimson and Griff's fuckin' moment," I argued. Griff is standing right beside Rashad but didn't break it up. He should've got his boy because this isn't the fuckin' place.

"Danielle, you already know what it is with me? Don't put on a front for this nigga. I've been telling you this shit for months. Wherever I see you at with him at. I'm letting that shit be known. Danielle I FUCKIN' told you. You can do it my way, or you can learn the FUCKIN' hard way. I gave you the option to leave months ago but you were fuckin' stalling. Crimson and Griff had their FUCKIN' moment but now it's my FUCKIN' moment.

You got TWO fuckin' options and you SHOULD pick the right FUCKIN' one. You can't and you FUCKIN' ain't about to continue to be with this nigga. You can leave this nigga right now and let him know your marriage is a FUCKIN' wrap. I ENDED that shit for you. What's it going to be?" Rashad asked. I wanted to fuckin run and hide. My purse and phone weren't too far from here.

"Hold the fuck up! Danielle please tell me you haven't been cheating on me with this fuckin' nigga? I'm not even fuckin' surprised, but I should've known better. I met this lil BITCH name Mya a few months ago at **Nik and Skeet's.** I guess it's his BITCH huh.

She said my FUCKIN' wife was FUCKIN' her man. Shawty said she had fuckin' pictures and everything but I didn't want to see that shit. Danielle, I know you would NEVER do me like that. I gave her my number and she sent them immediately but guess what I never opened them.

If I open this fuckin' message. I swear to God it better not be you," Baine argued. He opened his phone and went to retrieve the message. His eyes were trained on me. "DANIELLE don't FUCKIN' RUN." I took off running. I couldn't wait around and let him see that. I grabbed my phone and purse off the table and ran. I don't know where I'm going but I'm getting the fuck away from here. In all my years of living, I've never experienced anything like this. Baine is going to fuckin' kill me. I want to know why he gave her his number. I want to know what would make him entertain her and the conversation. I need to ask Nikki can I see the camera footage.

Baine's hangs out over there a lot, but she's never mentioned him chatting with any females. How did Mya know to find Baine over there? He shouldn't even know this bitches name. Mya has a fuckin' problem now because what she done should've never fuckin' transpired. I'll sue her. I never gave her permission to record me let along send it to my husband.

I've only seen this bitch a few times. I don't know shit about this bitch, but she's taken the time out to find out everything about me. I never forget faces. Her face is one that I'll never forget. I don't even know her fuckin' last name. It wasn't hard for her to find out anything about me because I own my fuckin' business. When you log onto my website, I'm the first bitch you motherfuckin' see. DANIELLE MAHONE!

I shouldn't have kept my composure because she violated me and Rashad. I should've given it to her, so she would've known better. I want to know how she got in my building because the door was locked. She came before business hours which indicates she's been watching HIM. Baine's fucked with a lot of women, but I've never took the time out to I SPY on these bitches. Whatever you do in the dark always comes to the light.

The first time I saw her was at the FUNERAL. The second time I saw this bitch, is when Rashad brought her to the clinic. Mya and I locked eyes with each other. She knew I was fuckin' him and I knew he was fuckin' her. We were both in love with the same nigga. The third time I saw that bitch is when she walked in on us making love. Rashad never fucked me he always made love to me.

I swear it's some crazy bitches out here. I can't remember if she was crying or not, but I think she was. I knew she was going to be a problem. I know Baine and if a bitch had some dirt on me. He wouldn't hesitate to look at it. I don't believe he held onto the pictures without opening them. It's a possibility it's true because he would've tried to kill me. I've never investigated any female before, but MYA I'll be at her front door soon passing out an ass whooping. She FUCKIN' tried me and I'm not the ONE to try.

Mya was better off taking that loss instead of exposing me. I always tell people be careful when you're messing with a child of God. Who covers me might not be the same person that's covering you? My faith is at an all-time high. My ancestors are standing in the paint with me. If you dig a ditch for me. I'll dig three for you. I want Mya to know get ready for these ditches. I'm not surprised because women these days do the most. It's too many niggas out here to be caught up one.

Chapter-1

Cheree

Crimson's wedding was so beautiful. She deserved that and more. I'm so glad Bone and I got to experience that with her. I knew Danielle and Rashad had something going on, but I didn't want to say anything. I could feel the love between them. whenever they're in the room with each other. I knew it, the day he came over to Mother Dear's house with Griff. I watched how he looked at her. I watched the exchange they had. Danielle was upset and distraught then. He shouldn't be looking at a married woman as if she's his woman. Who am I to judge? It's something deeper going on between the two of them.

Why else would he do that? He's in love too. I remember Camina telling me Rashad was in the bed with Danielle. Crimson and Griff need to have a sit down with Ms. Camina. I don't know what I'm going to do with her besides love her and spoil her. I love her little self so much. She can't be telling everybody's business.

My heart goes out to Danielle. I can only imagine what she's going through. The moment the argument started.

Everybody stopped what they were doing to focus on the three of them. Ms. Gladys was disappointed in Danielle. I saw her facial expression. You can't help who you love. I know that firsthand. True love never dies no matter who you're with. True love will trump any existence of your current love. She's my God daughter so of course I had to be there for her.

I don't know who ran out the church faster me or Danielle. Bone was looking at me crazy. Danielle made a run for it. I had to run for it too. I swear Crimson and Danielle are going to be the death of me. I ran to my SUV as fast as I could. I haven't run like this in years. I know it's about to get ugly. I can feel it. I need to call Daniella.

I had to catch my damn breath. I'm too old to be running. Bone's blowing up my damn phone. I can't answer right now. I got to get Daniella on the phone and swoop Danielle. SHIT!

I called Daniella she answered on the first ring. Thank God. I crossed my fingers and closed my eyes. I said a prayer to the highest.

"I'm surprised to hear from you this early Cheree? How was it? I know she looked Beautiful." I wish I could go into details about Crimson's wedding, but I can't. I'm calling about a serious matter. Danielle's in a crazy love triangle. I don't see it ending pretty. I don't know Baine. I know Camina's God daddy Rashad. I saw the look in Baine's eyes he was about to fuck her up. I couldn't let that go down. I'm glad Danielle ran to avoid any more confusion.

"Daniella it was so beautiful. I want that one day. I'm happy for her. That's not why I'm calling. BITCH we got a motherfuckin' DILEMA. I got to blow this joint right now. I need to crash at your spot for a few days. I'm bringing Danielle and maybe Crimson with me. Danielle's in some deep shit. She needs you Daniella it's time," I sighed. Our mothers raised our daughters the best way they knew how. I can't complain at all. Danielle needs Daniella and Gary. I can't tell her what to do because I've never been married. I can't speak on nothing that I haven't been through.

"Cheree is Danielle okay what happened," she asked? I can tell by Daniella's tone that she's concerned. Danielle isn't okay. Her world was shattered in front of the world in a matter of minutes.

"Daniella, she's been cheating on her husband. Her side piece told her husband at the reception. It's about to get ugly. She fled the reception."

"Say what now? Is she okay? Sure, come on. I've been telling Gary for months now. It's time. Get here I'll be waiting. I can only imagine how she feels." I know how she feels. I saw her facial expression. She wasn't expecting it. More of the reason why she needs to get far away from the city.

"She feels horrible. I'll see you in a few hours." Daniella and I ended the call. I cleared Bone out. I can't talk right now. Once I'm situated. I promise I'll call him. My only priority is to find Danielle and get her away from here. I know Danielle feels bad. I saw the look of defeat on her face. Rashad's wrong he shouldn't have done that. He knew she had a husband. I know he cares about her, but he shouldn't have blown up her spot. I swear it feels like Deja Vu.

Daniella can relate. She knows this situation all too well. I remember when Gary caught her cheating. I swear it was like Deja Vu. The only difference between now and then. Daniella wasn't married. She was creeping on Gary with another nigga and he caught her.

God is my witness and he can take me right now. Gary assassinated that man in front of us. I just knew he was about to kill Daniella, and I would be a witness to her murder. Yeah Daniella needs to school Danielle on this. It's time for Daniella and Danielle to reunite. This is the perfect moment. It's only so much I can do. I watch how Danielle watches me and Crimson interacts. I know she wants that. I want that for her. I swear it felt like Deja Vu watching that shit unfold. The only difference between now and then.

Rashad was Gary and Baine was the nigga Daniella was creeping with Tony. Unlike Danielle, Daniella couldn't get away. We watched Coop kill that nigga in front us. I've seen plenty of motherfuckas get killed, but Tony didn't deserve that shit. Daniella and Gary weren't even together when she was creeping with Tony they had broken up. Bone had us cornered in, he thought that was the funniest shit. Unlike Griff Bone is always with the shit. He had the biggest smile on his face watching the drama unfold. I knew he was reminiscing about some old shit because he looked at me and laughed. I love Griff for Crimson. I swear I do.

I'm glad she chose him to be her partner. They complement each other well. I can tell underneath Griff's exterior it's a beast lying underneath that.

I need a vacation. I can't do shit with Bone sniffing up under me. It feels good to be back home, but I need a vacation. I haven't seen Daniella in over five months. Now is the perfect time to see her. After that I'm going back home to California. I miss the beach, sand and my peace. My daughter and grandchildren bring me peace. I'm trying to shake Bone.

Rashad

I don't even know why Danielle is fuckin' surprised. I've already told her what the fuck it is between us. She knew I wasn't going to let that shit ride. I told her don't fuckin' bring that nigga, but she didn't listen. I don't give a fuck about their marriage. She should've kept Baine at home. I don't give a fuck. Her vows mean nothing to me. She disrespected the fuck out of me by bringing him here as her date. She had the nerve to fuckin' dance with him in my fuckin' face. It's not going down like that. She knew I would have a fuckin' problem with that shit. I'm not about to sit here and act like I'm cool with it because I'm not.

Danielle and I have been having this conversation for months. Whatever marriage she thought she had with Baine. It's a fuckin' wrap. I ended that shit. She had the fuckin' balls to bring him here. I ended them HERE. I don't give a fuck about this nigga looking stupid. If he wants smoke, I'll air this motherfucka out. Danielle will be a fuckin' widow.

"Pussy ass nigga you've been fuckin' my wife. You knew we were married. You didn't give a fuck though," he argued. I didn't bust a fuckin' move. Mya called herself being slick and telling Baine,

Me and Danielle where fuckin'. She did me a fuckin' favor. Baine swung at me. His fist connected with my jaw. We started going at it blow for blow. I grilled him and start laughing at his pussy ass. He swung again and missed. I've been wanting to fuck his ass up for minute though.

Today was the fuckin' day. I picked him up and slammed his ass. My foot was about to slam down on his face. Griff pushed me out the way. He grabbed Baine's hand and pulled him off the ground. Griff tried to stand in between us and break it up. If I don't get the chance to get at Baine here. I will get at that nigga wherever I fuckin' see him at. He knows that. Make no fuckin' mistake about it he'll get his.

"Come on Rashad and Baine don't do this here in front of my kids and family. It's not the place y'all got to move around." I understood where Griff was coming from. I slapped hands with Griff and exited out the reception. Where the fuck did Danielle run off too? She has nothing to be ashamed of. We did it, but we love each other. Nobody can change that not Baine or Mya.

Our story was already written and now it's time for us to pick up the pieces and live it. I can't wait to pay Mya a fuckin' visit. Leaving out the reception.

I jogged up the steps. My adrenaline was at an all-time high. I bumped into just the person I was looking for. She looked at me and smiled. I stopped in my tracks. I had to address her.

"What the fuck are you doing here? You weren't invited. Follow me because we got a motherfuckin' problem." Mya looked like she wanted to object. She came here to cause fuckin' problems. I grabbed Mya's arm and dragged her to my fuckin' car.

"Rashad you're hurting me," she cried. Hurting her is the least of my fuckin' problems. We finally made it to my car. She reached for the passenger side door. She wasn't getting in my car. It's a wrap. I stood in front of her. She folded her arms across her chest. I don't give a fuck about her having an attitude.

"Aye Mya you got some shit you want to tell me? I heard you're sending pictures of Me and Danielle around to her husband. What's up with that?" I stepped in her personal space. I wrapped my arms around her throat.

"Stop Rashad please you're hurting me," she cried. I loosened my grip on her neck.

"Answer my fuckin' question Mya? Danielle doesn't have shit to do with me and you. You and I aren't together. I never put a title on us. If you're doing grimy ass shit like this, I'm glad I didn't make us official." I mean that shit what the fuck does she have to gain by doing that.

"Rashad you don't fuckin' mean that. Yes, I showed her husband the pictures of the two of you. I don't give a fuck. She's married Rashad. What would make you want to mess around with a married woman? It's plenty of single women out here, but you chose to mess with a married woman. I don't even know why I'm explaining myself to you," she argued.

"You had no right to fuckin' take pictures of Danielle and send them to Baine. What I do is my business and it ain't your fuckin' business. Thank you for telling him." That bitch is crazy. I wish I never fucked her. I tried to get in my car. Mya grabbed my shoulder. I looked over my shoulder to see what she wanted.

"What? We're done here. Don't say shit to me and I won't say shit to you."

"Rashad I'm pregnant." I looked at Mya like she was motherfuckin' crazy. I know she didn't say what the fuck I thought she said.

I ran my hands across the brim of my forehead. Mya being pregnant by me is the last thing I fuckin' need.

"You're pregnant by who Mya?" I knew she was pregnant by me. I just wanted her to confirm it. Mya's a good girl. I just hate that we've come to this. It's my fault not hers. I strung her along with no intent to be with her until Danielle came back along and changed my life.

"Are you fuckin' serious right now Rashad? You know you're the only person I've been with. I can't believe you would say that to me. It's yours and I'm fuckin' keeping it. I just wanted to let you know that. I'll take care of my child. You can keep chasing a married woman. You can pay me child support.

I want $4,000 a month not including the living expenses you were already paying. I've been accustomed to that. I want let you or that bitch take that from me," she cried. Mya's upset and I'm not trying to upset her. If she's carrying my child. I don't want us to be at each other's neck because of my fuck ups.

"Mya stop crying. I'm not trying to hurt you. If you're pregnant with my child. You know I'm going to take care of my child never question that.

My children come before everything. I got; you stop tripping on me. We're better than that. I fucked up when it came to us.

I'll admit that Mya, but I'll never fuck up when it comes to my kids. I can promise you that. I'll never drop the ball there."

"I'll hold you to that Rashad. Are we done here? I wish you would've been honest with me. Instead you led me on and now I fuckin' hate you. Hate is a strong word to use. You played me and you knew about everything I went through. Do you know how hard it was to fuckin' trust you? After everything we've been through Rashad the only thing, I have to show for is a fuckin' child. It's the only thing you're willing to commit too."

"Mya I'm sorry what more do you fuckin' want from me? You told me you're pregnant. I'm okay with that. You gave me a list of demands and shawty I'm not tripping about none of that shit. Mya, we made a baby and I'll take care of it. If you don't want your baby when you deliver. I'll take it off your hands. Shawty you can live your life and you can hate me from a distance.

I've been hustling in these streets for a long time. I can take care of all my kids and grandkids. What more do you fuckin' want from me? You gave me your ultimatums and now I'm giving you mine."

"I want US Rashad that's all I ever fuckin' wanted was US. I hate that I love you.

Getting over you isn't the easiest thing. I don't care about your money Rashad and you know that. I want you. I want to raise our child together. We made this baby with love. Our child deserves to have both of their parents in their life," she cried. I cupped Mya's chin forcing her to look at me. I wiped her tears with my thumbs. I swear I don't want to hurt this girl any more than I already have.

"You WANT US Mya? How could we be together after the things you've done? What if I didn't know you told Baine; I've been fuckin' his wife and he had one up on me? You gave that nigga the upper hand on a drop with me. If he would've killed me your child would've been fatherless. I can't trust you. We can co-parent. I'll be at every doctor's appointment. I'll be there every step of the way. We can't be together.

You went out your way and you didn't have to do that. It's my fault and not yours.

I'm not trying to hurt you and I'm sorry for hurting you. It was never my intentions. I can't change that Mya."

"I've made one mistake Rashad and you've made plenty. You're holding that against me. I'm sorry can we move past that. After everything we've been through and I'm sorry is the only thing I can get. I'm not going to beg you. I don't even want your money.

I don't want my child to have any dealings with you. Fuck you Rashad! I hope Baine kills you for fuckin' his wife. I can't believe that I love you. I wish I can take it back," she cried. Mya pushed me off her.

"Why do you want me to fuckin' play with you Mya? I play a lot of games but don't play with me when it comes to my child. We don't have to deal with each other if that's how you want it. I'll take care of mine regardless of how you may feel about it." I'm tired of arguing with Mya. Why would you want to put yourself through that? I can already tell Mya's about to be a fuckin' problem.

"You said what you had to say Rashad and I said what I had to say. I'm respecting your decisions. What's wrong with you respecting mine," she argued.

“You came to the wedding for what to cause more trouble. You're telling me you're pregnant, but you want to keep my child away, from me because we're not together? Mya keep playing these games and let's see how that works for you. I'm out. You don't want me as a fuckin' enemy. You can take it however you want. Any enemy of mine ain't living to say that they're an enemy of mine.” I jumped in my car and pulled off on Mya. I grabbed my phone to call Danielle.

Chapter-2

Danielle

I can't believe Rashad done that to ME. Why would he fuckin' do that to ME? Now our business is out in the open for everybody to SEE. I thought we had an understanding that we would move accordingly. I thought he at least had enough respect for ME and decency to keep the peace until I figured how I was going to LEAVE. My feet are killing me. I don't give a fuck I had to leave the reception IMMEDIATELY. Looking at Baine and Rashad the fire igniting in their eyes. I could feel the fire and rage coming from the two of them. I knew it was about to get ugly.

My eyes were so heavy because the tears wouldn't stop falling from my face. My vision was clouded. Damn Rashad why did you have to do that? Today at our best friend's wedding of all places. I'm trying to keep my pace. I had to run away. My heart couldn't take it seeing the look of disappointment on Baine's face. My heart's aching and threatening to beat out my chest. My life is fuckin' over. The fact remains the same I swear to God I didn't want to hurt Baine.

"Danielle, get your ass in this motherfuckin' SUV now. We got to clear it. Crimson pick up your motherfuckin' dress," God momma Cheree yelled. She didn't have to tell me twice. God Momma Cheree whipped her BMW X5 in front of us. I'm so thankful for the ride. I just wanted to get the fuck out of dodge. I kicked my heels off instantly. I leaned down and massaged my feet. They hurt so bad. Crimson and I both hopped in trying to catch our breaths. I knew she had a ton of questions for me. I have no choice but to answer.

It's time I gave my best friend slash sister my truth. I know Crimson would never judge me. She's always loved me unconditionally. Cheree fled the premises. She looked at me and smiled. I don't have anything to smile about. I can feel Crimson breathing down my neck. I didn't want her to leave her wedding reception.

"Danielle Mahone or should I say COOPER? Bitch you know I'm out of shape. Do you mind telling me why in the fuck I'm fleeing my wedding reception? Please tell me you haven't been fuckin' Rashad," she asked? Crimson's trying to catch her breath.

I wiped my tears with the back of my hands. My make-up is ruined. I'm sure my face looked a mess.

Why would she say that in front of Cheree? I know I'm not innocent but damn. Crimson knew I did! Why else would I run? I've been doing it.

"Crimson don't do that! What's understood doesn't need to be explained. You could've stayed at your reception. You didn't have to leave."

"Danielle you won't be the first women or last women to cheat. No matter what you've done I support you no matter what. I got you. Dry your tears baby girl. It's going to be alright. I got you. This is a judgement free zone!" I appreciate God Momma Cheree for that. I needed that.

"Crimson I've been having an affair with Rashad," I sighed. I held my head down. I'm not ashamed because I wanted it. I know right from wrong. I just didn't think Rashad would get so upset and air it out at the reception. I love him and you can't help who you love." Crimson tapped me on my shoulder like she was the fuckin' police. I looked over my shoulders to see what she wanted. Crimson wiped my eyes with Kleenex. Her eyes were shooting daggers at me. She knew I done it. Why did she want me to admit it?

"Pick your head up Danielle because this is what the fuck you're not about to do. I knew it but why didn't you fuckin' tell me? I know you love Baine.

I know you never stopped loving Rashad. I would never judge you. I just didn't want to be caught up in the middle. I'm riding with you right or wrong. You and Baine have the perfect marriage to me. No matter what you choose to do somebody is going to be hurt even you.

Now whoever this Mya bitch is she's going to have to answer to me. Because whatever her and Rashad had going on has nothing to do with you," she argued. Mya knows a lot about me. How did she know I'm married to Baine? She went out her way to tell my husband I cheated on him, with a man that's not hers.

"I know Crimson trust me I know, and I've weighed every option, but I didn't tell you because I didn't want you to judge me. Because you've stated your opinion more than once. I don't need anybody judging me that's why I didn't want to say anything. Everybody and their fuckin' mother want, too fuckin' judge ME. I don't give a fuck how a motherfucka may feel about ME.

These MOTHERFUCKAS don't know shit about me. These motherfuckas couldn't walk a mile in my fuckin' STILETTOS. Excuse Ms. Cheree I'm sorry for cursing. I'm not perfect. I have plenty of imperfections. Don't fuckin' judge me off the reflection that you SEE.

On the outside looking in we're PERFECT. Sometimes we ARE. I love Baine I swear I do, and I never stopped loving Rashad. I made a mistake. I should've left the moment we got INTIMATE, but I DIDN'T. I don't regret it because you live, and you learn. Every lesson is a blessing in disguise.

On the outside looking in, what you SEE between Baine and me is perfect, but you don't know that half of what we've been through. It took a lot for us just to get to this point and unlike my previous relationship. I thought I wasn't making the same mistake twice and to be honest I should've left a long time ago. Our marriage ran its course years ago.

I've always ran from everything, and this time around I chose to stay. I wanted to see if things would get better. Instead of walking away like I'm accustomed too. That's just a part of my truth. On the outside looking in you don't know what BAINE MAHONE has took me through. Crimson Rose Griffey I don't look like what I've been through. I got SCARS CRIMSON." I cried. I'm not pointing the finger. It's two sides to every story. It's a lot of stuff people don't know about us. It is what it is.

"Danielle what do you mean by that? It's nothing that you can say to me that would make me think Baine has cheated on you. I don't get that from him. No shade but that nigga is the perfect fuckin' husband. I adore that." If Crimson only knew. More of the reason why I'm not going to tell her. She wouldn't believe it. I don't want to taint the image she has of him just to justify my wrong doings.

"It doesn't matter Crimson what he's done. You know what I've done. I don't want to change the way you feel about Baine based off what we're going through. You'll see. Trust me if Baine knows I cheated on him. You'll see the real him soon. You remember the account I had you open for me in your name. I saved it for a rainy day. Today's my rainy day. I'm sure when we come back, I'll need to cash in on that soon." Crimson grabbed her phone and scrolled to an app.

"What's that supposed to mean? Don't speak on shit, if you're not ready to disclose it Danielle. I'm riding with you right or wrong? Maybe what I said came out wrong. He's perfect in my eyes. You're everything to me. If Baine hurt, you. He hurt me too. I get it and I'm with whatever you're with. Don't keep whatever you went through to yourself.

I'm supposed to go through this with you. I fled my wedding reception for you. The bond we have is unbreakable no man come in between this. It's 2.5 million dollars in that account Danielle. I need to know the real. You know everything about me. There are no secrets between us. You're my personal diary and I'm yours. You've been with me through some of my darkest moments. I'm forever grateful for that. I need to know whatever he done. Fuck the image I have of him. I'm here for you no matter what."

"Thank you Crimson! I appreciate that. I need you," I cried. I wiped my eyes with the back of my hands. I hated the way Baine looked at me. I know Rashad was upset too. What the fuck have I done. I can only imagine what's on going at the reception. I'll tell Crimson what happened between Baine and me. Not tonight though. I just want to relax and unwind. My mind is in a million places.

"Danielle, I know it's a lot going on. Home is probably the last place you want to be. I'm going to Hawaii for a few days. I want you to come with me. It's a girl's trip. Everything is on me. We'll shop when we get there. I have someone I want you to meet. Crimson you're more than welcome to come. If not, we'll see you in about a week. I'll drop you back off at your reception."

Cheree didn't have to tell me twice. I'm out of here. I'm not ready to face Baine. I can't go home. Baine is vindictive. I'm sure my shit is packed up by now. I wish Rashad would've waited but he just had to let Baine know we were fuckin' around.

"I'm coming with y'all. Griff he'll be alright with the kids. I'm not staying here to face the music. Fuck that let Griff handle it. It's his fault anyway faking his death. I need a break from him and my three kids." Crimson swear she needs a break. Ms. Cheree is the bomb. I wish I could meet my mom. I would give anything to be in her arms. My phone alerted me I had a text. I looked at my phone to see who it was, and it's Rashad.

HIM-I love you. Where are you so I can come get you.

I left his message on read. I'm not about to respond. I love Rashad. He should've waited for me to make that decision and not take matters into his own hands. I made plans to leave Baine it wasn't going to be today or tomorrow. I needed to have things set in place. I need to let my staff know we're moving. I'm a businesswoman first. I need to conduct my business.

Chapter-3

Baine

Danielle Mahone not my FUCKIN' wife. Not my precious FUCKIN' Danielle. She's the only bitch that has the key and rights to my throne. Our house has always been a fuckin' HOME. I gave that BITCH MY MOTHERFUCKIN' last name. I gave up my WHORISH WAYS for HER. I did a fuckin' 380 for HER. She fuckin' EMBARRASSED ME in front of all these MOTHERFUCKIN' people. I gave that BITCH my FUCKIN' HEART she just tore it A PART. I'm going to fuckin' KILL HER.

I knew it was some truth to Mya pulling up on me. She went out her FUCKIN' way for me to see my wife's infidelities. Danielle's going to WISH she never FUCKED OVER ME. Everything associated with Danielle must DIE starting with Ms. Gladys I'm going to shoot that old BITCH in her left EYE. Until this day I still haven't looked at the pictures. I'm about too.

I don't need fuckin' too, because I'll fuck around and kill Rashad and Danielle both for fuckin' around on me. Danielle could've fucked any nigga she wanted but HIM?

It ain't no coming back from that. Danielle confirmed everything I needed to fuckin' know. When she ran, I knew it was some truth to it. I know I haven't been the best nigga to HER in the past but damn MY WIFE fucked up. She thugged it out with a nigga for years.

I had so many slip ups and Danielle she stayed down through all my fucks ups. She wanted to leave me plenty of times, but I wouldn't let HER. She knew I would fuckin' kill HER. She promised me, she would never CHEAT. She'll leave me first if she decided to cheat. After two kids and another possibility. She finally decided to cheat.

After all these fuckin' years we've been together. I wonder how long she's been creeping with Rashad behind my fuckin' back. I'm going to FUCKIN' kill Danielle. Rashad's going to fuckin' die too. Griff spared his nigga. I noticed he had some fuckin' pressure on his chest. I KNOW he KNEW Danielle was fuckin' Rashad.

"Are you okay," Griff asked? I looked at Griff like he was motherfuckin' crazy. A nigga my wife was fuckin' just exposed their relationship in front of hundreds of motherfuckin' people. To make matters worse my fuckin' wife just ran off on me instead clearing up any fuckin' doubts I had.

Me and Rashad got history and it has nothing to do with Danielle. The blood between us has always been bad. I'll never be good, and Danielle won't either. If she thinks she's leaving me for him. The only ways she's leaving is in a motherfuckin' casket. I will put her in a fuckin' body bag. I mean that shit. It's not a fuckin' threat. It's her fuckin' reality. I felt a small tap on my hand. I looked over my shoulder to see who it was. It's Camina. Camina's the prettiest little girl.

"Uncle BANG BAINE! I got pictures of Uncle Rashad and God mommy Danielle on my iPad. Look at them kissing," she laughed. Camina was jumping up and down trying to show me her pictures. I tried to brush that shit off. Danielle's so fuckin' sloppy a little kid got you on camera being a hoe. Griff grabbed his daughter and pointed to the table. Camina went over there to take a seat.

"Hell, no I'm not good. Did you know my wife was fuckin' him? Don't lie either Griff. I've never smiled in another niggas face and openly known my boy was fuckin' his wife. I know that's your nigga, but damn Griff that's my fuckin' wife. We've known each other way before you knew that fuckin' nigga." Me and Griff were close growing up. It's has to be some type of fuckin' loyalty.

My wife should've never been cheating with his fuckin' friend. I'm looking at all them sideways now.

"Come on Baine you know me fuckin' better than that. If he's my nigga or not that's still your fuckin' wife. I don't condone that shit. I got a wife. I wouldn't want my wife cheating on me. Hell, no I didn't fuckin' know." I don't believe that shit at all. I knew he knew. Rashad's his fuckin' nigga. I know where his loyalty lies and it's not with me. As close as they are. He fuckin knew and Crimson knew that's why she ran after Danielle.

"If you wouldn't have faked your motherfuckin' death. My wife would've never been in Rashad's fuckin' reach." Griff snarled his nose up. He's mugging me like he wanted fuckin' smoke.

"You know what Baine I'm going to tell you like I told RASHAD. My reception ain't the fuckin' place. My kids and family are here. I'm not your issue. You need to have a discussion with your wife and not me. You can leave because you two have caused a scene here. It's my wedding and I'm the only NIGGA that needs to cause a scene," he argued. Griff didn't have to tell me twice.

Fuck him we ain't FUCKIN' cool no more. Danielle needs to be at home by the time I get there. She knows I'm going to fuckin' hurt her.

I grilled Ms. Gladys. I pushed her out my way and she fell. Mother Dear grilled me on my way out.

"Motherfucka you're going to die behind that," she argued. I chuckled. Fuck all of them. The two old bitches knew Danielle was cheating on me. It's best I get the fuck up out of here before I hurt a few motherfuckas on my way out. Fuck Griff we're not cool anymore. His blocks ain't safe.

Every fuckin' block I wanted to setup shop on a few years ago. I'm about to setup fuckin' shop. I want Rashad to come at me with some motherfuckin' bullshit. I'm not even with no talking. Straight motherfuckin' head shots. If Danielle thinks she can ride off into the sunset with Rashad she's sadly fuckin' mistaken. She can forget about that shit. I jogged up the steps to leave the reception. I'm to fuckin' fly to be stressing. I bumped into someone.

"Excuse you! You need to watch where the fuck you're going," she sniffled. I looked up to see who the soft voice belonged too. We locked eyes with each other and it's Mya. My eyes roamed every inch of her body. I'm single now. Damn Mya's fine ass fuck.

"What's up! What are you doing here? Why are you crying," I asked? I stepped in Mya's personal space closing the gap between us. Her breasts poked my chest.

I had to adjust my dick. Mya got my dick hard as fuck. I cupped her chin forcing her to look at me. I can tell she's been crying. Our lips were damn near touching each other. She stepped back and I stepped up.

"Back up Baine you're too close. Why do you care? I'm leaving. I said what I had to say. Where's your home wrecking wife," she argued. Mya's still in her feelings. I am too, but I'm not going to act on it anymore. I do want to look at the pictures because when I divorce Danielle, she's not getting shit. I made her. I made that BITCH who the fuck she is. The building I brought for her it'll be vacated by the end of next week.

"Mya you want me this close. I get it you're upset, and you should be. I don't want to talk about my EX-WIFE. I asked about you. If you want to talk about Danielle and him, you can have that conversation by yourself. What's understood doesn't need to be explained." Mya wiped her eyes with the back of her hands. I grabbed her hands and wiped her eyes with my handkerchief. Mya's eyes were trained on me. "Stop crying over that nigga."

"Okay Baine it's nice seeing you. I'm glad you moved on too," she sniffled. Mya attempted to walk away. I grabbed her by her wrist. I wrapped my arms around her waist.

I had to feel her up a few times. I felt her body tense up. Mya and I have found ourselves in this position a few times. I whispered in her ear.

"Damn I want to hold you for a few hours. Look stop crying. You're too beautiful to cry. I haven't moved on yet, but I'm about to pick up the pieces. I'm not going to sit around and be miserable. It gets greater later. I'll see you around shawty." I couldn't entertain Mya.

I had to keep it pushing. It's too many bitches out here waiting on a nigga like me to slide through and bless them with some dick. Unlike Danielle I'm not making permanent decisions on temporary emotions. I just hope she'll be able to deal with consequences that came along with her cheating. I finally made it to my car. I hit the key fob to unlock my doors. I grabbed my phone and scrolled to Mya's name.

I've been curious for months now. Today's the day. I opened the message. It's a video of Danielle and Rashad fuckin' at her clinic. I'm burning that motherfucka down. She was fuckin' this nigga in some shit I brought her.

Raw at that. She's disrespectful as fuck. I need all the camera footage to see how long they've been fuckin' around. I refused to look at it anymore. I sent the video to my attorney and told him to draw up the divorce papers. Danielle ain't getting shit.

I'm going to give her clothes to my two baby mommas and I'm going to bless my new bitch with her fuckin' jewelry. Danielle didn't want to have my baby because she was too busy fuckin' on Rashad. Our divorce is just the beginning. She's going to fuckin' feel me. I sent Mya a text.

Me-Good looking out. How much do I owe you?

Mya-$4000.00

Me-Alright where can I meet you? Does that come with a date also?

Mya- Maybe

Me-Send me the location and I'll pull up.

I need to relive some fuckin' stress. I wouldn't mind fuckin' on Mya on some get back shit. I made my way to the Northside. It's about thirty minutes from here. I had a faithful bitch waiting on me to slide through.

I swear I'm going to FUCKIN' hurt Danielle. I checked the fuckin' cameras and she wasn't at home. She should beat me to the FUCKIN' house or it's going to be some extra FUCKIN' problems.

I pulled up at my spot. I keyed in. I kicked my shoes off. I made my way upstairs. I stopped by son's room. He's asleep taking a nap. I made my way towards Nova's room. We locked eyes with each other. A small smile escaped her lips. She ran her tongue across her lips.

Nova's my son's mother. We've been fuckin' around for about six years now. Nova's fine as fuck. She's one female I could never shake. I had no plans too. She always played her position. She acts up from time to time. Her skin is the color of vanilla bean. She always wore her hair in crazy colors. I love the way that shit looks on her.

Her breasts sat up and her thighs were extra thick. I loved that shit. She stood about 5'4. She weighs about 142 pounds when she's not carrying one of my seeds. She motioned with her index finger for me to come to her. She didn't have to tell me twice.

Nova's pregnant with my daughter. She just started showing even with a baby bump she's still bad as fuck. I want to dive deep in that pussy without any repercussions.

"Baine what are you doing here. I thought you had a wedding to attend with your precious Danielle," she asked? I'm not trying to feed into what she's saying.

I want to feel her pussy and I want to fuck her mouth. Nova started undressing me. I stepped out of my pants and tossed my shirt on the floor.

"You're worried about the wrong shit. Undress me and let's get to it." Nova looked at me with wide eyes. I'm not with the foreplay and shit. I need Nova to do less talking. I just want to fuck without the extra shit. She knows why I'm here. I want to see my son and to dig in her guts for a few hours.

"Really Baine?" Nova rested her hands on her thick ass hips. "What are you going to do when I get married to someone and he accepts your son, daughter and me? We won't be able to do this anymore. Baine I'm so tired of doing this shit with you. I'm good enough to fuck when you want and however you want.

Why am I not good enough to LOVE? Our son he's five years old. Our daughter she'll be here in six months. He knows what's going on. When you leave here Baine and go home to HER. He cries when you leave. He wants to go home with you. Yes, we live a nice life because of you. Damn Baine Danielle is ruining our fuckin' family. Our son can't come to your house on the weekend because of her. Our holidays are cut short because of HER. We can't pull up on daddy when we want too because of HER.

I'm pregnant with our daughter and it's about to be the same shit because of HER. I can't keep doing this with you. It's time for you to choose it's either going to be US or HER. Why does my child have to SUFFER BECAUSE OF HER? As bad as I want to fuck you right now.

I'm going to pass. Everything that you made with HER you were supposed to make that with ME. I'm sick of it." Nova's been tripping EVER since she's been pregnant with RAINE. I don't know why Nova's in her feelings. The whole time we were at the wedding. She was sending me VIDEOS begging me to come fuck her. I'm here now and it's a motherfuckin' problem.

"What the fuck are you trying to say Nova? Are you cheating? Are you fuckin' another nigga?

The baby you're carrying is she mine or is she someone else's? What the fuck do you want from me Nova? Anything you want. I fuckin' get it. You don't work. You don't pay any fuckin' bills. I take very good care of you. I don't complain about nothing I do for you. Danielle knows about our son and she knows I take care of him.

I leave my house every fuckin' morning at 6:00 a.m. to take my son to fuckin' school. I'm at every fuckin' football and basketball practice or game. Whenever he's fuckin' sick I drop whatever I'm fuckin' doing for my son. What's your problem are you worried about me or you're worried about HER? She doesn't even fuckin' know I take care of you too.

She doesn't know that you're living in a house WE own. What's changed Nova what's up with you?" I've never been pressed for pussy. I don't have too. I always had options and I always kept a few hoes, in my pocket. My phone alerted me I had a text from Mya with an address.

Mya-6970 Lake Forest Drive. Sandy Springs, GA 30328

A small smile was etched on my face. I grabbed my pants off the floor. I pulled up my pants. Fuck having this conversation with her.

If she wants to argue about some shit that's under control. We'll talk later. I'll get up with Nova another day. I love Nova. I swear I do. I'm not in the mood for this conversation.

"Baine where are you going? Who is that texting your fuckin' phone? Is that HER. You just got here and you're leaving for HER. You know what I'm sick of you and HER. Does she know about RAINE? I'm done keeping quiet about US. I'm telling HER and I don't give a fuck how she may feel." I ignored Nova. I'm out of here. I guess she didn't like being ignored. She jumped out the bed and ran up on me. She punched me in my back. I looked over my shoulder. I punched the bridge of my nose. I closed the gap between us.

"What the fuck do you want from me? Nova you've stated your demands. We ain't got to fuck. Do you know how many bitches out here that want to fuck me? It's plenty of them. I don't give a fuck what you to tell Danielle. I'm the fuckin' bread winner. I pay for all this motherfuckin' shit. If you got a nigga that can do what the fuck I do; Nova go be with that nigga.

You're one less bitch I got to take care of. I'm obligated to take care my kids.

I'm not obligated to take care you. So, what the fuck do you want to do? You can leave Nova. Your services are no longer needed. You can shut the fuck up and keep enjoying this fuckin' ride. You're a side bitch and you're winning. What's the fuckin' problem? Do you know how many bitches that want to be in your shoes?" It's plenty of bitches that want to be in her shoes. She started crying. She started this shit. I just fuckin' finished it.

"Baine don't leave. I'm sorry," she cried. I grabbed Nova's hand and led her to the bed. She sat in front of me with tears in her eyes. I pulled her panties down and unfastened her bra. My face found its way between her legs. Nova had a tight grip on my dreads.

"Stop crying before you wake my son up. You're going to upset my daughter. I got some shit going on Nova. The last thing I need is for you to be at my neck about a situation that's under control. Keep playing your FUCKIN' position and the top spot maybe yours sooner than you think."

"I love you Baine and I'm trying but it's hard. We're about to have our second child. I want you here all the time," she moaned.

"Get up here and ride my face." Nova did as she was told. I don't know what more Nova wants from me. She has my son and she's pregnant with my daughter. I see her every day. We might not go to sleep with each other at night, but we lay up with each other in the daytime.

Mya

I don't know where Rashad and I went wrong? We went from spending time with each other to me spending my nights all alone. It's like I barely even fuckin' know him. If somebody would've told me a few years ago we would be here. I wouldn't believe them. Rashad and I were never supposed to be here. He used to be so fuckin' perfect. He played me for a fool not once but twice. I never would've been open and submissive to him.

I would've never let him lead me down a tunnel of heart ache and pain. I thought he was worth it. Rashad and I never really spent any time together in the daytime. He hustled all day and I worked from 7:00 a.m. to 7:00 p.m. Our time together was always at night and it was always intimate. After he left the streets, he was always coming home to me. I cherished that. Part of those moments defined us. We were supposed to raise our child together and give him or her what we never had.

Rashad promised me when he was ready to settle down, I was the only one promised that spot. I thought me telling him I'm pregnant things would change between us. He knew how I felt about having a child with him and we weren't in a committed relationship. That's the last thing I wanted was to be his baby mother without any clear understanding of what we're doing. It's the very thing that's landed us here.

I wanted Rashad to fight for us. I've been the only one fighting for us. He played with my heart. Even after my demands he didn't budge. He really didn't give a fuck about us. He accepted all my demands without a fight. He'd do anything I say just so I want interrupt whatever he has going on with her. I can't be brought. I won't be brought.

My living expenses and what I want for our child was nothing to Rashad but chump change. I thought about fuckin' with Baine for get back. It wouldn't make me feel better, but it would ease the pain. I want Danielle to feel how I feel. I sent Baine my home address. We'll see where things lead too.

I want this baby, but I won't have it if Rashad and I aren't together. I don't believe in abortions either. He's okay with me having it. He didn't tell me to have an abortion. I pictured my pregnancy different than this. I want him there every step of the way.

Not just at the doctor's appointments and when I call him. We need to talk because I have some more things I want to discuss. I grabbed my phone to send him a text.

Me-Can we talk I have some more things I want to say?

Rashad-I thought you said everything you had to say. I'll get up with you before the week is out.

Chapter-4

Crimson

If it ain't one thing it's something else. We can't catch a fuckin' break. Rashad fucked up my wedding reception. I'm not even surprised. Danielle and Baine were doing them. Of course, Baine was going to dote on his wife. He always does that. Rashad couldn't take it. I watched Rashad from afar. His eyes were trained on Danielle. He's still in love with her.

He never stopped loving her. I heard Danielle and Rashad going back and forth in the food pantry last night. I didn't think it was too much. I should've known better. Journee asked me was it something going between the two of them. I denied it. I knew but I didn't want to believe it. Griff has called my phone a million times. I had to answer. Danielle was in the living room asleep. Our flight leaves in two hours.

"Hello," I sighed. I'll miss Griff and my babies for a few days, but I'm going to be here for Danielle for as long as she needs me. He should understand that. He won't understand. He's selfish when it comes to my time.

"Crimson what's up with you? I've been calling you for the past three hours and you haven't answered the phone. You can't be doing that shit. Anything could happen and I won't know because you're not answering.

I know you're with Danielle but shawty you got to let a nigga know something. How is she and when are you coming home," he asked?

"I'm sorry Carius. It's not intentional. I should've answered but it's a lot going on. I'm okay! She's not okay. Why did you allow him to do that? I told you don't let him fuck up our wedding reception. You let him do it. You could've stopped him, but you didn't.

I'm upset because not only did he ruin our moment, but he fucked up Danielle's life. That's the only thing people our going to remember about our wedding is Rashad and Baine beefing behind Danielle.

Whatever happened between the two of them should've stayed between them. It shouldn't have been leaked at our wedding reception. I'm not coming home Carius. Danielle needs me. I'm not leaving her side. We're going to Hawaii for a few days. I'm going to be with her for as long as she needs me too. Mother Dear said she'll help with the kids while we're gone." He's pissed! I can hear him making those little noises that he makes when he's pissed off.

"Crimson! I'm not about argue with you about shit that doesn't concern us. We don't have shit to do with the two of them. I went down there to defuse the situation like you asked me too. No matter what, it was bound to come out. Am I sorry that it happened at our wedding reception?

I am. What the fuck do you mean you're going to Hawaii for a few days Crimson? We're supposed to be on our way to celebrate our honeymoon. Danielle's more than welcomed to come with us.

I let you do a lot of shit Crimson. You're not going to Hawaii for a few days. Bring your ass home I'M waiting." He didn't do shit. I should've gone down there myself. Carius he's about to be so mad at me. I'm not coming home. We'll talk about it again when we see each other.

"Carius why are you cussing to prove your point? We have everything to do with the two of them. If you wouldn't have faked your death. They wouldn't have crossed paths with each other. Yes, they would've saw each other at our wedding but that's about as far as it would've got. I'm not coming home. We can postpone our honeymoon. She needs me. Once I help her put herself back together again. I'll be home." I heard Carius huffing and puffing in the background.

"Crimson! You can't hide from love. You can't help who you love. Stop pointing the finger at me. I didn't tell Rashad and Danielle to FUCK or whatever you want to call it. They're grown they both wanted each other. Can't you fuckin' see that? If she didn't care about Rashad, why would she avoid seeing him? Danielle should've never married, Baine if she knew she was still in love with Rashad.

Danielle knew this. If she didn't want it to happen, she should've said NO. I'm sure she did.

I'm sure Rashad made it real hard for her. They did it Crimson and it can't be undone. I'm not postponing our honeymoon. Where are you because I'm coming to get you?" Carius and I never argue but we're about to have a real argument because I'm not coming home.

"Two wrongs don't make a right. You should've corrected Rashad because he was wrong. It's not on Danielle, because Rashad knew she was fuckin' married. Give your nigga the same speech you're giving me. Carius cancel out trip because I'm not coming home. I said what I said. I'm going to Hawaii and I'll see you when I come back home. Rashad still shouldn't have done that. I agree they love each other.

He should've respected her enough to not do that there. He didn't give a fuck he just wanted to let Baine know he was fuckin' his wife. What's the real beef between Rashad and Baine it's deeper than Danielle? Rashad can't be mad. Danielle is married what does he think is happening when she's at home with her husband?

He couldn't handle it. He just had to make a point. You don't want to speak on that Carius. You could've ushered Rashad out the reception, but you didn't. You're going to be mad at me Carius, and I'll just deal with the consequences when I get back home. I'm going to Hawaii and I'll talk to you soon." I hung up the phone. I cut my phone off because I'll argue with him all night.

I don't have time for that. Danielle walked in the room and smiled at me. Even through all the bull shit that just happened she's still smiling.

"Go home Crimson! You just got married. I'll be fine," she smiled. I know Danielle was just saying that to keep confusion down. How could I go home and she's going through all of this? I can't do that. If she's good, she'll take her ass home. Carius he'll be alright. He knows I'm coming back home to him.

"I'm not going home Danielle. I'm staying with you no matter what. Carius ain't going nowhere. I know we just got married but he needs to respect what I just said. He knows how close we are so he should expect that. I'm not leaving your side. You've never left my side. I'll be less than a woman to take my ass back home and I know you're dealing with all this. Girl bye."

"I don't want to cause any problems between your marriage Crimson," she sighed. I understand where Danielle's coming from but it's already problems. Griff and I are in the middle of it no matter what. Our best friends are back fooling around. We're the cause of it.

"You're not. My husband needs to understand you're going through something. I'm going to be here. Part of me being here requires me not being at home. I'll call him when we land. It's nothing he can do to change that. NOTHING.

I know me and Griff will have some problems when I get back home it's just some shit that I'll have to deal with. I grabbed my phone to send Cariuna a text.

ME-Princess Cariuna. I love you and I'll see you soon. I'll be gone for a few days I'm with your God-mommy Danielle. Look after your brother for me. I know Camina will be fine. Help your daddy as much as you can. I'll call you tomorrow Princess.

Danielle tapped me on shoulder. I looked over my shoulder to see what she wanted.

"What did he say Crimson? I can't believe you hung up in his face like that." I had to hang up because I would've kept talking and he would've pulled up and I didn't want that. I shrugged my shoulders at Danielle. I know Griff's pissed but oh well.

"I'm not texting him I'm texting Cariuna. I'll deal with him when I get back. I'm sure he's going in on Rashad because I left. I can't wait to give Rashad a piece of my mind. He wouldn't care."

"I feel you. I wish Cariuna and Carius can come with us. Your demon spawn Camina she can stay at home with her daddy and Rashad. I swear Crimson your daughter has out for me," she laughed. I pushed Danielle she needs to leave my baby alone.

“Look Danielle leave my baby alone. I don’t know why you and Camina don’t get along she’s done nothing to you. It’s not her fault she’s Team Rashad.” My mother brought me and Danielle some changing clothes out. I’m ready to get out of these clothes.

Griff

Crimson's tripping and it ain't shit I can do about it. I respect her for standing her ground. I knew when she ran, she was going to ride with Danielle. I expected her too. It's our fuckin' honeymoon and she's trying to run off with Danielle. What the fuck am I supposed to do with Camina and Carius besides spoil them. Cariuna my princess she'll help daddy out for a few days. Crimson knows we're going to have a few issues when she comes back. Danielle could've come with us for a few days. I wouldn't have told Rashad shit.

I'll admit what Rashad done was fucked up. He's in love and he doesn't know how to control his emotions. He's always wore his heart on his sleeves. Danielle's breaking him down, she's his weakness. His pride wouldn't allow Danielle to enjoy her night if it wasn't with him. Danielle has his heart. She's had it for years and didn't even know it.

It's about to be a war out here in these FUCKIN' streets. I can feel it. I saw the look in Baine's eyes, and he saw the look in mine. I swear to God that nigga doesn't want no FUCKIN' smoke with me. Yes, I knew Rashad was fuckin' his wife but that ain't my FUCKIN' business. Baine and I grew up together, but we grew apart. My loyalty lies with Rashad. Baine's never been loyal to me. I let a lot of shit slide because of our father's history.

Our fathers are dead and I'm not letting shit slide. He's done some slick ass shit one too many times. I don't give a fuck about Keondra. I always had eyes on her because I never trusted her. When we were married. He was trying to fuck her. He's never been loyal to me. She should've been off limits. I got Danielle's back no matter what. She always had mine and Crimson's.

Baine's a spiteful ass nigga. I know he's going to try and do whatever in his power to hurt Danielle. I got her though. She's my wife best friend and I'll never let anything happen to her. Camina and Cariuna were asleep. Carius he's looking around for his mother. He won't go to sleep without her. My phone rang. It's a Facetime from Rashad. I answered on the first ring. I had to make sure that nigga ain't out here about to do some crazy shit.

"What up," I asked? Rashad's silly as fuck. I can tell he's high ass fuck. I can see the smoke cloud in front of him. I need to roll up some of that shit.

"Where the fuck is Danielle? I know she's over there with Crimson. Put her on the phone." Shit I wish Danielle was here because my wife would be here too.

"I wish I could. Crimson and Danielle are gone to Hawaii for a few days on our fuckin' honeymoon. I'm taxing you behind that shit. My wife she's mad at me and you. She ain't coming home. She told me she'll see me in a few days. Rashad, she cut her phone off so I can't track her location. You know you started a war out, here right?"

Rashad wanted to kill Baine and Ike years ago, but I stopped that shit. It's a new day and some different fuckin' beef added on top of the other shit.

"I know Griff, but I don't give a FUCK. I'm aware of my actions and it is what it is. If Baine wants to shoot it out behind something that was never his; than he's ready to FUCKIN' die. Anybody can get touched even me. It's FUCKIN' murking season MY NIGGA. That pussy ass nigga should vest the FUCK UP. You know I'm going to kill him, right? You ain't his fuckin' lifeline no more don't even try to stop me.

I'm not even asking you to be on the gun-line with me because I started this shit and I have every intention on finishing this shit. I want that nigga to FUCKIN' try me when it comes to my FUCKIN' blocks. I pulled his FUCKIN' hoe card. I would've killed him at the reception, but my babies where there. If our kids weren't there Baine would've died in front of his EX-WIFE. I swear to God Griff I'll burn his MOTHERFUCKIN' ass. Lights off no FUCKIN' mask MY NIGGA." Rashad's still hot about that shit. I know Rashad and I know he had every intention on killing Baine.

"I hear you and I'm listening. You've been my nigga for years. I've never had to question your loyalty. I'm on the gun-line even if you don't want me too. You know I'm not standing down. Me and Baine had a few words after you left. I need you to bring your ass over here and help babysit these kids since my wife is gone."

Rashad already knew what it was between us. I'll never let my brother go to war by himself with any nigga. What's understood doesn't need to be explained. I'm here regardless. I had to let him know that for reassurance.

"I got you. I'll scoop Camina and Cariuna tomorrow. I'm going to do right by Danielle this time around Griff. I swear to God I am. She FUCKIN' tried me. It took everything in me not to push Baine's shit back while he was feeling her up. I ain't NEVER respected their marriage. I know he only wanted to FUCK with her because he knew I used to FUCK with her. I know I'm not a saint. I'll never pretended to be. You and I both know Baine isn't who Danielle thinks he is." It's true but it's not my business to expose him. If she hasn't seen the real him by now, she will. "I got another dilemma. When I left the reception. I ran into Mya she came to start more shit. She's pregnant Griff. I swear every time I'm trying to live right one of these females end up pregnant."

"Damn Rashad! Every fuckin' time. Stop fuckin' all these chicks. You think Danielle wants to rock with that. What arc you going to do? You need to watch Mya. I don't trust her. Why would she be coming to my wedding if she wasn't fuckin' invited? I understand she's hurt. Hurt people hurt people. She went out her way to expose Danielle. She went to go find Baine and show him the pictures. Why you didn't tell me she caught y'all fuckin'. You need to settle down. I can't fuck with that. I'm glad I never been that nigga to juggle multiple women," I chuckled.

Mya caught that nigga with his pants down and she's fuckin' lost it. Damn Rashad always has the craziest shit going on with his choice of women.

“Aye stop fuckin' laughing at my expense, that's why I didn't fuckin' tell you. You know how I feel about kids. If I make them and they're mine, I'll take care of them. I didn't tell her to have an abortion. It's her choice. I can't lie I cared about Mya. I got mad love for her, but I've never been in love with her. I know I need to watch her. I got Slap following her around. I heard Baine say she pulled up on him at Nik and Skeet's. I know she's about to be problem.

She wants us to raise our child in a two-parent home. She's already threatening me about not letting me see my kid. I need Danielle to roll with the punches. Me and Mya were fuckin' around before me and her. I don't know how far along she is, but I swear this shit feels like Deja Vu Griff. This time around I'm not letting anything come between us. Mya can act stupid if she wants to that bitch will end up dead fuckin' with me.

You and I both know I don't care about raising my kids on my own.” I finished rapping with Rashad. We made plans to link up tomorrow. My nigga has a lot on his fuckin' plate. He can't win for losing. I hope Danielle rocks out with him despite the shit he has going on with Mya. Mya's a fuckin' problem for Rashad. If she’s pregnant by him.

I hate to say it, but Danielle isn't going to want to be bothered with that. I finally got Carius to sleep. My mind traveled back to Crimson. I miss the fuck out of my wife with her stubborn ass. If she isn't home in a few days, I'll find her and bring her ass home. I grabbed my phone to send her a text.

Me-Crimson Rose Griffey! You know I'm mad at YOU. I understand it's some shit YOU had to do. I don't have a problem forgiving YOU. It's our wedding day. It's the day WE said I DO. I should be lying next to YOU. Damn SHAWTY I miss YOU. If you ain't home in three days I'm coming to find YOU. I LOVE YOU Mrs. Griffey.

Rashad

I can't FUCKIN' sleep even if I wanted too. Sleep is the last thing on my mind. Danielle's invading my FUCKIN' mind, but she won't even answer the phone or respond to any of my FUCKIN' texts. I know she's mad at me, but what the fuck did she expect. My feelings are involved too. See that's the problem with females they think niggas don't have feelings, but we do. I'm not a PUSSY ass nigga and I'll never PRETEND to be one. I could never watch Danielle be affectionate with another nigga that's not ME and not say shit. I'm not built like that.

She dipped on me and fled the FUCKIN' scene on a nigga. I've been tossing and turning all FUCKIN' night. She didn't have to run. I would've killed that motherfucka if he would put his hands on her. I'm an observer. Danielle's scared of Baine. She was too FUCKIN' fidgety which leads me to think he's put his hands on her before. I didn't think she would run. I thought she would've at least denied it. She ran off to Hawaii.

I crashed at my mother's house tonight. My son and my nephew where in their rooms asleep. We locked eyes with each other. I smiled at her. I swear my mother's my heart. She just trips on a nigga too hard sometimes. I don't want to hear her preach to me. I want to sleep but I can't.

“What's up son? I knew you were still up. You got it bad huh? I can't believe you did that shit at the wedding. Let me guess that's Danielle she's beautiful. Rashad what are you doing trying to pursue a married woman? It's a lot of single females out here why her?” I knew my mother wanted to come in here and fuck with me. I had to choose my words wisely. More of the reason why I didn't answer when I heard her knock at the door.

“Ma I'm not trying to justify my actions to you. What's understood doesn't need to be explained. I'm sorry for embarrassing you. I LOVE HER. WE LOVE EACH OTHER and nobody can change that. Not even her husband. She belongs to me and I belong HER. She knows that. Her marriage means nothing to me. She was never supposed to marry him. She only did that to get over me and look where it's landed her. She’s the one that got away. One day we found our way back to each other ma. I’m not letting anyone come in between that. She was divorcing him I just sped up the process.”

“I hear you RASHAD and I get it. You're a hot head just like your father. I never seen you act that way. Hell, yeah you embarrassed the fuck out me. Lil Rashad and BJ put their heads down. I'm a woman before anything. I haven't met Danielle, but I want too. I can't judge her. At the end of the day you can't help who you love. The two of you are playing a dangerous game. You love HER and her husband loves HER. I witnessed that. You ruined her marriage Rashad.

She's a damsel in distress. I just want to reach out to her and hug her. I feel so bad for HER because you're my son and I witnessed what you did to her. I hope you're serious about her. I hope you didn't ruin her marriage just to fuck over her. I know you, but I've never seen this side of you. I know it's serious. It's time for you to settle down Rashad. Your son needs a mother."

"Ma, I know I'm working on it. I want to settle down. I'm not playing with her. I've been there and done that. I don't want to do that anymore. Danielle is the only woman I want. She wouldn't have to be a damsel in distress if she would've told him it was over sooner. I want to make an honest woman of her. Danielle knows me." I finished rapping with my mother. I heard everything she said. I'm not the same nigga I used to be. I'm older now and little bit wiser. I want to be with Danielle. It's not a BITCH walking or a NIGGA breathing that's about to come in between that. I grabbed my phone to send Danielle a text.

Me-Danielle, I know you see me fuckin' calling you. I know you've read my text. I know you're in Hawaii. Drop that location so I can pull up. Shawty you can't fuckin' hide from ME. I'll FIND YOU. How much do you want to BET? You know I love you. I'm not going to sweat you though. Let me know if you're okay? What more do you want from ME? I want to be with you.

I thought that's what you wanted too? I'm tired of playing this game with you. I'll chase you and run you down until I get the fair chance to be with you.

I swear Danielle has me tripping so FUCKIN' hard. I know she's alive, but I would prefer to hear it from her than the read message on our phones. I swear this shit me and Danielle got going on is far from fuckin' over it's just the beginning. I know Baine wants smoke and I got that shit for him. My fuckin' clip stay loaded. I don't mind shooting out with that nigga behind something that belongs to me. I'm coming the worst fuckin' way.

He only married Danielle to fuck with me. I'm not saying that he doesn't love her, but his intentions were never good. Griff saved that nigga because if he didn't pull me off him. I would've stomped his ass out until I saw his brains lying on the floor. I would've been waiting at his trap to air Ike's ass out. I live by and die by that shit.

I heard my door open again. I swear to God I'm never going to get any sleep between my mother and Danielle evading my mind, but she refuses to answer the fuckin' phone. My son walked in. I swear every time I see my young bull a smile comes to my face.

"Daddy I didn't know you were here. I thought I heard Mimi talking to you. Can I sleep in here with you," he asked? I nodded my head in agreement. My nephew BJ came in right behind him. BJ he's my sister's son. God bless her soul we were eleven months a part.

He's my son too whatever I do for my son I do for him too. As soon as the climbed in the bed the grabbed the fuckin' remote and took over my shit.

A FEW HOURS LATER

Chapter-5

Danielle

I'm tired but I can't sleep. Every time I close my eyes, I keep replaying the images of what happened to ME. I feel so empty and alone the facts remain the same; I may never be able to go home. Judging by Baine's tone. I know he'll never call me Mrs. Mahone. My feet are swollen and aching. My heels did a number on my feet. I think Crimson noticed because she put my feet in her lap and started massaging them. I appreciate her so much. She didn't have to do that. Nor did she have to leave her reception, but she did anyway.

I can't seem to wrap my mind around my INFIDELITIES being LEAKED. My heart's caving in. I can barely feel my heartbeat. I can't get over how Rashad and Baine both looked and talked to me. I can only imagine what happened after I fled the scene. I had to run because I felt like my life was in danger. I know Baine wanted to lay hands on me. He didn't give a fuck who was around.

He was ready to CLOWN. I hated the look of disappointment on my grandmother and Mother Dear's face. I know she's ashamed and embarrassed because of my actions.

I wiped my eyes with the back of my hands so many times. My eyelids hurt. My nose is stuffy. God momma Cheree had to pop me. Every time I close my eyes tears pour out the brim's. I'm sure my eyes are puffy. I know I look a hot mess. My life's a mess right now and I don't think I'll ever be able to pick up the pieces. I'm smiling through the pain to stop from crying. On the inside I'm dying. My heart is broken. I don't think I ever felt like this before. Rashad sent me over twenty text messages. I read them all, but I never responded. Not one time did he say he was sorry.

I'll never respond because once again Rashad has fucked over me. It's a wrap. I feel like the same twenty-two-year-old, who's boyfriend abandoned HER without any reasoning. Rashad exposed us because I didn't agree with his REASONS. If he gave a fuck about me, he wouldn't have done this to ME. Why did this man have so much FUCKIN' power over ME? God, I wish you'll release the HOLD he has on ME. I should've never allowed Rashad to get next to ME. He's fucked ME over one to many times.

Yesterday was the last FUCKIN' TIME. I can't fuck with Rashad PERIOD. I'm blocking him and changing my number. He wasn't a mistake. I made a FUCKIN' mistake. I should've never had sex with HIM. I thought he's changed, and he hasn't.

Mya's proof of that. I've never stepped on anybody's toes. Mya can have Rashad. I'm giving her to him. I swear she's going to regret the day she ever ruined my FUCKIN' LIFE to EXPOSE ME. Everything she's done can't be undone. I've never been a malicious person, but THAT BITCH she's going to regret the day she ever mentioned my FUCKIN' name or took any pictures of me. I can promise you that. I know she loves Rashad.

I saw that at my clinic. I don't have anything to do with what the two of them had going on. More of the reason why I stayed out of it. She never addressed ME she addressed HIM. Had I known she recorded us. I would've beat her ass in my clinic. Rashad broke my heart once. I know what that feels like. My head's lying on Crimson's shoulder. She ran her hands through my hair. I know she's trying to calm me but it's not working. My nerves are a wreck.

"Danielle are you okay? Are you at least going to respond to any of his messages," she asked? I looked at Crimson like she's motherfuckin' crazy. Fuck Rashad. I thought I would never say those words again. Sometimes some shit ain't meant. I don't think we're meant. Rashad ended US. He doesn't deserve a conversation from me. I cut him off once and I'll do it again.

"Are you FUCKIN' SERIOUS right now? Rashad just filed MY divorce for me without my FUCKIN' signature. No Crimson I'm not okay! Please stop asking me that. Fuck Rashad.

I don't give a fuck what he has to say. He's said plenty already. What more does he have to say? The moment we land. I'm changing my number and please don't give it to him. I don't mean to take it out on you. I'm sorry Crimson my life is fuckin' ruined.

My husband hasn't even fuckin' texted me. I've always took the good with the bad. I've always bounced back from all the bullshit I've been through. This time I might not be so lucky." I want to give up so bad, but I can't. Bitches have been rooting for me to fail since day one. Failure isn't a fuckin' option. I know why Baine hasn't called. We need to talk about it. I'm sure it won't be a civil conversation. I know it's no coming back from what I did. I don't have a problem with leaving.

"Danielle, I get it! Real women never tap out. We've been through a lot of shit in our life and this is another obstacle that WE'LL have to overcome. I agree with you one hundred percent. I know you're mad and I get it. I'm not going to bc your punching bag. It is what it is. It's not my fault you put your pussy on the wrong nigga. Rashad he's in love with you Danielle. I know you love him too. You don't mean that. How do you think Rashad felt Danielle? He's human too. Let's be honest bitch you should've left after you gave the speech.

You knew you were playing a dangerous game. I'll give you that. If you had NUTS them motherfuckas was heavy tonight.

When Baine was in the room you acted like you didn't see Rashad. I think that's what hurt him the most. Men can't keep the same composure as women.

Why do you think it's so many side bitches? They're willing to be quiet. A man won't do that. Have you heard from Baine? What are we going to do? You're human we all make mistakes. I think Baine will forgive you. Do you still want your marriage? If so, are you going to fight for it?" I haven't thought about any of the questions Crimson asked about my marriage. I don't have any fight in me.

"I'll be honest with you Crimson. I love Rashad and I love Baine too. I don't care about his feelings Crimson. Why should I? It's CLEAR that nigga didn't give a fuck about MINE. Let's be honest he's NEVER cared about MINE. This isn't the first time he's fucked me OVER but it's his last. I've been married to Baine for five years. I couldn't pretend to not be Baine's wife just to accommodate him. He's knows I'm still married.

When he decided to force his dick between my legs. He knew I was still married to Baine. He knew that. He also knew that I was going to leave Baine. I didn't want to continue to creep with Rashad behind Baine's back. I wanted to leave on my terms and not Rashad's. Baine and I will never be able to be together. Maybe if I cheated with anybody else but Rashad. A man can cheat on a woman and expect us to forgive. Let those tables turn a man won't be as forgiving. I know we're done and I'm okay with that." I know my husband. I know this divorce will be nasty.

"Two wrongs don't make a right. You don't know what's going to happen Danielle, but you need to have a conversation with your husband.

Don't just leave without letting him know. He deserves that much. If you were willing to leave Baine, you haven't been telling me everything. You've been keeping a lot of secrets. If you want to be with him. I have faith that y'all can work it out."

"I wish it was that simple Crimson but it's not. You have more FAITH than I ever will. Baine and I need to have conversation and we will. I already know it's the END. It's something I have to come to terms with." Baine and I have been over for a few years now. I've been the only one keeping this marriage together. He's stepped out on me a few times throughout our marriage. I wanted to leave years ago. Baine wouldn't allow me too. He begged me to stay. He threatened to kill me if I left. I'm tired of pretending.

Over the years it got better, but he always reverted to his old ways. The moment he found out I did him, how he did me. He wouldn't let that ride or forgive me. I cheated and he has too. We'll never be even. I wouldn't dare tell Crimson what I've went through with him. I wouldn't want her to look at me differently. I found myself crying just thinking about all the shit he's put me through. Crimson wiped my tears.

"It's okay Danielle to cry. I know it's a lot going that you're not ready to speak on. I love you and I would never judge you. I'm here.

I hate that you don't feel comfortable enough to tell me. I swear if Baine ever fucked you over. He won't have to worry about Rashad killing him. He'll have to worry about me." I looked at Crimson with wide eyes. She didn't blink once.

I know how Crimson feels about Baine. I cheated on him and everybody knows. She'll see the real him. He's cheated on me numerous of times. He has plenty to show for that can't be taken back. I'm not ready to speak on that. I want to enjoy this trip and clear my mind. Even if it's only for a few days.

I felt a soft tap on my shoulders. I wiped the sleep out the corners of my eyes. I didn't realize I dozed off. I needed the sleep especially after all the crying I've been doing. I'm glad sleep took over me. It's God Momma Cheree. I gave her a faint smile. I appreciate her so much for coming to my rescue.

"Wake up baby we're here," she smiled. I didn't have anything with me, but my purse and shoes. I brought a pair of flip flops and charger from the airport. God momma Cheree gave me and Crimson some clothes to change into. Damn my feet still hurt.

"Crimson can you please cut your phone on and call your husband. Camina's called my phone from her IPAD ten DAMN times looking for YOU. Your husband has called my phone twice this morning.

I understand what you're doing Crimson and I respect it but cut your damn phone on and call your husband and kids." Camina's bad as hell.

I'm sure she tried to call my phone. I blocked her bad ass. I can't stand her little bad ass. I locked eyes at her on my way out. She rolled her eyes at me and stuck her tongue out.

"Ma, Camina doesn't want anything she has her father. I know she's fine. As long as he's around and her Uncle Rashad she doesn't need me."

"Crimson call your husband and check on your kids. You don't know what Camina needs. You and Griff have great communication don't lose that being stubborn. You need to check on my grandson he's a baby and he needs you." Crimson was stubborn as hell. I'm glad God Momma Cheree checked her ass. Crimson did as she was told.

"Ma have you called my father. He's called my phone a few times too looking for you too?" Cheree looked at Crimson and rolled her eyes

"Crimson your father can't clock my moves. He's not my man and he's NEVER been my husband. I'm so glad to take this trip because who knows when he'll see me again." Crimson looked at me first then Cheree.

"What are you trying to say ma? Why are you leaving me, and I need you?" Crimson's spoiled as fuck. A big smiled appeared on Cheree's face. I knew she was fuckin' with Crimson.

I love Crimson and Cheree's bond I want that. I could use my mother right about now. I envy what Crimson and Cheree are building.

"I'm not leaving you Crimson. I need a vacation. I'm sick of your father. To avoid me killing him. I need a few weeks to myself. Don't worry I made plans to take Camina with me because you and her father can't handle her."

"Oh okay," she sighed. Crimson checked Griff's ass last night. I was surprised. I don't care about Griff knowing where we are. I just didn't want Rashad to know. I checked my phone. I didn't have any missed calls or texts from Baine. Which leads me to believe he didn't go home. I'm not even surprised. If this was years ago, I would've cried, but I'm all cried out. Baine finding out that I cheated gives him the opportunity to cheat. I looked at the clock it's a little after 6:00 a.m. I still have a business to run. Baine's very spiteful.

We finally made it to Hawaii. Our flight just landed. We've been cleared to exit the plane. It's time to handle business. I got to be two steps ahead of Baine. When you've been with a man for so long you know how he moves. The flight was eleven hours. We had a layover in LA. On our way back I want to go to Crenshaw and Slauson to pay my respects to **Nipsey Hussle The Great.** I need to call my office manager. We walked through the airport. I don't know if Cheree had a car, but I couldn't really talk how I need to because it's loud in here. I know she's up.

"Come on follow me! Our ride is out here waiting on us," she explained. Cool me and Crimson followed Cheree out the airport. My phone had enough juice to complete the call I need to make. We finally exited the airport. Cheree sat up front. Me and Crimson climbed in the back. Cheree's friend is pushing a fuckin' Maybach Benz. She kept looking at me out the corner of her eyes. I waived and gave her a faint smile. I grabbed my phone to call Madison. She answered on the first ring. Thank you, Jesus.

"Good morning Danielle! It's early! Is everything okay? Do you need me to do anything," she asked? I swear Madison is everything. She knew I wouldn't be calling her this early if I didn't need her.

"Good morning! My love yes and no. I know it's early, but I need you to do something for me," I sighed. Damn I can't even talk in peace. Cheree's friend is creepy. She keeps looking at me through the rear-view mirror. I hope she isn't a lesbian. I like DICK! The DICK is the reason why I'm here.

"Sure, boss lady! Let me get my planner so I can take some notes." Madison she's always on it. I'm blessed to have her. Me and Madison have a great bound. It's not even our business and she's about to get to it.

"Okay! I'm going to be out of the office for a week or so maybe. I need you to hire some movers right FUCKIN' now Madison. I need everything moved out the office today. All the office equipment must go.

EVERYTHING I don't want to leave anything behind. I have a storage facility. I'll text you the gate code and they'll give you the keys to my units.

Call all the staff and let them today they're off with pay until the end of the week. Let Michelle know to reschedule all clients until further notice.

I've been looking at a few spots. I need you to meet with the realtor and Facetime me while you're there so I can check out everything." I saw two properties that I'm interested in. My realtor has two more that she wants to show me before I make my final decision.

"Boss lady what's going on is everything okay. Why are we moving suddenly? It's 6:00 a.m. I don't know where I can find some contractors this early. I know some hood niggas who can get this stuff moved in about two hours but it's going to cost you," she explained. I really didn't want to say what's going on because I don't know Cheree's friend. Oh well she doesn't know me to judge me.

"Madison it may be the beginning of a nasty divorce. Call them I'm paying. I just need it done ASAP. I just want to have things in order because I still have a business to run. I help my staff feed their families and live comfortably. Nobody's going to come in between that."

"Are you serious? I'm sorry to hear that. I'm praying for you, boss lady. I'll have this shit moved. Oops I meant stuff moved before we're scheduled to open.

I sent Michelle a text and she's on it." I knew Madison was hood chick it slips out sometimes. I'm forever grateful for her.

"It's okay! I appreciate you for everything you do! Once you get that handled. Tomorrow I'll have you meet with the realtor to look at few suites." I trust Madison she has great taste. I'm not that picky. I can always hire a contractor to make all my dreams come true.

"I'll do it today! See if she'll be free after 1:00 p.m. Boss LADY we can't drag our feet. Let's close a deal today if we can. You pay me to assist. I'm here to assist. I love our staff but ain't nobody getting a free check off you. They can use their PTO time, or they can charge it to the game. Get yourself together and I'll handle everything else. Call me if you need me. Send me the code and I'll call you once everything is moved. I'll call and get the utilities disconnected."

"Thank you, Madison, I love you so much. What would I do without you?"

"Boss lady I love you too. You don't want to find out but that's neither here nor there. Relax I got you. Enjoy your vacation which I know you want. You were there for me doing my divorce. I got you. I have a ZERO TOLERANCE FOR FUCK NIGGAS." I finished talking with Madison we ended our call. Crimson wrapped her arm around my neck. I looked at Crimson and we shared a smile with each other.

“That's my best friend! Handle your business. BOSS,” she beamed. My business is my baby. I won’t let anyone interfere with that. I worked hard for this. My staff depend on me. I employ a lot of single black women and Baine won’t stop us from eating. I know how he operates.

“I'm trying girl Madison is on it. I got to call my realtor in two hours so Madison can view some suites. I need a computer like right now.

Excuse me God momma Cheree I need a laptop. Can you take me some where later to buy one PLEASE?” I asked. I need a computer ASAP. I can do a lot from my phone, but I need a laptop. Before Cheree could speak up. Her friend answered for her.

“I have a MacBook Pro. I never used it before. You can have it,” she explained. She looked at me through her rear-view mirror. It’s like her eyes were trying to read me. This lady is creeping me out. I get the gay vibe from her it's making me nervous. I don't know if I can stay at her house for a few days.

“Thank you but I can't accept that. I wouldn't feel comfortable. I prefer to buy my own,” I explained. What woman you know is giving out MacBook Pro’s just because? I think I need to get my own place for a few days.

“I hear you, but it's a gift rather you want it or not it's yours.”

"Okay thank you." I elbowed Crimson and she looked at me. Our eyes had their own conversation. I sent Crimson a text. I've never been a good whisperer. The last thing I need is for this lady to hear me talking about her behind her back.

Me-Bitch your momma's friend is creeping me out. I don't like the way she's looking at me. I'm uncomfortable. I'm getting the gay vibe. Your momma ain't gay is she lol!

Crimson's stupid ass couldn't even hold her laugh in. I elbowed her ass so she can shut the fuck up. The lady looked at me again through her rear-view mirror and smiled at me. I couldn't even take in the scenery like I wanted too, because I started handling business the moment I got in the car. Hawaii's a beautiful place.

"Excuse me! Is it okay if I roll down the windows and let some air in," I asked?

"Sure, it's fine." I rolled down the windows. Hawaii's beautiful. I just want to lay on the beach and relax. The wind is blowing my hair all in my face.

Chapter-6

Daniella

Danielle's so beautiful. I can't stop looking at her. I can't believe I created something so beautiful. I know I'm creeping her out, but I can't help myself. I had to blink twice to stop the tears from falling. She looks exactly like me and Coop. The pictures Cheree sent me of her a few months ago didn't do her any justice. My baby is a BOSS. I can tell she's been crying because her eyes were swollen. She's a survivor even through whatever bullshit she has going on with her husband she's still making moves and handling her business.

I admire that. It shows my blood flows through her. I had a strong feeling when Cheree went back home for Crimson. I knew our time would be coming soon. I didn't raise Danielle because I couldn't. I wanted too but my mother didn't want Danielle with me and Coop because of the life we lived. I did a lot shit that I'm not proud of. I can't change none of it. I wouldn't. We always took care of Danielle she's never wanted for anything. My mother never worked Coop made sure of that.

My mother called me and told me what happened at the wedding reception. I play a lot of games but MOTHERFUCKA don't ever touch my momma. I don't know Danielle's husband.

I didn't think to do a background check on him because my mother never gave me the vibe that he's abusive. I knew the Rashad guy broke her heart my momma told me that. I wanted to kill him for that. I understand that you're mad. You ain't the first nigga to get cheated on and you won't be the last. Mr. Mahone will fuckin' see me. Whenever Danielle decides to touch down in East Atlanta, I'll be right by her side. I got a bullet with his fuckin' name on it. He touched the wrong fuckin' one.

Coop's called me over twenty times asking when are we coming? I know he's anxious to see Danielle. I didn't want to tell him why she was coming. I had to make up a lie. His crazy ass would start having flash backs of when I cheated. Nigga that's over twenty years ago. I'm kind of nervous, but it's now or never.

Cheree told me how Crimson flipped out on her when they reunited. I laughed for days. I don't know Crimson, but she looks like Cheree and acts like her too. I don't know what she Cheree expected Crimson inherited her ways from her mother. I know Danielle and Crimson where talking about me I can feel it. It's crazy our daughters are as tight as we were back in the day. It's one of the reasons, I kept looking at her and Crimson interact. I forgot to congratulate Crimson on her union.

"Congratulations Crimson on your union. Marriage is a beautiful thing if it's with the right one," I beamed. I looked through the rear-view mirror at Danielle.

She had a smug look on her face. I smiled at her. She gave me a faint smile.

I swear to God if that motherfucka has been fuckin' over my daughter, he'll regret it. I put that shit on his MOTHERFUCKIN' momma. I can guarantee you a BITCH don't want to fuckin' see me behind DANIELLE COOPER. I didn't raise Danielle, but I won't hesitate to kill anybody behind her. I don't give a fuck. I've committed a lot of crimes. I'll do to jail time behind MINE. The moment she stepped in the car I listened to her conduct fuckin' business. She didn't have to do it, but she did that shows a lot about her character.

"Thank you!" I can tell my baby is going through it. I can feel her pain. It hurts even more that she doesn't even recognize who I am. I can only blame myself and nobody else. I hope she allows me to be in her life. I've never been afraid of anything in my life, but I'm scared of Danielle's reaction when she's finds out I'm her mother. My mother assured me I'll be fine. Danielle will welcome me with open arms. I hope so. I just want to hug her.

We finally made our way to my house. I don't care how much money we had. Coop was still a hood nigga. He didn't give a fuck who knew it. I keep trying to tell him he's not a young nigga anymore. He's an OG he hated that. Coop hasn't aged that much.

He had the salt and pepper look going on. I wasn't surprised to see him outside waiting on the porch waiting on us. I rolled my eyes at him. I pulled in the garage. I didn't want him to scare Danielle off.

I don't know who wanted to see her more me or him. I couldn't even get out the car good this nigga was at my door already. He snatched it open. I wanted to smack the shit out of his impatient ass. I'm sure Cheree could sense I was irritated. I heard her laugh.

"What's up? I know you saw me outside. What's up Cheree long time no see. I heard you've been running around with Bone. Tell that nigga I said what's up." Cheree waived at Coop and rolled her eyes. I know she had something smart to say. I wish she would stop playing with Bone and give that man what he wants. I really wish Coop and Bone could go back to how they use too.

"Coop I've never been the messenger. He ain't hard to find tell him yourself," Cheree stated. Coop grilled Cheree and focused his attention back on me.

"Don't start! We have company. Can I get out the car or can you carry me out," I asked? I swear Coop loves to show out. He leaned in the car. He looked around. I know he locked eyes with Danielle. I can feel it. He picked me up and carried me out. I swear this is not the way I wanted our daughter to see us.

"Put me down Coop you're embarrassing me," I blushed. He bit my neck. I tried to swat him away. He wasn't budging.

"I don't care you've been gone for a long time. I thought you were never coming back. You saw me outside waiting on you." Coop whispered in my ear. "She's beautiful she looks like her mother. I'm ready to introduce myself."

Coop opened the back door. Danielle stepped out and Crimson followed suit. Crimson she's Danielle's keeper. She's very protective of her.

"Come on ladies follow me you have to excuse my husband. He doesn't know how to act." They followed us in the house. Damn I'm nervous as shit. I guess Coop noticed. He grabbed my hand for reassurance. The moment we stepped inside the aroma filled my nose.

Coop cooked us breakfast. My mother told him all of Danielle's favorites. I guess I should do this now because it's awkward. We made our way through the kitchen. I'm sure they're hungry. The flight was eleven hours. I know Danielle didn't have any clothes.

My mother told me her size. I went out and brought her things that I think she would wear. I'm still fly. Whenever me and Coop step on the scene all these young niggas out here be checking for me. All these young bitches be hating.

“Hey, would y'all like to eat first before you get situated.” Cheree and Crimson nodded their head in agreement. Danielle was kind of hesitant. I’m sure she wanted to freshen up. She needs to eat first. After she eats, we’ll have a talk.

“Sure,” she sighed. They took a seat at the table. Cheree washed her hands and fixed Crimson's plate. I grabbed three plates to fix mine, Danielle’s and Coop’s.

“Danielle what do you want,” I asked? She looked at me.

“Everything,” she sighed. Coop took a seat right beside her. I swear I remember the day I had her. He would dote on her so much. He’s doing it now and I can tell she’s uncomfortable. I looked at him. My eyes poured into his begging him to back up, but he wouldn’t. Coop don’t give a fuck she’s his baby girl. I swear he can never follow my lead.

“Excuse me can you back up please your making me uncomfortable,” she argued. Coop looked me and gave me a stern look. I put our plates in the oven warmer. I know he’s going to fuckin’ ruin it. Cheree looked at me. I guess now is the time. It’s now or never.

“Danielle can we talk to you in private,” I asked? Danielle backed up from the table. She stood up and looked at me and Coop. I can’t really read her. It’s time I let her know who we are.

"No, you can't! I'm sorry God momma Cheree but your friend and this man are creeping me the FUCK out. Anything you need to say to me. You can say in front of them we're family." Cheree and Crimson looked at me with wide eyes. It's to be expected. She doesn't know us.

"Okay." I grabbed our plates out the oven. I slid Coop his plate and gave Danielle hers. I don't know how she's going to take this. I can tell she's already on the fence. I can't blame her. She doesn't know us and it's not her fault. It's ours.

"Danielle, I'm Daniella Cooper your mother, and this is your father Gary Cooper," I smiled. I can't read her. Tears flooded her eyes. I just want to hold her, but I'm scared. Danielle tried to get up, but Crimson held her. Coop stepped in and grabbed his baby girl. Danielle wrapped her arms around him. Coop's crying too. I swear I've never seen this man cry since the day she was born.

"Danielle baby girl I'm sorry. I'm excited to see you. I didn't mean to creep you out. I haven't seen you since you were about four years old. I love you. I NEVER STOPPED. I've been telling your mother for a few months now it's time. I don't know what happened and why you're here. I'm glad you're here.

If you don't ever want to go back home, you don't have too. I want to be a part of your life if you would allow me too. Daniella why are you standing over there and our daughter is right here," he asked?

I made my way over to Danielle and Coop. I knelt in front of Danielle. I removed her hair from her face. I wiped her tears with my thumbs. Danielle's eyes were trained on me.

"Danielle, I know I'm sorry isn't enough but I am. I'm sorry! I've made a lot of mistakes in my life. You were never a MISTAKE. I don't have many regrets in life but ONE! The only regret I have is not being able to raise you and watch you grow up. When your father and I went on the run. I wanted you to come with us. My mother and Mother Dear wouldn't allow it.

I've been living with a broken heart for years. I'm so glad you're here Danielle. I want to be a part of your life if you would allow me too." Danielle wrapped her arms around me. She hugged me so tight. She started crying again. I tried to hold my tears in for as long as I could. I couldn't hold them anymore. "I love you so much Danielle." I've wanted to do this for years. I'm so happy Cheree called me and setup up the opportunity to make it happen.

"I love y'all too. I want y'all in my life. I need you two right now. Thank you, God momma Cheree for bringing me here," she cried. My mother knows my child better than I do. I'm glad she accepted us with open arms. We ate breakfast. I showed Danielle upstairs to her room. I sat the laptop on her bed with the charger. Coop and I cleaned the kitchen. He walked up behind and wrapped his hands around my waist. He bit my neck. I swear I can never get tired of this man.

"Coop stop please! We have guests in the house, and I don't want our daughter to see us like this," I moaned. Coop grabbed my hand and led me to the table. He took a seat in the chair and pulled me onto his lap.

"Daniella, there are no secrets between us. I'm going to ask you again. Why is my daughter here? I want her here and you know that? What the fuck happened to her. She didn't bring any clothes with her. I find that odd. She didn't have to bring any because I'll buy her whatever she wants. I may have not raised her. I know something is going on.

You can either tell me right now or I'll catch a flight to East Atlanta and find out what the fuck is up with my child. I'll ask the nigga that gave her his last name what the fuck is up. I'm from East Atlanta and my face card is still good. So, what's it going to be. I heard you talking to your mother and you mentioned killing somebody what's the fuckin' address and I'll handle that." I swear I can't get away with nothing without Coop finding out. He's needs to sit down. I can't enjoy the moment. I expected it. Coop wants to know everything. I know he'll ask Danielle himself. If he feels that she's not telling the truth. He'll go to the source which would be her husband.

"Coop calm down and listen! Your daughter cheated on her husband. She didn't tell me that Cheree did. The guy she cheated with he's Crimson's husband best friend. He exposed Danielle at the wedding. She ran and she came here. I got an issue with her husband because he pushed my momma and she fell.

I'll show that nigga myself how it feels to be pushed in the fuckin' dirt." Coop started sizing me up. He gripped the bridge of his nose. I know he was about to say some shit that I wouldn't like.

"She cheated I wonder where she gets that shit from," he smirked. I pushed Coop up off me. I smacked him in his fuckin' face. I'm not beat for his shit. "Watch your hands Daniella. I ain't done shit. I'm just stating facts." I swear I'm going to fuck Coop up in this kitchen.

"Watch your fuckin' mouth? You cheated too. I know you didn't FUCKIN' forget. What the fuck are you trying to say? I cheated on you ONE MOTHERFUCKIN' time compared to you cheating on me numerous times. MOTHERFUCKA we ain't EVEN. You could've left way back then and we wouldn't even be having this conversation. I wasn't even married to you then! Don't fuckin' try me Coop. I've always owned up to my shit. Own up to yours. It's one of the reasons why I didn't want to say shit, because I knew you would bring up some old shit.

It's too much like fuckin' right for you not too. It doesn't matter where she got it from. She cheated so fuckin' what. It's not the end of the fuckin' world. BITCHES get cheated on every day and suck it up. He can move on OR HE CAN forgive her. If not FUCK HIM, he can be replaced." Coop stepped in my personal. He cupped my chin roughly. I knew he felt what the FUCK I SAID. I wanted him too. We all make mistakes nobody is perfect we're all human.

"Lower your motherfuckin' voice Daniella! You said what you had to say. Now listen to what the fuck I have to say. I made a mistake. I shouldn't have said what I said. I'm sorry I can't take none of it back. She cheated okay I understand that. You mean to tell me it was so bad she couldn't stay at home and work it out? I'm a man and I know women. Women only run if they're scared. You cheated on me and you didn't run when I caught you. I want to know why my DAUGHTER ran from that nigga?" I swear Coop is the worst. I couldn't fuckin' run if I wanted too. Shit Bone had me and Cheree cornered in.

I just knew I was about to die when Coop found out I cheated on him. I swear Cheree wasn't even fuckin' with Bone because they were into it as usual. He didn't give a fuck she was still his no matter what. Niggas can dish it, but they can't take it. I don't know why Danielle ran. I care. I'm going to find out. I'm glad she decided to come home to see us. Her father is so fuckin' crazy if he finds out her husband has done anything to her. She won't be leaving this house. He meant what the fuck he said about her never leaving.

"I hear what you're saying Coop. I don't want to think the worst of this nigga. She ran because she wanted to run let's leave it at that. Our blood flows through her. I hope she wouldn't stay with him if he did. IF A NIGGA ever BEAT my DAUGHTER, he wouldn't live long enough to catch his next breath. I don't want to talk about it anymore. Ask her whatever you want because I don't like bullshit lingering on my mind." Coop knows I'm always on a hundred.

I'll go to one thousand really fuckin' quick. I ain't never beat my child or whoop her. I be damn if a nigga does it.

“Daniella. Make this shit make FUCKIN' sense to me. Danielle is always welcomed home. I always wanted her home. You know that. I should've never listened to your fuckin' momma. I protected you. You think I wouldn't protect my fuckin' child. I would give my life any day to save hers. The day I check out from this FUCKED UP place. EVERYTHING is FUCKIN' hers.

Face the fuckin' FACTS DANIELLA. You ain't never been blindsided to nothing. I ain't saying the nigga beat her but it's a FUCKIN' Possibility. I hope it's all in my mind but if it FUCKIN' AIN'T. DANIELLA YOU SHOULD PRAY IT AIN'T. I swear to God I'll stop that nigga from FUCKIN' breathing. She said she needed US. In all my years of living. I ain't never ran from NANN NIGGA and GUESS WHAT MY DAUGHTER AIN'T EITHER. WHO IS THIS FUCKIN' NIGGA AND WHERE CAN I FIND HIM? I'LL BE GONE FOR A FEW DAYS.”

“I understand that you're concerned, and you have every right to be. You're not going any fuckin' where. Don't let that nigga rain on our fuckin' parade. Enjoy your daughter while we can. When she leaves, we'll be right behind her? You're not about to fuck up the city if I'm not with you. You can sit down I know you're anxious but not more than me.” Coop bit down on my neck. I know he’s mad but oh well deal with it.

Chapter-7

Danielle

I'm emotional in a good way. I can't stop the tears from falling if I wanted too. I can't think of the last time I've cried this much. It's been a minute. The tears that are escaping from eyes are tears of joy. I can't believe what just happened to me. It's going to take a minute for all of this to sink in. I've prayed for this. I wanted this for the longest. God finally answered my prayers. I know my parents weren't there for me growing up physically.

I know they took care of me financially. Anything I wanted I had growing up. I knew my Gigi couldn't afford it, so it had to be coming from somewhere. Now I know my parents were the source. I've never been the type of person to judge anyone not knowing their circumstances. I'm not holding that against my parents because they weren't there. I'm focused on the right NOW. I need them right now.

I should've known something was up. I didn't know my parents lived here. It's crazy because Cheree gave me a hint. She said she wanted me to meet someone. I didn't think I would be meeting my parents. I forgot she said that. It makes sense now why she kept looking at me. I'm forever grateful for her setting this up because she didn't have too. My mother and father were still together that's amazing.

My mother she's so beautiful. She doesn't look forty-eight. She could past for my sister. I couldn't stop looking at her either now that I know who she is. My father he doesn't look that old either. The grey hair in his beard are the only signs of his age. I'm a mixture of the two of them. I think it's cute how my father dotes on her. I adore that. It warmed my soul to witness that. I guess true love does exist somewhere. I'll never know I think it's a little too late for me.

Their home is so beautiful! Shit my room is fuckin' beautiful. It looks better than the master suite at my house. My mother set my room up nice. The moment I stepped inside. I couldn't help to admire the décor. She has amazing taste. I might have to take them up on their offer.

My closet is flooded with nothing but FUCKIN' designer shoes, purses. Everything a woman like me would need. I'm like a kid in a candy store. I can't stop thumbing through my closet. The vanity in my room is nice. I had bottles on top of bottles of perfume, lotions. I had panties and bra's that are my size. How did she know all this?

My mother has great taste. I have no complaints. I need to call my Gigi. I'm sure she's worried about me. My phones fully charged. I blocked Rashad. I got to get over him. He's bad for me. It's been proving on more than one occasion. I'm not fuckin' with him anymore. It's a wrap. I love him but I got to him let him go. If he loves me, he'll let me go. What we had and what we started it's over. It could never be us.

Baine still hasn't called or sent me a text. I can't lie, last night my mind was clouded with visions of him. Today I'm thinking about reaching out to him to see where his head is at. He didn't care about me cheating. He just hates people found out. He's not calling because he's out cheating, I can feel it. I grabbed my phone to call my Gigi. I can't worry about what Baine's doing.

My Gigi she's more important than him. She answered on the first ring. A huge smile appeared on my face. I'm sure she'll kill me if she knew I fled the city because of my infidelities. My Gigi told me to never run from anything. Normally I wouldn't but either way my life would be still be a mess. I didn't see a way out.

"Good morning Danielle! I've been waiting on you to call me. Are you okay? I've been worried sick about you. You can't FUCKIN' do that. You're grown but you're not to grown enough to NOT pick up the phone," she stated. I knew my Gigi would worry and that's the last I wanted her to do. I'm going through some things. I don't want to hear the I told you so and you know better. I can't change the past and I don't want too. I could've gone about it a different way, but I didn't.

"Good morning Gigi! I'm sorry it's a lot going on. I'm trying to cope with everything. I'm sorry for embarrassing you yesterday. I didn't mean for that to happen," I sighed.

I'm sure Gigi and Mother Dear's friends were talking about my ass. I swear old folks gossip more than young people. Gigi and Mother Dear, do it all day. I swear Mother Dear cut her eyes at me so quick it was crazy.

"Danielle you didn't embarrass me, you embarrassed your husband. You don't have to apologize to me. It was very entertaining. I wish you would've stayed instead of running. I understand why you ran. Danielle I've never spoke on your marriage. If you're happy I'm happy.

If you love him, I love him. What I will say is The MOTHERFUCKA that you CALL YOUR HUSBAND pushed me on his way out and I fell. You know and HE FUCKIN' KNOWS I find that very disrespectful and inappropriate. I saw aside of Baine that I've never saw before.

I never would've expected that coming from him. I'm glad RASHAD beat his ass. Your mother called me last night. She told me you were coming there with Cheree. I'm guessing you've made it already. I wish I could be there to witness the two of you reuniting. I know you're happy to see your mother and father Danielle.

Don't let them spoil you and trick you into not coming back home. I know how they operate. I'll be honest with you I told your mother what happened with Baine and she wasn't happy about it.

I would've preferred to speak with you first, but you didn't call me like I expected you too. I didn't go into details about what happened at the wedding. It's not my business to tell. It’s yours. If you feel comfortable enough to talk to her feel free to do so. Your mother she holds grudges and she doesn’t forgive so easily.

She doesn’t forgive or forget. I didn’t want that for you. Let me put a little bug in your ear. Your mother and father are very dangerous and that’s a fuckin’ UNDERSTATEMENT. I can’t believe I gave birth to that.

I didn't want you to get caught up in their lifestyle. What you have now is what I always wanted for you. I don't know how much you love Baine because I know you do. Danielle if your father gets a whiff of this, you'll be a FUCKIN’ widow. Gary, Goldie or Coop whatever he calls himself now. He’s a fuckin’ monster trust me he’s going to pry. Every action doesn't need a reaction but that should've never happened.

I know your mother. I raised her and molded her into part of the woman she is today. She's not going to let that slide. I understand he's hurt but he fucked up when he touched me. Hurt people hurt people. I hope that he’s never hurt you Danielle.

I knew you and Rashad had something going at Mother Dear's house when you ran out of there crying. I knew then it was something going on between the two of you. I saw it you love him, and he loves you.

I wish you would've divorced Baine before you decided to pursue him again Why do you keep running from him? You love him Danielle because if you didn't you wouldn't keep running. Stop FUCKIN' running. RUNNING ain't never solved SHIT. If it did you wouldn't be there. You can't help who you love. You can't hide from love. I'm not saying what Rashad done was right, but he didn't give a DAMN about your HUSBAND knowing about the two of you.

He knows what he wants, and he doesn't care who knows it. Instead of Baine trying to figure out from him if you cheated. He should've been running after you. Why didn't he run after you? Danielle if you love Rashad baby let that man know because he doesn't give a damn about fighting for you. If you love your husband fight for your marriage too. I raised you to make the right decisions. I hate to say it but you're playing a dangerous game.

Somebody is going to end up hurt and I don't want it to be you." I found myself crying again Baine had no reason to touch my fuckin' Gigi. He has me so fucked up. I don't give a fuck what WE HAVE going on. My Gigi she's off fuckin' limits. I would never do that to his fuckin' mother. I knew this shit was about to get ugly. I swear this is just the fuckin' beginning. It makes sense now why he hasn't called. He's seeking revenge.

"Gigi I'm sorry he shouldn't have done that. I haven't heard from him. I'll handle it. I don't want my parents getting involved with my problems."

"Don't be sorry Danielle. Don't ever apologize for his actions. You've done nothing wrong. I want you to enjoy your mother and father while you can. Relax Danielle and think about what I said about Rashad. How many times are you going to run but you keep running back into him?"

"I hear you Gigi! Rashad and I will never work too much stuff happened then and too much stuff happened now. I'm going to let it go." Rashad and I can't be together. He ruined us by not following my lead.

"I hear you Danielle, but do you hear you. If you want to work, it out with your husband I support that. Two wrongs don't make a right. The first time he made a mistake it was on him. This time it's on the both of y'all. Hey what do I know. I'm sixty seventy years old. Enjoy your vacation baby you need it." I swear if it ain't one thing it's something else. Baine got me fucked up. I grabbed my phone to call him. He answered on the first ring. I knew he was out moving around his background is loud and noisy.

"What the fuck are you calling my phone for DANIELLE? You need to take your motherfuckin' ass home? Where the fuck did you stay at last night. I never thought MY fuckin' wife would be a slut. BITCH you out here giving my fuckin' pussy away to Rashad, in a fuckin' building I brought you. Danielle you're so fuckin' stupid that nigga couldn't take you to a room to fuck YOU. His broke ass had to fuck you in my shit. Bitch I'm going to fuckin' hurt you.

It makes sense now why you stop giving me the pussy. He cheated on you once he'll cheat on you again." I had to pull my ear away from the phone. It's plenty of reasons why I stop giving him the pussy. I knew he was in front of some people that's why he's showing out. I never thought he would stoop this low.

"Are you done yet," I asked?

"What the fuck do you mean am I done yet. Danielle, where are you? You got a lot of motherfuckin' heart today. Yesterday your sneaky pussy ass ran. Keep that same fuckin' ENERGY TODAY! When I see you Danielle, I'm going to put my hands on you. When were you going to tell me you FUCKIN' cheated? You made plans to leave me for him? Danielle, if you think I'm going to let you run off and be happy with RASHAD. BITCH you're sadly FUCKIN' MISTAKEN.

I will FUCKIN' KILL YOU and you'll watch me from your grave love another BITCH that ain't YOU. It ain't going down like that." I pulled my ear away from the phone. I swear I don't want to do this with him. I know we need to have a conversation, but he's going in. I have no choice but to defend myself. He wants to kill me because I cheated on him. Baine's really showing his ass because I cheated on him.

"BAINE, I don't give A FUCK how you may feel about me. I ain't never been a FUCKIN' SLUT. I ain't NEVER BEEN A FUCKIN' HOE.

My PUSSY ain’t got no MILES on IT! You got me confused with them BITCHES you use to fuck with. It’s ONLY ONE NIGGA in this world that could say HE fucked ME besides YOU. Whatever me and you got going has nothing to do with my fuckin' grandmother. I can't believe you would push her down. You got too much fuckin’ pride to take the high road. Why are you putting our business out in the streets,” I asked?

I hate to even take it there with Baine but he’s forcing my hand. I cheated one fuckin’ time and this is how he acts. I know he’s in front of Ike. I didn't want my mother or father to hear me. I be damn if I let Baine talk to me like I'm an average bitch out here in these streets because I AIN'T. Damn I can't believe this nigga is getting me out of fuckin' character.

“Danielle, SEE that's the motherfuckin problem you want to gloat about how you fucked that NIGGA. You let him put some MILES on your PUSSY. How come you couldn't tell me TO MY FACE you fucked him? Any BITCH I EVER FUCKED YOU KNEW ABOUT HER. Them bitches made sure you knew about them. The best thing you could've EVER done was run in the fuckin' SHOES I brought you.

I hope you broke your FUCKIN' ANKLES. MY MOMMA always told ME NEVER BUY A BITCH A PAIR SHOES, THAT HOE WILL WALK ALL OVER YOU. She ain't never lied.

You ain't REAL you FAKE as FUCK. I do what I want Danielle, you know that. I know your Gigi knew you were fuckin' Rashad her eyes told it all. Rashad put our business out in the streets when he wanted everybody to know he's fuckin' my EX wife," he argued. It's pointless to even have a conversation with him. I hung up the phone in his face. He called my phone back. I answered. I didn't say anything.

"Why did you hang up in my face," he asked? Why else would I hang up? He's not talking about shit I want to hear. I swear niggas are funny. I always knew If Baine and I divorced it would be ugly. To make matters worse he wants to throw it up in my face about him fuckin' other bitches.

I swear Baine's being a typical nigga. I know he's fuckin' other bitches because his nasty ass would always fuck the wrong bitch and bring me back some SHIT. It's funny now he wants to GLOAT about it in front of his NIGGAS. Tell your niggas how them hoes you were FUCKIN' burnt that friendly dick up.

"What more do I need to say Baine? You've said enough. I said what I had to say. I've listened to you downgrade me and show out in front your friends. You shouldn't even do that. I've never done that to you. After all the things you put me through. I should've left you a long time ago." I mean that. I've took plenty of loses fuckin' with him.

"Yeah and you would've died a long time ago. Rashad would've never had the chance to fuck you. Think about this Danielle and I'm hanging up. Bring your motherfuckin' ass home today or it's going to be some FUCKIN' problems.

You know you'll never see Rashad again the last time you fucked him was the last time. Your cute little clinic I paid for I'm burning that shit down. I'm divorcing you because I don't fuckin' trust you. You slept with my FUCKIN' enemy. Get you a lawyer because I want a fuckin' divorce. The only thing you're getting is whatever you came with. Which is nothing. BITCH I fuckin' made you and I'll be the nigga to break you.

Every joint account we have together you don't have the rights to it anymore." I hung up in Baine's face. I'm not even surprised. He's divorcing me. I slept with his fuckin' enemy. If he wants a divorce, I'll see his motherfuckin' ass in court.

I swear men can dish it, but not take it. People would be surprised what Baine and I've been through. I never put my business out in the streets because what goes on in our home is between us not anyone else. I don't want anything from Baine. If he wants to divorce me that's fine.

If he thinks he can leave me without anything. He's sadly fuckin' mistaking. I heard a knock at my door. I swear I didn't feel like being bothered. Baine just gotten under my skin in less than ten minutes.

He didn't want to talk about anything. He just wanted to argue. I'm glad I'm two steps ahead of him. Baine ain't never gave me shit without throwing it up in my face. Gigi always told me to never put all my trust in a man. I never wanted Baine to buy my building. He needed to wash some money. My business was perfect.

"Come in," I yelled. I'm so fuckin' annoyed right now. Crimson walked through the door. She looked around at my room. She had the biggest smile on her face. I can't even enjoy the room in peace because of this fuck nigga. I've never had a problem starting over. It's my fault though and I own up to it.

"Look don't cuss me out! How are you? I'm so happy for you. At least you know she isn't trying to sample some pussy," she laughed. I'm not even on that anymore. I can't believe Crimson brought that up especially after she outed me in the car.

"Shut up." I pushed Crimson. I can't stand her. I swear I can't. If she keeps it up. I'm going to drop Griff the location to pick up his wife. I appreciate Crimson for coming but I can't keep her away from her family that long. I want to stay out here for a week or two.

"She set you up nice Danielle. I just knew you were about to trip. Shit you did. I wanted to laugh so bad, but I couldn't. I'm glad I came with you. You took that very well better than I ever could. Damn your daddy is fine as fuck. It's good to finally meet old Daniella and Gary Cooper.

You look just like your momma. You got it honestly. She's so beautiful! My momma is sneaky too. She never told me she keeps in touch with her. I guess we got it honestly. I'm glad she set it up. I know you're going through some shit, but Danielle don't get comfortable and end up moving here. Shit this room is better than my room at home. It's time for Griff to upgrade us. Danielle I'm sleeping in here too. I don't give a damn what you say. I wonder if I could squeeze into some of these clothes."

"Crimson you wish you could squeeze into my clothes. The moment you started fuckin' Griff. You got pregnant your ass and hips have been spreading ever since." Crimson rolled her eyes at me shit it's the truth. We used to wear the same size, but she's way thicker than me.

"What are you trying to say," she asked? Crimson rested her hands on her thick ass hips. She pursued her lips together. I flipped middle finger at her.

"Shit I said it. You got more ass and hips than me. The only thing that stayed small on you is your breasts. You look good though. I want to get to thick. I swear these niggas ain't MOTHERFUCKIN' ready. You remember how I was after Rashad and before me and Baine made it official. A MOTHERFUCKIN' MESS." Crimson looked at me and rolled her eyes. "What I do now shit I'm telling the truth." I climbed into my bed. I rested my arms behind my neck and laid my head back. Crimson climbed in right beside me.

"Danielle, OH I remember. I'll never forget it. I don't think that you need to try and date anyone. You have too many doors open already. Did you hear what I said about not staying here? You got to come back home and focus on your marriage. Hawaii is too far. I don't think Rashad's going to let you get away that easy." I don't know why everybody is rooting for Rashad.

"I'm bullshitting Crimson damn! Can I have my moment? I know I can't stay here forever, but I can. I plan on staying out here for two weeks. My marriage was over the moment Rashad opened his mouth it's a wrap. I just spoke with Baine he wants a divorce. He told me to lawyer up."

"Are you serious Danielle? He's doesn't want to move past it. He doesn't want to work it out. It's over." I nodded my head in agreement.

"Pretty much! It's cool though. I need you to ride with me because this divorce is about to be real nasty. I can feel it. He's made it clear that, he's not giving me anything. Baine and I don't have a prenup. I don't need anything from him, but if he thinks he could leave me without. He's sadly FUCKIN' mistaken.

Everything he doesn't want me to have. I'm taking it. I wish your husband didn't take it upon himself to vacate our old spot. I got to find me somewhere to live." Baine and I acquired a lot of property together.

I could stay at one of those properties, but I don't want him to have access to me. It's best that I find on my own spot.

"I'm starting to not like him. You can come and stay with us," she offered. I looked at Crimson like she's fuckin' crazy. I'm trying to shake Rashad. I'm not trying get back in bed with him. If she only knew the real Baine Mahone. I've never been the type of person to tell someone negative things about a person for them to dislike them. I want Crimson to see what Baine is like for herself. At this point he'll do anything in his power to hurt me.

"Girl my days of staying at your house are over. NEVER will I EVER! Your house is the reason why I'm headed for divorce now. I'll be alright. I'm okay with starting over. When you know a person better than they know themselves. A lot of things they do, doesn't even surprise you." Crimson and I kicked back and caught up.

I'm still not ready for Crimson to know about everything that I've been through with Baine. It's deep and I don't want to cry. I've cried enough and revealing everything that he's done to me. It's going to open old wounds I've kept hidden. I need to call Nikki back she's been calling me since we fled the reception. I need to have a conversation with Nikki.

Me-Hey pudd! How are you? I'm good I'm not avoiding you. We need to talk. I'm going through some shit. I need to have a conversation with you. I'm going to call you in a few.

I know Nikki has questions that only I have the answers for! I'm not ready, but what I will say about Nikki is since we've been cool, she's never been the friend that I hit you with the I told you so. I'll fill her in on what's going on in my life in a few. Madison she's supposed to meet with the realtor in a few hours.

I need to charge this computer and set it up because I need to work. I'm not worried about paying my staff for the days we'll be closed because their patients pay their salary and they're doing well this month. A few insurance claims that we've been waiting on are set to pay this month. According to my reports they're dropping Wednesday which will help us exceed our monthly quota. My phone alerted me I had a text.

Nikki- PUDD! I'm miss you. I'm just checking on you. I don't want to talk about me. Yes, we're overdue for a conversation. I miss our morning talks. I'm expecting to hear from you.

Crimson tapped me on my shoulder. I looked over my shoulder to see what she wanted.

"You've called Baine don't you think it's time for you to call Rashad," she asked? I really need Crimson to stop promoting Rashad. I turned back around and faced the opposite direction. I'm not thinking about him. After I read that last text message from him, I'm done. "Danielle, I know you hear me talking to you."

"Crimson I'm not calling Rashad. The only reason I called Baine is because he put his hands on my Gigi," I argued. I wouldn't even called him if he wouldn't have done that.

"What you mean by he put his hand on Ms. Gladys," she asked? I swear I don't know why Crimson always wants me to break stuff down for her.

"He pushed her, and she fell." Crimson looked at me with wide eyes.

"I swear I don't even know who he is anymore. He's doing a lot over one fuck up."

Chapter-8

Daniella

My baby she's been upstairs in her room all day. It feels good to have Danielle in the house with me and Coop. It's a dream that I thought would never come true. I can't stop smiling. The only thing that's separating us right now is a few walls. I just want to smother her. I know she's been handling her business all day. I didn't want to interrupt or distract her from that. I'll never stop her from handling her business. It feels good to catch up with Cheree we haven't seen each other in months.

I want to spend some time with my daughter before she cuts her stay short. My mother gave me and Coop a list of Danielle's favorite foods. Tonight, Coop's cooking Jerk chicken, baked macaroni and cheese, cabbage and corn bread. It'll be a few hours before dinner is ready. I want to catch up with Danielle before it's time to eat. I saw Crimson just come out of her room. Now is the perfect time for me to speak with her. I knocked on her door.

"Come in," she yelled. I opened the door and made my way inside the room. Danielle's face is still buried in the laptop that she didn't want. She peeked around the laptop to look at me. She's needs to take a break she's been working since she got here. I want her to relax. If she needs someone to assist her, run her business and find a new space I'll be glad to help with that.

“Hey, are you busy? I just wanted to check on you. I haven’t seen you since breakfast this morning. Are you hungry do you need anything? I brought you something to drink and something to snack on.” When Danielle was a little girl, she loved fruit. Apples, grapes and strawberries where her favorites. Her birthmark on her right arm is shaped like a strawberry.

Danielle closed the laptop and gave me her undivided attention. I know she hasn’t eaten since breakfast. I’m sure she could use some water or lemonade and something to snack on. I brought her all three. I sat the tray in front of her she started feeding her face.

“Hey! I’m kind of busy, but my work isn’t going anywhere. I can stop and put this away. I’m fine. Thank you for everything. I can’t believe you know my size. I don’t need anything you set me up pretty nice,” she smiled. I took a seat on the bed right beside Danielle. I sat the laptop on the nightstand. Danielle’s a workaholic just like her father. She gets that from him. I make him stop working and take a break. Danielle needs to do the same.

“No thanks needed. Your grandmother told me everything I need to know about MY precious Danielle. Before I got pregnant with you. I couldn’t gain any weight. I was your size for the longest. I think I’m still fly for a forty-eight-year-old. I think you could use a break. How are you? I know you have a lot going on.

I've been watching you work since the moment you stepped foot in my car. We don't know each other and that's my fault, but I want to get to know you. I know you're going through some things, but I'm here for you. What do you need me to do to make your transition a lot smoother?" I know Danielle's thinking about what she wants to say, but no answer is the wrong answer. We got to start somewhere.

"I love my Gigi she's everything to me. I spoke with her earlier she told me she ratted me out. It makes sense now why all my favorite foods where cooked for breakfast. I understand because you're her daughter she has no loyalty to me now. Gigi is sneaky. I think you're fly as hell to be forty-eight. I hope I'm as fine as you when I reach that age. I can't gain any weight either, but I know it's because of stress. I want to get to know you too. I've been wanting to meet you for the longest. I'm excited too. I hate it's under these circumstances, but it is what it is," she sighed.

"I love her too. Trust me her loyalty is with you. She's cursed me out at least five times today telling me don't try to kidnap her baby. I told her I'm not making any promises. I love you Danielle more than you would ever know. I love the woman that you've grown into be. I'm proud to call you my daughter. No matter the circumstances it's perfect timing. Stress isn't good for you. I don't want you to stress or worry about anything while you're here. I know you have an assistant allow me to allow my people to assist your assistant."

Danielle looked at me with wide eyes. I know she's hesitant. I can't make up for lost times, but I can step in and help my baby because she's in need.

"I love you too. Are you sure? I can handle it, but if you insist than I won't say no," she smiled. I can't believe my baby she's here in the flesh. I'm so proud of her. I can't help but to dote on her.

"I'm positive. Tell me a little bit about yourself Danielle. I can only imagine what you're going through. I'm team you. Do you think that you and your husband can work past your differences? Since we're being honest with each other. My mother told me what he did. I've never been the female to play games.

The only games I ever played was Connect Four and Candyland with you. I don't mean to come at you like this because we're trying to establish a relationship. My mother is off fuckin' limits. You're off fuckin' limits. I'll kill anybody behind YOU TWO!

I've been with your father since I was seventeen. He knows to not to fuck with me. No relationship or marriage is perfect. It's a lot of work take it from me baby I know. I don't sense that you've been abused because in my eyes you're perfect. What kind of man is your husband?

I've never felt the need to investigate your husband because my mother always made him seem so perfect. I haven't been around the block, but I know NIGGAS. I done seen it all. I done it all.

A perfect nigga doesn't operate like that. I cheated on your father once. He showed his ass, but he didn't put his hands on my mother. A scorned nigga is far more dangerous than someone that's hurt. I take it that Mr. Mahone isn't as perfect as the picture he paints," I asked?"

I read Danielle like a fuckin' book. I watched her facial expression. Her body language changed. She might not let me in because she doesn't know me, but I'm on Baine's ass.

In matter of hours I'll have everything I need to know about him. I'm not saying I'm the baddest bitch walking, but a nigga can't touch my momma without any fuckin' consequences. I don't give a fuck about Danielle being married to him, the moment he put his hands on my momma. He signed his fuckin' death certificate. What would provoke him to do that? I'm not saying that he's beating Danielle, but if she ran from that nigga things had to be physical.

"Ma your right no marriage or relationship is perfect. I'm sorry about Gigi that should've never happened. Baine's ego is bruised. I'm not perfect I have flaws and my EX husband has them too. I cheated and it's nothing I can do to change what I've done. I know right from wrong. I tried to fight temptation, but I couldn't. I should've ended my marriage before I crossed that line, but I didn't. I love Rashad I never stopped loving him. I kept my distance from him for seven years.

The moment we got in the room with each other. Our hearts and soul had a private conversation that I couldn't control. So here I am in Hawaii with you. I had no clue Rashad would disrupt the wedding. He warned me but I didn't think he would act on it. Now I know," she sighed. She admitted that no relationship or marriage is perfect.

She was already thinking about leaving. If she was going to leave than there had to be problems.

I'm not going to pressure her anymore because she said enough. I can read in between the lines.

"Fuck him Danielle. You can't hide from love baby. It'll always find you when you least expect it. I support whatever you do. Let's enjoy your vacation. If you cheated on him, he didn't fuckin' deserve you. In my eyes you'll always be PERFECT never forget that.

Your father and I are proud of you. I want to meet this Rashad. I've heard about him. I heard about when he broke your heart. I wanted to kill him behind that. I heard about him professing his love to you at Mother Dear's house. I hate to say it Danielle, but he got it bad.

He reminds me of your father. I swear history repeats itself. I met your father through Cheree and Bone at first, I didn't want to deal with him because I knew he was crazy if he was friends with Bone, but he won me over. The best gift he could've ever gave me was you. I need to make sure Rashad is the right one for you.

I don't want you circling back if his intentions aren't pure. I want to make sure that he can protect you from this situation that he's created. I'll protect you with my life and I'll give mine any day to save you." Danielle buried her head in my chest. She's so embarrassed. I didn't miss the smile that she had on her face. I ran my hands through her hair. It's so pretty the blonde looks good on her.

I got my people on the phone to let them speak with Danielle to hear her vision to see what they can come up with. They emailed a list of properties over that fits her qualifications. Me and Danielle finished talking getting to know each other. After dinner we made plans to get a massage and wine down.

Chapter-9

Baine

Danielle thinks this shit is a motherfuckin' game and it ain't. I ain't never been the nigga to play a game with NANN bitch and I'm not about to start. The only fuckin' games I play is with my son's. I meant what the fuck I said. I told that bitch to bring her motherfuckin' ass home and she hasn't. I got a fuckin' problem with that. Even though we have a fuckin' disagreement you don't have to run. I know you fucked him. Just deal with the fuckin' consequences. I'm burning every fuckin' thing. I made her into the bitch that she is and I'll fuckin' break her. I put that shit on GOD I will. I wonder where the fuck she's staying. It shouldn't be with Rashad. I'm going to kill that nigga once and for all.

I'm sick of his pussy ass. I know he's still salty about the shit that happened between me and his sister. Yeah, I killed the bitch. He knows I did, but that pussy ass nigga ain't got the fuckin' heart to get sideways with me. If he wants smoke I fuckin' got it. The only reason he did that shit at the fuckin' funeral was to show out. I got something for niggas and bitches that want to show out. I knew the baby his sister was carrying was mine, but I told that bitch I wasn't ready for a baby and she took it upon herself to fuckin' have it anyway.

I killed her because any motherfucka that doesn't listen to what the fuck I tell them needs to go. Rashad's so busy trying to save my wife. He should've saved his fuckin' sister. It's too late to save Danielle. She fucked over the wrong nigga. I swear she fucked over the wrong fuckin' nigga. Ike tapped me on my shoulder. I looked over my shoulders to see what he wanted. I've been waiting on my shooters to pull up for a minute now to get this shit on the motherfuckin' road.

"Baine are you sure you want to fuckin' do this. You're taking this shit too fuckin' far," he laughed. I pushed Ike off me. I've never been the nigga to say I'm going to do something but never does it. I don't give a fuck about her clinic. I got plenty of bitches that want to help me wash my money for free. She ain't keeping this shit. She was fuckin' this nigga in the spot I fuckin' paid for. I can show a bitch better than I can fuckin' tell them.

"I'm dead fuckin' serious. She took it too far when she decided to fuck another nigga and give him somcthing that fuckin' belongs to me. I got papers on Danielle. I gave her my last name. Ike this bitch really fuckin' played me. I know she started fuckin' him when Griff died because she stopped giving me the pussy. To make matters worse I knew the nigga had an issue because I felt that shit.

Every time I would look over my shoulder at the wedding, he was staring at us. This is just the beginning he's going to feel me too.

He can't fuck my wife break up my marriage without any consequences. Consequence is middle name. Baine Consequence Mahone."

Ike nodded his head in agreement. My shooters finally pulled up. I looked at my watch it's a little after 12:00 a.m. They were right on time. I pulled my ski-mask down. I slid my gloves on. I'm ready to get this fuckin' show on the road and over with. I got better shit to be doing besides burning down a clinic. Danielle's workers where here yesterday. Those bitches won't have anywhere to fuckin' work tomorrow. Ike picked the lock. We made our way inside of Danielle's clinic.

"Douse this bitch wet with gasoline. That's the only fuckin' thing I want to smell." My shooters came to do their job. Gasoline was dripping through this shit. I made sure everybody cleared it before me and Ike threw the matches. The moment the match hit the floor a flame instantly sparked. Ike tapped me on my shoulder. I looked over my shoulder to see what he wanted.

"Baine bring your motherfuckin' ass on before the smoke alarm goes off," he argued. I waived Ike off. I grabbed my phone to Facetime Danielle she didn't answer. I called that bitch again and she finally answered. I knew she was sleep, but I didn't give a fuck. She wiped her eyes with the back of her hands.

“What Baine what the fuck do you want? It's late and I'm bed,” she argued. A small yawn escaped Danielle's lips. The camera's facing Danielle. I can tell she's in the bed by herself.

“Danielle, I don't give a fuck about none of that shit. Get that nigga's nut off the side of your mouth. Trust me I'm not calling you because I want too.

Ain't shit about this fuckin' call friendly. I just want to show you something. It's late I know hoes like you got your legs up. Stupid ass bitch you're letting that nigga put a dent in your pussy. Check this out,” I argued. I flipped the camera so Danielle could watch her fuckin' clinic burn to the ground. “I busted my ass to buy you this shit, just to make you happy. I guess me busting my ass wasn't enough for you. The first chance you got.

You couldn't wait to open your legs up and fuck the next nigga in my shit. Your granny’s next. I’m going to kill everything around you until you come home.” Danielle started crying. Her tears don't fuckin' move me. “What the fuck are you crying for? When you were fuckin' that nigga you weren't crying.” I exited out her clinic and made my way toward my car. I don't give a fuck how she feels. I'm not in the business to spare her fuckin' feelings right now.

“You're so fuckin' spiteful. My clinic ain't got shit to do with me and you. Out of all the things you've done to me these past seven years; nigga I ain't never scooped that fuckin' low.

I swear Baine you better leave my fuckin grandmother out of this shit, because it ain't nothing for me to touch your ugly ass MOTHERFUCKIN' momma and I mean that shit."

"Aye bitch you got some fuckin' heart now? Where the fuck is you at? We ain't even got to do this shit over the fuckin' phone. Drop that location and I can pull up. Keep my momma's name out your fuckin' mouth. You know what Danielle she ain't never liked you no fuckin' way.

She always said you were slut and a cum drinking hoe. My momma ain't never lied about you hoe. She always said you would be my fuckin' downfall.

Word to my mother I'm going to always ball; falling off ain't never a fuckin' option. I'm the reason why you were fuckin' balling HOE." I hung up the phone in her fuckin' face. I'm going to show this bitch two reason why I'm not the nigga to fuck with. I took my ski-mask and gloves off. Home depot open twenty-four hours.

I want that bitch to show her motherfuckin' face. Fuck all that talking bring your motherfuckin' ass home and say that shit to my motherfuckin' face. Home depot wasn't too far from Danielle's clinic right off Snapfinger Road. Fuck it they're closed.

I'll go to fuckin' Walmart and get some shit. I want the world to know my wife cheated and she's a fuckin' HOE.I don't give a fuck. I finally made it home. I grabbed all the shit I needed from Walmart.

A bitch can't humiliate me in front of the fuckin' world without no fuckin' consequences. I grabbed the white tarp out the bag. I shook the spray paint can a few times. I knew exactly what I wanted to say. Danielle got these neighbors fooled. I'll expose you hoe. I spray painted the fuckin' sign. **Welcome Home Cheater. My Wife Danielle Mahone Is A Hoe. I Want A Divorce Hoe.** I went outside to hang the tarp up. I cut a few pieces of rope so I could tie it to the trees. I'm proud of my work. I grabbed my phone to call her.

I want Danielle to see this shit. She answered the phone on the first ring. She didn't say anything she just looked at me. "Say something Danielle! I'm begging you too. I want you to pull up. I want you to talk that hot ass shit you been talking. I want to talk about this shit. Where are you, because you ain't been at home in two fuckin' days. I got something for bitches that don't want to bring their motherfuckin' ass home. Look at this shit Danielle. I want the whole neighborhood to know my wife ain't shit but a cheating ass hoe."

"You know what Baine. I'm all cried out. You want me to come home so bad WHY? Our house hasn't been a home in years. You're doing everything in your FUCKIN' power to FUCKIN' hurt me. You're slandering my fuckin' name for the world to see. You and I both know you didn't marry a hoe. I married one though. You're putting our business out in the street for the world to see.

You're going to pay for that. We can get a divorce you don't have to do all that. Have your lawyer to call mine and we can handle that. You want me to fuckin' bend and break, but MOTHERFUCKA I AIN'T. MOTHERFUCKA I AIN'T cut like that.

Real BITCHES NEVER TAP OUT! I remember many of nights when I stayed up late at night waiting on you to come home and you never came. I kept my cool. I didn't fuckin' TRIP but I should've. Everything you're fuckin' doing can never weigh up to what I did. I don't have many regrets in my life. The only thing I regret is loving you and saying I DO. I gave you all of me and I've never had all of you.

I had to share you for years with plenty of bitches. I never gave a fuck about your riches I always came with mine. Get the fuck off my line you're trying so hard to embarrass me, but you're embarrassing yourself," she argued. Danielle hung up the phone. I knew she was going to do that. I grabbed my phone and sent her a text.

Me-You regret saying I DO Danielle. Tell me to my face you fuckin' regret it. Oh yeah, I regret that shit TOO. I cheated throughout the whole fuckin' marriage. I'm glad I kept some loyal pussy on the side. You embarrassed yourself the moment that nigga aired out your business out for his friends to see. He embarrassed you so what's the problem with me doing it? You want me to keep quiet. Never that slut. My EX WIFE is a HOE. I want the world to know.

Danielle left my message on read. I ain't got time to stress myself out over no bitch. I walked back inside of the house. I went into the kitchen. I grabbed five garage bags. I went upstairs to our room. I snatched all her fuckin' clothes off the hangers. I tossed all her shit into the fuckin' garbage bag. She left it here and she hasn't come back.

I guess she doesn't need this shit. She wasn't walking out this house with this shit. I started bagging up all of Danielle's shit, shoes, make-up, jewelry every fuckin' thing. I wish she would attempt to come back to our house to get any of this shit I brought her. I'll fuckin' drag her stupid ass.

I'll give this shit to a bitch that deserves this shit. It took me a minute to pack up all Danielle shit, but I did. I wouldn't dare give this shit to Nova, but I'll give this shit to Bre'Elle she's been calling my phone like crazy. I know she's on her good bullshit. I was supposed to slide through there earlier, but I had to handle my business.

I'll slide through tonight since I ain't got shit to do. Bre'Elle stayed out in Powder Springs. I had her ducked off. She hated it too, but if I'm footing the bill you do what the fuck I say do. Bre'Elle and Nova both stayed at each other's neck and whenever they saw Danielle, they always caused fuckin' problems. I ain't have time for that shit.

It took me about forty-five minutes to get over her house. I had a key to Bre'Elle's house. I dropped the bags on the living room floor.

I made my way upstairs toward Bre'Elle's room. I stopped by my son's Baieon's room first. My young nigga is asleep. I'll see him in the morning. I made my way toward Bre'Elle's room. I knew she wasn't asleep. I hope she's not pregnant. I don't want another child. Nova's pregnant too. Bre'Elle's so fuckin sexy.

She knows that shit too. She stood about 5'4. Everything about her is nice. Her skin is the color of hot cocoa. Her lips are plump, and her thighs are thick like I like them. Her ass is fat. Her pussy is GRADE A. I knew she was up waiting on me.

I've been fuckin' with Bre'Elle for forever. When I first started fuckin' with Danielle me and Bre'Elle used to kick it. She's from my hood. We never stop fuckin' around. She ended up having my kid two years into me and Danielle's relationship. I always had a soft spot for Bre'Elle I guess it's because I've known her the longest. She gives me the most problems.

I guess it's because we have the most history. I've made her a lot of promises that I've never kept. She's never switched up on me. Even after I said I do she stayed in my corner. The timing was never right when it came to us. She's posted up against her headboard with her arms folded across her stomach.

Her breasts were sitting up in the red bra begging for me to free them. Yes, I wanted to feel all that. I just want to get my dick wet and my balls sucked.

Bre'Elle looked at me and rolled her eyes. I unbuckled my pants they dropped to the floor. I tossed my shirt on the chaise. I flexed my back muscles. My shoulders are tense.

I need a massage bad. I can feel Bre'Elle staring a hole in me. I swear I'm not beat for her shit. I should've gone over Nova's. She would appreciate a nigga being in her presence. Bre'Elle's been tripping all fuckin' week. I turned around to face her. I grilled Bre'Elle I hope she takes my facial expressions to heart.

"What the fuck are you looking at me like that for?" I swear I'm not in the mood for her shit. It's late I just want to fuck and that's it. Bre'Elle threw the remote at me. "Aye you better watch your fuckin' self. I don't know what's your fuckin' problem, but I'm not for it. Can I sleep here, or do I need to go somewhere else?" I turned around to face Bre'Elle I don't give a fuck about her having an attitude. I got one too and trust me she doesn't want my fuckin' attitude. She knows I'll do some shit that I'll regret later. I swear I'm not trying to handle her like that, and my son is in the next room.

"I got plenty of fuckin' problems Baine and you're the cause of all of them. Don't come in my house talking shit. I called you earlier to come through. You can't fuckin' stay here. It's rules to this shit. It ain't my fuckin' fault your wife cheated. How does it feel to be the side nigga to your main bitch?

She should've cheated on you a long time ago. Don't take your fuckin' problems out on me. I'm tired of being a convenience. I'm good you can leave. It's plenty of niggas that want to come through to fuck me when I tell them too. I just choose to fuck you. I got a nigga that's about to swing through any minute now. Nova may be cool with this shit but I'm not. I'm sick of it," she argued. I stepped in Bre'Elle's personal space. The smile that once was etched on her face instantly turned into a frown. I grabbed her fuckin' neck. I swear I'm not trying to handle her like this. Bre'Elle likes for me to handle her like this.

"What's your fuckin' problem? You've been blowing up my phone all fuckin' day. You think it's funny Danielle cheated. You knew my wife was cheating? What exactly are you sick of Bre'Elle? You don't fuckin' work. I do everything that you fuckin' ask me too. You got a nigga that can fuck you and provide for you? Go be with that nigga Bre'Elle. I got plenty of bitches that want to live like you. Pack your shit right fuckin' now.

My son can come and live with me, because I'm sick of you too bitch. I'm not in the business to keep nann bitch that don't want to be fuckin' kept. Choose your fuckin' words wisely because this might be the last fuckin' time you speak. I've killed bitches for less. You don't want to be one of those bitches," I argued. I didn't let my grip go on Bre'Elle's neck. Tears seeped through the corner of her eyes. Her tears don't fuckin' move me.

She should've kept her fuckin' mouth shut and continued to play her position until I tell her otherwise. Bre'Elle's eye were trained on me. Tears coated her chocolate skin. I swear I didn't want to lay hands on her but she's always fuckin' pushing me. I wiped her tears with my thumbs. "Why do you always got to fuckin' take me there. I didn't come over here for this shit. I got enough shit going on out here.

I don't need extra shit coming from you. You think I want to hurt you Bre'Elle because I don't. Let me leave before I do some stupid shit. I got a lot of anger built up. I swear I'll take that shit out on you if you fuckin' provoke me." I heard footsteps enter the room.

"Daddy what are you doing to my mommy," he asked? I looked over my shoulder to see my son. I released the hold I had on Bre'Elle's neck. I grilled her. I haven't seen Baieon in two days. He's a light sleeper whenever I come over, he's always wakes up.

"Son, son what's up. I stopped by your room and you were sleep. I'm just admiring how beautiful your mother is. I love her but she's been giving me a hard time." Baieon walked over to me and gave me a hug. I swear I missed my young nigga. He walked over to his mother to look at her. I swear my son is protective of his mother.

Every time me and Bre'Elle have a disagreement and he's asleep. He wakes up and hears us. It's one of the reasons why I didn't want to argue with her because I knew he would hear us.

"Mommy my daddy loves you. I told you stop being mean to my daddy. Can I lay in here with y'all," he asked? I wouldn't dare tell him no. Bre'Elle looked at me and rolled her eyes.

"Of course, baby you can stay in here with me. I'm not being mean to your daddy. I'm just expressing myself," she stated. Bre'Elle grabbed her night shirt and shorts and through it on. She left the room. I couldn't help but to watch that ass when she left the room. My son climbed in the bed with me. He laid his head on my chest.

"I missed you daddy." I miss him too. I make sure I see my kids at least five days out of seven. I wish I can have all my kids under one roof.

"I missed you too." Bre'Elle walked back into her room. Her hands where on her hips. I wanted her the worst fuckin' way. I can't wait until Baieon takes his little ass to sleep. I got plans for Bre'Elle. She knows it too. I'm going to handle all that fuckin' attitude. She looked at me and turned her lips up. I can't wait until Baieon takes his little ass to sleep.

"Baine what's all this shit you got in my living room. I hope you don't think you're moving in," she argued. I didn't want my son to hear us argue. I got up out the bed.

I walked over to Bre'Elle. I grabbed her hand and led her into the hallway. She looked at everything but me.

"What are you doing Baine? I'm sick of you, stop using our son against me. You ain't never going to change," she sighed. I cupped her chin forcing her to look at me. I backed her up against the wall. My hands roamed every inch of her body. I wanted to feel something else.

My hands found its way in her shorts. I had her attention. I finger fucked Bre'Elle wet. I can tell she's at her peak. Before she could nut on my fingers. I pulled out. Her face was flustered.

"You want me to take you down through tonight, don't you? Your mouth is saying one thing, but your body is saying something else. Did you look through the bags? I think it's some things in there you might like," I asked. Bre'Elle still refused to look at me. I leaned in and gave her kiss. She didn't hold back. She wrapped her arms around my neck. I grabbed a handful of her ass. I bit down on her neck. "Why do we have to argue just to get to this?" Bre'Elle broke the kiss. She placed her hands on my chest. Bre'Elle grabbed my beard.

"Because you're never going to change. Don't you think I deserve to be happy Baine? What about Baieon he's confused. I don't want him to think it's okay to do this to the women he decides to date.

We've been doing this for years. I'm mad because I know you were with Nova yesterday, she sent me a picture this morning of the two of you. You were in her bed beating her back in. She's pregnant. Go be with her Baine. I promise, you have my blessing. I'm tired of hurting. I was with you before Danielle, you chose her and married her. I've been with you all through your marriage. We have a son together I wouldn't trade him for nothing in this world.

I won't keep continuing to play the background. It'll never be us, because you can't commit to one person. I'm willing to give up the house, cars, clothes and whatever your money can buy for my sanity and peace. I stayed down through it all. The only thing I'm good for is a late-night fuck. I'm your drug mule when you need something moved quick. I know you'll take care of Baieon," she cried. I pulled Bre'Elle into my arms. I swear I don't think I've ever heard her cry this much. The last thing I need is for my son to come out here to see what I've done to his momma. I picked Bre'Elle up and carried her into the living room.

"Stop crying because I'm not trying to upset you. I'm going to be honest with you. I slipped up a few times with Nova and she got pregnant. I can't change that. Shawty I had plans to tell you, but I didn't know how because I was afraid of this. Bre'Elle I'm not perfect and you know that. You accepted me flaws and all. Danielle cheated and I want a divorce. I want to be with you. You stayed down through everything when the divorce is final.

I want to marry you. I don't want you to leave shawty. A nigga would be lost without you. I'm begging you Bre'Elle please don't leave me."

"I've heard this before Baine actions speak louder than words. Show me and I might consider changing my mind. What's in the bags," she asked? I know Bre'Elle's getting tired of my shit. Leaving isn't a fuckin' option.

"Look and see." Bre'Elle looked through the bags. She looked at me and smile. I knew she would want this shit. Majority of Danielle's stuff still had tags on it. Whatever she didn't want she could sell it. Danielle brought clothes just to be buying shit.

If she thinks she was leaving with this shit. She's sadly fuckin' mistaken. Every black card and every bank that her name was attached too. She no longer had access.

"She's going to kill you. I hate you but I love you. I'm keeping this shit. Every piece of it. It's over huh. I get to keep the jewelry too?" I nodded my head in agreement. I just want to see Bre'Elle smile.

"Yeah it's over. You can keep everything. I want you to have the jewelry since you picked it out. Whatever you don't want you can sell." Bre'Elle wrapped her arms around my neck. She placed a kiss on my lips. She started to mount me. "Aye don't let them lips get you in trouble." Bre'Elle kissed me again. I wasn't about to stop her.

I wanted her as bad as she wanted me. I can feel the heat coming from between her legs. I'm dying to knock the fuckin' flame out. I tugged at her shorts. "Take them motherfuckas off. I don't want Baieon to hear you fuckin' screaming."

"He's asleep or else he would've come down by now to see what you're trying to do to his mommy," she moaned. I slid down her shorts. I tossed her shorts on the floor.

"Sit on my face." Bre'Elle did as she was told. I smacked her on her ass, on the way up. We both had something to prove. I tongue fucked her wet. Her legs were shaking. Her juices were coating my face. I wasn't easing up. She had a tight grip on my hair. I knew she was at her peak. I wanted to dive in that pussy and bury a few fuckin' seeds. I lifted Bre'Elle up and tossed her on the couch.

I threw her legs over my shoulders. Her pussy was extra wet. I call her SUPER SOAKER. I made my way inside of Bre'Elle. She started squirming and shit. She knew better than to ever give my pussy away. I started stroking her long, deep and hard. I worked up a sweat instantly. I can't stop looking at her juices coat my dick. Her juices and the sounds of her moans drove me insane.

"Baine slow down please. It hurts so bad, but it feels so good," she moaned.

"I'm not I owe you one. Get used to this." Bre'Elle's eyes rolled in the back of her head. I sped up my strokes. Bre'Elle started throwing that pussy back at nigga.

I felt her cum all on my dick. I went in overdrive. The tears she was holding poured down her face.

“I love you Baine,” she moaned. Bre'Elle clamped her pussy muscles down on my dick. I buried my seeds all up in her shit. Bre'Elle jumped up quick and tried to run.

I had a death grip on her waist. I want her to have another child for me.

“Baine did you bust a nut in me,” she asked? I don't know why she wanted me to answer a question she already knew the answer too. “Yeah I want you to have another kid. You said you love me. I told you we were going to be together. What's the problem Bre'Elle?

We just had a perfect moment don't ruin it with the questions. Come on and let's go take a shower so I can clean you up. You said actions speak louder than words. I'm trying to show you.”

Chapter-10

Danielle

I've been tossing and turning for a minute. I was sleeping so good until Baine ruined it. I tried to go back to sleep but I couldn't. I shouldn't have answered the phone when I saw him calling. Hawaii's time is totally different from ours they're five hours ahead of us. It's 5:00 a.m. Baine knows I hate to be woken up out of my sleep. He wouldn't care because he's in his feelings. He's going out his way to try to fuckin' hurt me. He has every right to be mad, but he should understand how I feel. I knew he was going to fuck with my clinic. I didn't think he would burn it down. I swear he's so fuckin' spiteful.

I grabbed my phone off the nightstand. He sent me a text message. I can't believe him. I didn't even realize I started crying. I wiped my eyes with my sheet. I didn't want Crimson to hear me because she's lying next to me. "I fuckin' hate him and that's a strong word to use," I cried. He cheated throughout the whole relationship. I swear when a nigga is pissed his true colors will show. A few times I weighed my options. I thought about staying and telling Rashad that I'm going to work on my marriage. I'll never scoop to Baine's level. I don't even need this for court. The babies he had on me during our marriage is proof of all his infidelities.

“What's wrong Danielle, why are you crying,” she asked? I'm not ready to tell Crimson what happened. I don't have the heart too. I ignored Crimson because no matter what I said it wouldn't change anything. I'd still have these tears. A few wounds that I patched up due to his cheating would reappear and I'm not ready to deal with that. I loved Baine so much.

I swear I lost myself behind him. I felt stupid a few times, but I really feel fuckin’ stupid now. Crimson tapped me on my shoulder hard as fuck. I refused to even look at her. She got up out the bed and stood in front of me. My hands were covering my eyes. I didn't want to look at her. Crimson removed my hands from my face. We locked eyes with each other. She pointed her finger in my face.

“Danielle, I love you, but I'm fuckin' sick of you. Look tell me what the fuck is going on with you. I left my fuckin' husband and three kids to be here with you. Why won't you tell me what happened. I swear it feels like I don't even fuckin' know. You're crying what the fuck did he do. I heard y'all arguing. I want to cry with you. I want to hate that nigga too.

I can't feel your pain if you won't fuckin' allow me too. After everything we've been through Danielle, I've never turned my back on you. We've kept each other secrets. I thought we were better than this,” she cried. It's now or never because the last thing I wanted to do was get Crimson upset. I wrapped my arms around her.

"Crimson don't cry! Please don't I'm sorry. I know you love me. I wouldn't trade you for nothing in this world. You know I'm a very private person and I like to keep things to myself. Since we're up. I might as well tell you everything now." I grabbed some Kleenex off the nightstand. I cut the light on. I tossed Crimson my phone so she could read the text Baine sent me.

Crimson read the long ass text he sent. Baine ain't never sent me no shit like that. He put in a lot of fuckin' effort. She looked at me with wide eyes. Her cheeks turned red. I knew she was about to trip. The moment her left eyebrow raised up, and her top lip turned her face into a frown.

"Danielle is he serious or is he bull shitting," she asked? A small laugh escaped my lips. Maybe it's better to get this shit off my chest. I don't know even know why I've been holding this shit in, because I shouldn't even be walking around with all this bullshit on me.

"He's very serious Crimson. Baine has taken me through so much. Bitch I think you're going to need a tall glass of coffee for this." Me and Crimson grabbed our robes and may our way toward the kitchen. My parents had an Expresso Machine built in the kitchen. Crimson grabbed the cups and I got the machine started.

I made sure we both had an extra shot. We headed back upstairs to my room. Me and Crimson took a seat on the bed.

I took another sip of my coffee and made myself comfortable. I grabbed the comforter and through it over me. I wanted to be as comfortable as possible.

"Talk Danielle and stop stalling," she sassed. I threw my middle finger up at Crimson. I had to relax because what I'm about to tell Crimson I've never told a soul. Now that I think about it, I don't know why I didn't tell her because she's my confidant.

"I'm not stalling Crimson. Trust me I'm not. I've should've been told you this, but I've never had the courage to tell you. I finally found my voice to reveal this. It's time. I've never told you any of this before for more reasons than one. I never want to taint the image you have of him. I didn't want you to judge me. By me not saying anything it's like I'm protecting him, and I shouldn't.

He called me on Facetime earlier just to show me he burnt down my clinic. If I was spiteful, I could've recorded it and showed the police, but I'm not that type of person. He'll get his. Baine and I have been together for seven years. We've been married for five years.

You've witnessed or highs, but you've never heard about our lows. Do you remember when Baine and I first started dealing with each other," I asked? Crimson nodded her head in agreement. I'll never forget the date I first met him. I knew he was a street nigga and I knew he wasn't perfect. I've always been attracted to niggas in the street.

Shit I'm from the hood and I never wanted to be a product of my environment.

"Keep talking because I'm listening. You know I remember." Crimson sipped her coffee.

"One of the reasons why I didn't want commit to Baine because he was a whore. I knew that about him that's why he stayed in the friend zone. We were okay with being friends with each other. He did his thing and I did mine. The moment he saw Rashad at Maria's party and he figured out we dated. He changed Crimson. Baine became everything I wanted and ever needed in a man. You know that I told you about it. He wined and dined the fuck out of me. He was a totally different person. You know how my Gigi use to always tell us, some men do everything to get you and once they get you, they switch up?

You and I wouldn't know about that because I've only been with two people and you've only been with Griff. Baine he's that type of man Crimson, On the outside looking in he's perfect. Tall dark and handsome. He's wealthy and he's well kept. What woman wouldn't want that. I wanted it, but I never wanted to share it with anybody else. He's been putting on a front for years as if he's the perfect husband and sometimes he is, that's slim to none.

Throughout our marriage he's cheated. He probably cheated more during the two years we dated. I wouldn't put it past him. The first time I found out he cheated, it was right after we got married.

It was our six-month wedding anniversary. We were going out to celebrate. I slid in the car and put my seat belt on. I found a used condom in his car. Not the wrapper the fuckin' condom. He lied and said Ike used his car. You know I wanted to call Ike to confirm it. He lied and said Ike and Keondra went to Jamaica for the week they left the night before.

They wanted us to come with them, but he knew I had to work. I felt he was lying, but I took his word for it. My heart ached so fuckin' bad. A special night was ruined in a matter of minutes because of him. The whole ride to the restaurant was silent. He kept trying to touch my hand and apologize. I didn't want him touching me.

This bitch was so fuckin' disrespectful. First it was the condom, it didn't stop there. The moment we got to the restaurant my phone started alerting me. I had messages and emails. I stopped to check my messages. I just started doing my internship at Emory. I had to check my phone to make sure I wasn't on call.

I was so fuckin' disturbed by everything. I don't know how she found my email and I don't know how she got my phone number. She sent me pictures of her and Baine having sex. I couldn't keep my composure if I wanted too. I can't believe he would just lie in my face like that. It wasn't just one it was multiple.

Baine sat in front of me. He had the biggest smile on his face.

The waiter had just brought out my glass of red wine. I threw it in his face. He was pissed because I embarrassed him.

Everybody was looking at us, but I didn't give a fuck. I slid him my phone. He had an excuse for everything those pictures were before my time. He lied to my fuckin' face. I knew they were recent because, the tattoo of my name on is neck was very visible. He had just gotten that, but it's before my time. Our dinner ended there," I cried. I started shaking Crimson held me.

I never wanted to relive these moments because it triggers me. If I don't speak out on it, I'm protecting him. Why should I protect him because clearly, he doesn't give two fucks about me? My heart started hurting all over again just thinking about it. Crimson handed me a Kleenex to wipe my eyes. I grabbed my phone to show Crimson the email from all those years ago. I kept every email. Crimson threw my phone on the floor.

"I don't want to see that shit," she argued. My phone rang interrupting me and Crimson from our conversation. I answered the phone it's the Dekalb County Fire Department. I placed the phone on speaker.

"Hello," I yawned.

"Hi, I'm trying to contact Danielle Mahone the owner Cooper's Women's Health and OBGYN," he asked?

“This is she how can I help you,” I asked? I've been waiting on this call. It's one of the reasons why I couldn't go to sleep either. I knew the police and the fire department would be calling. I hope this shit doesn't bite him in the ass. He's so fuckin' vindictive it's crazy. I hope Baine knows there’s cameras. I should've recorded his ass when he did it, but I didn't have the fuckin' energy to do it.

His stupid ass wanted to Facetime me from the location. The police are going to investigate it. It already looks suspect because I moved all my things out of there prior to the fire. Baine's stupid ass didn't need to know that.

“I'm calling to let you know that your fire alarms went off in your in your building, by the time we got there everything was burned down. We suspect arson because your door was unlocked, we were unable to save anything. Can you come down so we can ask you a few questions? Do you have any enemies that would want to arson your building? The fire damaged the other office spaces around,” he explained.

Baine is really fuckin' low. I don't want anything from him. I made plans to move out the clinic. He's so fuckin' petty and vindictive. I can't wait to cash out on the insurance policy. His name isn't even fuckin' on it. All funds will be distributed to me. Crimson looked at me and shook her head.

“I'm unable to come down sir. I'm in Hawaii for the week. You can call Mr. Mahone he should be able to come down and answer any questions or concerns that you may have.

"I'm sorry Crimson before I was rudely interrupted. Nova's her name and ruining my marriage was her game.

I thought my night couldn't get any worse. Your anniversary is supposed to be special. The moment we got back into the car and he pulled off. It got worse. No words were spoken between us. He was in his feelings and I was in mine. She called his phone and he didn't answer. She called my phone and I answered. I wanted to hear what this woman had to say. He got her pregnant Crimson and she was keeping it. We fought in the fuckin' car.

He couldn't deny it, his facial expression verified everything I needed to know. I ask the bitch was she getting an abortion. She laughed in my fuckin' face.

She told me she was three months fuckin' pregnant and he's been accompanying her to every fuckin' doctor's appointment. We fought again I tried to take his eyes out. He kept swerving because I wouldn't ease up. I couldn't believe he would do me like that. My heart ached so bad. I cried the whole way home. I couldn't even look at Baine. The moment we got home I started packing up my shit. He put a gun to my fuckin' head and told me I wasn't going any fuckin' where. He unpacked all my shit. He said he didn't believe in abortions. He's going to take care of his child, but I'm your fuckin' wife. He never considered my feelings.

I married you and the bitch you were fuckin' with on the side has your first child before I do? I tried to walk away but he wouldn't let me. He promised me he would stop cheating, and he did for a while. A few months later we were at the Mike Epps comedy show.

It was right after Valentine's Day. You know the whole city had come out. Always trust your women's intuition. I had a funny feeling the whole the show. I brushed it off we were having a good time. I just wanted to enjoy it. The moment the show was over. We walked to his car. It snowed the concrete still had black ice. He had just brought the black G-wagon. It's cold outside.

He carried me to the G-Wagon. Crimson it was a bitch at the G-wagon waiting on us with a pregnancy test. Girl she had the biggest smile on her face. It made sense why I was feeling like this because she was here lurking. The bitch had the nerve to say I want to congratulate your husband and my baby daddy we're expecting. Three months later another bitch popped up pregnant by him. I tried to get down off his back so fuckin' quick. He had a death grip on my legs. I grabbed his dreads with so much force. I pulled a few of them motherfuckas from the scalp.

He had no choice but to let me down. Crimson I drug that bitch. I took off my Manolo Blahnik boots. I beat her ass. Baine had to pull me off her. I fucked his ass up. Everybody was watching. I didn't care Crimson because at this point. I was over him. It's nothing he could say to me that would change my mind.

I snatched the keys out of his hands and pulled off. I rushed home to pack my shit. Twenty minutes into me grabbing majority of my stuff. He walks in the front door. No words were spoken between us.

I thought he was going to let me leave because at this point Crimson it's nothing he can say to me to make me fuckin' stay. Two fuckin' babies and they're only a month a part. I noticed I didn't hear him walking.

I felt him fuckin' watching me. I kept walking. The moment my hand touched the fuckin' door. He snatched me up so quick and threw me up against the wall. You know it's a fuckin' mirror right there in the hall. I hit the mirror and glass shattered every fuckin' where," I cried. I raised up my shirt to show Crimson the scar that covered the top of my back. Cocoa and Shea butter couldn't heal that.

"I couldn't believe he did that He grabbed the AK-47 out the hallway and told me I wasn't going any fuckin' where. Crimson I thought he was going to fuckin' kill me. He cocked the gun back and asked me was If I was still leaving because if I was, he'll leave my body leaking right here. I shook my head no. I was so fuckin' scared. I just knew my life was about to end. He smacked me in my face so hard, blood started leaking from my mouth. He told me I'm a kept a bitch. I can either get with the program or die."

I couldn't even get my words out. I started shaking. Crimson wrapped her arms around me. She was crying too I went through so much with him and that's only the half.

“He took his belt off and beat my ass Crimson. He beat me like a fuckin' slave. He was mad because everybody saw us. I wasn't in the fuckin' wrong. He fuckin' embarrassed me and I was fuckin' sick of it. He never apologized for his actions. He finally stopped, after that he carried me upstairs and tried to have sex with me. I wouldn't let him. He forced himself on me.

He thought sex would change things, but it didn't. Baine not being able to keep his dick in his pants is what led us to this situation. I was a prisoner in our home for months. Remember every time we would go somewhere; he would drop me off and pull up unannounced that's why because he was afraid that I was going to leave. He had two babies on me. They both are the same age five years old. They’re both boys. His baby mommas are fuckin’ scum. I despise those bitches. He's gave me every fuckin' disease except for aids and herpes.

The babies stopped but the diseases kept coming. Every time we would have sex, he would bring me back something. He gave me so many STD's I lost fuckin' count. The only way I could get him to stop having sex with me and giving me diseases. I had to act like I was on my period. I brought so many bottles of ketchup to make it true. It got so bad Crimson. Baine never wanted to wear a condom with me.

I used to massage his dick with KY Jelly and place a plastic sandwich bag over it, so he wouldn't touch me bare. I prayed every night that I wouldn't get pregnant by him. I couldn't see myself carrying his kids and two other women were given that privilege before me. I put myself on the Depo shot. His dumb ass didn't know. Baine was a nasty nigga. He was fuckin' anything walking. Please don't look at me like I'm a weak bitch because I'm not. I wanted to leave Crimson, but I couldn't. Rashad was my way out. When Rashad told Baine that I had to run because if I didn't, I might not be here to tell my story," I cried.

"Stop crying Danielle. It's over now you don't have to ever worry about him. I'm sorry for saying what I said about him. It's true you really don't know a person. He's a fuckin' monster. I fuckin' hate that bastard and that's a strong word for me to use.

You've should spoke up instead of protecting him all these years by not saying anything. I'm not a killer but I swear I would kill him. I can't believe you went through all that. I wish you would've told me Danielle. I feel like I failed you as sister and a friend. Why wouldn't you tell me? I would never judge you.

He could've killed you Danielle. Stop fuckin' lying to me. I asked you about the fight at the comedy show when the video was floating around on Facebook. Everybody was saying that was you and Baine and you fuckin' lied about it. He needs to die. He's so fuckin' selfish. He only married you so you and Rashad wouldn't get back together.

Damn you can keep a fuckin' secret. Where's the kids and these baby mommas so I can pass out a few ass whoopings for the old and the new," she asked?

"I'm trying to stop crying Crimson, but it's hard. I swear I never wanted to open these old wounds. I didn't want to tell you I was fighting his baby momma. You would've told me to leave and I couldn't leave. Them bitches are around. No offense I'm not a part of his kid's life. If he made me stay, his kids had to stay away from me. Call me selfish but I couldn't act like I accepted his kids, because I didn't. The babies were made during our marriage. I didn't want to stay. I wanted to walk away willingly." It felt good to get everything off my chest and tell Crimson what's been going on with me. Our good days never outweighed our bad days. I know no relationship is supposed to be like this.

Baine thought because he brought me everything it would suffice for his cheating, but it didn't. It made me resent him even more. Me and Crimson laid up in the bed neither one of us were tired. She was on the phone caking with Griff. I swear their relationship is so dope. She needs to take her ass home. My phone rang. Crimson looked at me. I wasn't about to answer it, if it was Baine. I need to put him on the block list.

"It's your property manager calling from the sub-division you live in," she sighed. I grabbed the phone and answered it.

"Hello!" I put the phone on speaker so Crimson could hear what was going on.

"Mrs. Mahone, I don't know if you're aware or not, but it's a sign in your yard that I refuse to repeat what it says. It needs to be taken down. It's offensive and your neighbors are complaining," she explained.

"I'm aware you would have to have Mr. Mahone to take it down. It's out of my control," I explained. I hung up the phone in her face. I hate to be rude, but I can't do anything. Call him he did it.

Chapter-11

Rashad

Danielle's still gone and won't return any of my fuckin' calls. Griff said they were in Hawaii. I'm thinking about going out there on a limb to find her. I just want to hear her voice and to make sure she's straight that's it. I heard Baine's been acting and talking reckless about a nigga, but it is what it is. I snatched up your wife. I'm not hard to find if you want smoke. If he has beef, behind something that never belonged to him. I'll cook it. He's the last nigga I'm worried about. I made my move. I'm waiting on him to retaliate. I can't believe my lil baby is hiding from a nigga. Fuck her EX husband.

Griff wanted me to stay out the streets for a few days, but I couldn't. I ain't never ran from nann nigga. I damn sure wasn't about to start. Fuck Baine and Ike, I should've killed those niggas years ago. I've been patient but this year is the year. I got to get up and pick up Rashad and BJ from school. I'm supposed to pick up Camina too. My phone started ringing it was Slap calling me on Facetime. I answered to see what he wanted. I just left the trap about three hours ago it was straight when I left. I know nothing's popped off since I left.

"What up," I asked? Slap ran his hands across his face. I knew he was prolonging what the fuck he had to say. I'm not trying to beat around the bush.

A nigga got shit to do. The last thing I want to do is to be holding this phone waiting on this nigga to say what the fuck he needs to say.

"Aye you remember that little thing you wanted me to do," he asked? I swear I hate when this nigga gets to talking in fuckin' circles I need him to get straight to the fuckin' point. Why wouldn't I remember, and I told him to do it.

"I remember talk. I need to scoop my young bulls up and Camina." I got to swing by Sam's Club or Costco's to get this girl some fuckin' snacks before these kids start fuckin' tripping. Danielle got me slipping I haven't done shit I need to do because she's been invading my fuckin' mind.

"I've been watching shawty's crib since last night. You wouldn't believe who just pulled up. Aye Mya's sneaky as fuck cut that hoe loose," he chuckled. Mya's sneaky tell me something that I don't know. I never got that from her until now. It's one of the reasons why I got my nigga watching her to see what the fuck she's up too.

"Who pulled up Slap it wouldn't be a nigga I know?" I already know who pulled up. I just want Slap to confirm it. If Mya wants to fuck with Baine, I'm not mad at her. Do what you got to do my nigga. I haven't been checking for Mya since I laid eyes on Danielle.

"Baine pulled up. I'm thinking Mya had to be fuckin' with him. You just don't give anybody your fuckin' home address. How about that nigga had roses and shit?

He wasn't too mad about Danielle cheating; If he's bringing another female a rose? He's been here for a minute. You want me to get my hands dirty or should I save that shit for you," he asked? I knew Slap wanted to do his ass in, but Baine is on me. Ike's on me too.

"We all know who Baine is. I'm just surprised that Danielle doesn't know they can have each other. I don't trust Mya. Hit wire up when Mya leaves. I need him to put a bug in her spot. No camera just a bug. I want to hear what Mya and Baine have going on. Anytime a bitch could fuck with my enemy. I can never trust her."

"Say less." I finished chopping it up with Slap. I need to call Griff. I always got to run my moves by with my nigga. I called Griff and he answered on the first ring. He couldn't move around like he wanted too because he has his young bull too. Crimson know she needs to bring her ass home. I'm real fuckin' close to have Wire track her cell phone so me and Griff pull up. I let Danielle get away once and I refused to do it again.

"Stop calling my phone. Crimson hasn't dropped the location yet. Aye you're still getting Camina from school, right? I got to scoop Cariuna and take her to dance practice. Mother Dear she's going to get Lil Griff. I don't know what you did to my child, but she had the teacher to call me to make sure you were picking her up from school?" Griff has his hands tied with Camina. She's not like that with me. I want a daughter.

"I'm headed to her school now. I think you and Crimson should start paying me to watch her. I didn't call you to ask about Danielle. I got Slap following Mya. He said Baine pulled up over there tricking. Check it. I want Wire to bug her fuckin' house so I can see what her and Baine are up too. I just want to run it by you. When I kill him, it has nothing to do with her but everything to do with him." I know Griff's trying to get his words together. I'm not asking for permission. I'm just fuckin' telling him.

"Oh yeah? Damn he's over there that soon. I agree with you, wire that bitch up. Are you sure you don't want any cameras in there? If Mya's pregnant with your seed what's the point of her keeping company with Baine. Are you cool with that? I never thought she was vindictive, but you fucked shawty up bad. I told you a long time ago about juggling multiple women." I know Griff was going to bring up old shit. He always does.

"I got mad love for Mya, but I've never been in love with her. Danielle always had my heart and you know that. She still has it. If Baine and Mya want each other that's on them. I just want a fair shot with Danielle that's it. I'm done with the games and shit." Me and Griff ended our conversation. I pulled up at Camina's school.

Mya

I looked at my watch it's a little after 2:00 p.m. I worked a 12 hour shift last night. I shouldn't have even opened my fuckin' door. I gave Baine my address two days and he's just coming by. He came baring gifts, so I welcomed him in. I wish I would've known it was him. I would've put some clothes. He brought me some roses and the money that I've asked for. I counted the bills to make sure it was all there. It's $4000.00 like I asked. I stuffed the bills in my bra and tightened my robe. I placed the roses in vase in a kitchen. Baine walked up behind me and wrapped his arms around my waist. He bit the crook of my neck.

"You're a little too close don't you think," I asked? Baine unfastened my robe. His hands roamed every inch of my body. His touch alone sent chills through my body. My robe dropped to the floor. He picked me up and sat me on the countertop. He stood in between my legs. We locked eyes with each other. He's so fuckin' fine. Damn he's everything. Why would Danielle want to cheat on him? She's so fuckin' stupid.

"Mya you're worried about the wrong shit. We both want each other. Tell me you don't want me how I want you? The only difference is I'm separated from my wife now, so we no longer have prolong that we want each other.

It's somethings I want to do with you. Can I do them Mya," he asked? Baine threw my legs over his shoulders. Hit bit the creases of my thighs. I want him so bad and right now I don't have anything to lose.

"It's some things you want to do to me Baine. It's something I want to do to you, but I don't want to be a rebound. I know you're only doing this to help you get over your wife, but I'm not trying to take it there. Sex only makes things complicated and I don't want to complicate us. I'll fight temptation for now." Baine wasn't trying to hear anything I had to say. He started finger fuckin' me wet. I almost came on sight. "Baine you're not listening to anything I'm fuckin' saying right now."

"Mya I'm not fuckin' with you on a rebound. Danielle and I have been over for a few years now. I just didn't approach you because I knew you knew who I was, and I thought you wouldn't be cool fuckin' with a married man. You ended my marriage for me. I need a good woman like you. I think a good woman like you needs a faithful nigga like me. I wanted you before I knew Rashad was fuckin' my EX wife. You came into Nik and Skeet's a few times peeping me before you told me about their affair.

Our chemistry has always been there. Are we going to keep talking or can we go ahead and take it there? Your pussy is already wet. I want to see if I can get it wetter," he asked? Baine said all the right things. It's crazy he felt everything I felt. I feel like he's being sincere about his intentions.

Fuck Danielle and Rashad. Danielle didn't deserve Baine. I wonder if I could make him my husband. I opened my legs giving him easy access. I pointed to my pussy. Baine ran his tongue across his lips.

"Please don't make me regret this," I moaned. Baine ran his tongue up and down my thighs. He made love to my pussy with his mouth. His tongue felt so good. My legs wouldn't stop shaking. We made a mess on the countertop. I ran my hands through his dreads. I held onto them for support. Baine raised up from between my legs. My juices coated his beard. I ran my tongue across my lips. He stood in between my legs. I leaned up and placed a kiss on his lips. Th kiss we shared is so passionate. Baine picked me up. I wrapped my legs around his waist. I wanted to feel him so bad.

"Where's your room?" I pointed upstairs. Baine carried me upstairs to my room. He tossed me on my bed. My body bounced a little. He grabbed my legs and pulled me to the edge of the bed. It's been a minute since I had sex. Baine's dropped his pants and boxers to the floor. Damn he's so fuckin' fine. Baine forced his way inside of me. His dick was medium length, but It was so fuckin' thick and wide it had a lot of weight to it.

It had three veins that were very visible. Two on the sides and one in the middle. He's being very gentle with me. It took him a minute to get in, because I'm tight. I haven't had sex in a minute and I'm pregnant. The moment he got inside of me. I gasped.

He started stroking me long deep and hard. I couldn't even move. I squirmed a little bit and he started picking up the pace.

He knew what the fuck he was doing. I laid there and took everything he was serving. I wanted to ride him. I came so many times I lost count. My eyes rolled in the back of my head. Baine's dick was so hard. I just wanted to ride it one time. He pulled out.

“Get up there I want you to ride me,” he asked? He didn't have to tell me twice. I'm about to put on for this nigga. I mounted him. He took both of my breasts in his hand and started sucking them. I started squatting and riding. His hands where rested on my ass and my breasts suffocated his lips. I'm almost at my peak and I can feel he's almost at his. “I'm about to cum Mya damn this pussy feels good.” A small smile appeared on my face, I wanted to make him cum. I sped up my pace Baine and I both came.

Mother Dear

I don't want to smoke around these kids, but I need something strong to calm my nerves. I haven't had this much company since I put everybody out. Sherry came through here with Jermesha's kids. Rashad dropped off Camina, Lil Rashad and his nephew BJ. I made him give me a sack of weed. I know he had some on him because I could smell it on him when he walked through the door. He said it's Gelato It might be too strong for me. Shit I snatched the weed and $100.00 out of his hand. I told him my house isn't a daycare. The kids were up front playing with Sherry. I had to keep an eye on Camina. I know Sherry didn't care for Crimson's kids. I came back into my den to smoke a little bit of this Kush. I passed the blunt to Gladys she didn't want to hit it. I rolled my eyes at her.

"I'm good, you know my doctors test me for drugs. I don't need them folks up in my business." she laughed. More for me. I knew Gladys wasn't about to hit this shit. I was I need it. Camina hasn't been here five minutes and she's getting on my damn last nerves. I love her to death, but she talks too damn much. She's nothing like her momma, but every bit of her grand momma.

"Don't say I ain't never gave you shit. Gladys have you heard from Daniella and Danielle. I know I told Crimson that I would help with her kids while she was gone, but damn her and her momma need to come home.

They're on vacation and I'm here babysitting these damn kids. I could've sworn Troy said she would watch her. I ain't seen one damn funeral in the paper that she's sung at this week, but every time I call her ass, she ain't answering the damn phone.

I called Shanden too her motherfuckin' ass said she's teaching her fitness class. Shit take Camina she can teach them people. Shanden said Camina was calling people fat the last time, so she can't come back. They wanted refund since Camina embarrassed them. I can't even call Willie Earl over here to break me off because Camina's too damn nosey. I don't need her telling my business to everybody.

Your grandson in-law Rashad dropped off Lil Rashad and his nephew, talking about he had to meet Griff at the Trap. Griff's supposed to be with Cariuna at dance practice. I knew he was lying. He better be glad I like his ass or else I would've told him no. Are you sure you don't want to hit it Gladys this is some good shit," I asked? Shoot this weed had me coughing. I had to pound my chest a few times.

"I like Rashad too, but you know Danielle isn't trying to hear that. I haven't heard from them. I'm trying not to bother her too much because I know Coop and Daniella are smothering her. I wouldn't be surprised if Danielle didn't come back. I know how much she's missed them. Rashad asked me had I heard from her. I lied and told him no. I know he didn't believe me. Cara do you hear somebody knocking at your door," she asked? Who's knocking at my damn door.

“Sherry get the damn door,” I yelled. I hope it's not them damn Jehovah Witnesses. I’m trying to smoke my shit in peace.

“Momma It's the police. I'm not getting the door you know I got warrants and they don't expire,” Sherry yelled. I jumped out my chair quick as hell. I grabbed the air freshener and started spraying this Febreze to kill the weed smell.

“Gladys light some damn incense no burn that damn sage. I can’t let the police come up in here and I’ve been smoking this weed. Shit, fuck, damn.” I emptied the Febreze can trying to kill the smell. It says it’s an odor eliminator. I still smell weed damn it. I shouldn’t have fired this shit up. I went to the door to see what the police wanted.

“Hi, we received a call about a loud smell,” The officer stated. I know this weed was loud but DAMN. Who in the fuck called the police over here? I know damn well they didn’t smell this shit outside. I swear if Lou Ann called the damn police over here because I didn’t invite her to smoke.

I’m going to jail. She needs to buy her own damn weed. I looked at the police like he was fuckin' crazy. I started shaking. I know he could tell I’m nervous. I’m suing Febreze because this damn spray ain’t eliminated shit.

“Where did the call come from. What kind of smell was it,” I asked? The police looked at me and smiled. I looked over my shoulder and Camina was standing right behind me smiling.

I swear if this little damn girl tells the police I'm smoking some weed. Crimson will have two kids and not three.

"The call came from this house. The dispatcher said it was child." God the cute little girl you sent down here for me to love I'm about to kill her. Why in the hell would she call the damn police? I told her about touching my damn phone.

"Camina did you call the police," I asked? I know Lil Rashad and his cousin didn't know where my house phone is. Camina knows. She CAN'T come back over here if she did. I mean that shit.

"Yes, Mother Dear, Auntie Sherry cootie cat stink. I called the police. My momma said your cootie cat ain't supposed to stink. Yours don't stink Mother Dear. I didn't know who else to call. They can lock her up, so I won't smell her cootie cat," she whined. Camina fanned her nose. The police officer busted out laughing.

"I'm sorry sir. I do apologize for the inconvenience." The police officer left. "Camina I should beat your little ass. You don't call the police because somebody stink. Sherry bring your motherfuckin' ass down here right now." Sherry marched in the living room. She did have a strong stench. "I don't know what man you fuckin' but you need to stop. Camina called the police because your cootie cat stink.

Go sit your ass in the tub with some Epsom salt, a little bleach and Apple cider vinegar. You need some antibiotics." Sherry started to say something. I pointed upstairs.

Danielle

Despite all the bullshit that happened earlier. Today's not so bad. I finally got a few hours of sleep. I needed it because my night was the fuckin' worst. My mother planned us a dope spa day. I've been smiling ever since I got here. Crimson and Cheree joined us. I thought me and Crimson were close but my momma and Cheree are worse than us. It explains why we are the way we are. I didn't realize I was so tense but I am. It felt good to kick back sip and unwind. I needed this.

I've been trying to clear my mind from everything that Baine has done so far but I can't. His text fucked me up. He finally admitted he's cheated throughout the relationship for some reason I can't seem to get over that. I didn't even realize I started crying. I wiped my eyes quick. I didn't want anybody to catch it. I might have wiped them too late because my mother came over quick.

"Danielle are you okay baby," she asked? My mother got up from her masseuse table to come and check on me. She's so attentive to me. I wrapped my arms around her. I'm so thankful because I need it.

"I'm okay momma. I just had a moment. I just got a lot of things on my mind that I can't seem to shake. I'll be okay. I'm taking it one day at a time. I appreciate you,"

I beamed. I'm really enjoying being in her presence. It's peaceful she brings me peace.

"You don't have to thank me that's what I'm here for. I'm supposed to do this. Thank you for allowing me in and welcoming me with open arms," she smiled. I wiped my eyes with the back of my hands. My mother placed a kiss on my forehead and went back to her masseuse table. I grabbed my phone. I need something to get my mind off Baine and his actions. I haven't been on social media in a few days, now would be the perfect time to catch up with the world to see what's going on out there besides what's happening in my fucked-up life.

I logged into my Facebook account first. I need to fill my kindle. I need to see if any of my favorite authors have dropped a new book. I checked my notifications. Someone tagged me in a live video. It's from Bre'Elle why would this bitch be tagging me, and I don't even fuck with her? My page is public, but I could've sworn I blocked her years ago after I beat her ass. Baine wants the world to know that we're not together. I see now these bitches want to get beside themselves since we're not together. I don't give a fuck what me and Baine have going on, but I won't tolerate the disrespect at all.

I looked at the live and shook my head instantly. I swear this nigga ain't shit. This bitch had the nerve to say **"My baby daddy's wife cheated. I used to be the side bitch now I'm the main bitch and his wife is the side bitch. My baby daddy gave me all his wife's shit."**

I swear Baine is so fuckin' low. I don't even know why I'm surprised. He hates me this bad that he did this. He gave this bitch all my fuckin' clothes, shoes, purses, jewelry. I swear he keeps a classless bitch on his arms. I would never take a man's wife's hand me downs. I don't give a fuck if the shit had tags on it or not. I won't do it. She really thought she was doing something. I swear she's trash.

"Crimson," I yelled. She looked at me to see what I wanted. "Come here I want you to see something." Crimson walked over to me. I tossed her my phone. She looked at the video and shook her head.

"Danielle, I swear he's no good. Here I am thinking he's a good man and he's a fuckin' monster. I swear he's acting like a real bitch. Excuse my language but that's not cool. What type of chick would do that? I know you didn't marry him for that but get him for everything. He needs to suffer. I swear he deserves it. He needs to pay you in cash and in tears. Girl did you see Jermesha stank ass in the comments laughing. She's been a fan too," Crimson explained. I swear he's the devil in disguise. I tagged my lawyer in the video so she could record it for proof adultery. I'm not even going to scoop to Baine's level.

"Crimson I don't even want his money that's the crazy part. He can keep it. I just want to be free from all the bull shit. I just want to be by myself I'm sick of him," I argued. I've been sick of him. My mother walked up to me. She snatched my phone out my hand. I guess she wanted to see what has, me so upset.

I put my head down because I can't win for loosing. I swear it never ends. His job is to make me miserable and uncomfortable. I can feel my mother staring a hole in me. She cupped my chin forcing me to look at her. I had to blink my eyes twice so the tears wouldn't fall. My mother wiped my tears.

"Danielle let them tears fall baby but make this the last time you cry over that fuckin' bastard. You don't have to put on a front for me or them. We're family. Baby he's not worth your tears you've cried enough. I hate that you've been dealing with this. Whatever he took I'll replace it and some. You don't need a motherfuckin thing from him. She can have it; she needs it more than you.

I don't understand these females she wants to embarrass you but she's embarrassing herself glorying somebody's husband gave her his wife's stuff. She's just as stupid him. They deserve each other. Find you home to live in right now. I'm fuckin' buying it. Your husband he fucked over the right one. Send this to your lawyer because he's going to pay you for deformation of character," she argued. My mother is pissed.

He wants a reaction out of me, but he'll never get it. My mind traveled back to Rashad. A small smiled appeared on my face. In a perfect world we could be together, but it's too bad we don't live in a perfect world. Baine would never let me, and Rashad be happy. I think this time around I'm going to choose me fuck what anybody else thinks it is what it is.

THE NEXT DAY

Chapter-12

Nikki

I've been calling Danielle for a few days now, and she's yet to answer. She sent me a text two days ago, but she didn't call me like she promised. I know she's embarrassed, but she's has nothing to be ashamed of. I would never judge her. I swear it's not like her at all to not call me. We talk every fuckin' day. The same conversations me and Journee have in the morning are similar too, the conversations me and Danielle have. I just want to make sure she's straight. I can't believe what happened at the wedding myself. Everybody's talking about it. I don't know who leaked the fuckin' video, but it's been buzzing on Facebook, Instagram. Media-takeout, The Shaderoom. Crimson's wedding reception that motherfucka went up.

My bitch was a trending MOTHERFUCKIN' TOPIC. A few hoes where in the comments talking their shit. I made sure I checked all those bitches and talked my motherfuckin' shit until they fuckin' blocked me.

Those bitches knew what's up, they reported my comments. I logged in from Journee and Alexis page and still went on them bitches and pussy ass niggas that had something to say. I started to go by her house, but Journee and Alexis said not too. I don't even know why I listened to those bitches. I love Danielle she's cool, as fuck. It's rare that I befriend females. I met Danielle through Journee and Crimson at Julissa's a few years ago. We clicked instantly. I think it's because we had the same sign.

Every month we all get together for Ladies night. We're close I fucks with her. She's good people. I consider has as my friend. I think we connect because we've been married the longest out of our circle of friends. I know she's going through a lot. I got her back and her front. I knew something was going on between her and Rashad. The moment he snatched her up and pulled her into the pantry. I knew it was more to it than she made it out to be. I swear she was on her phone with him all night at the bachelorette party.

I don't know Danielle and Rashad's history, but it reminds me of Journee and Juelz. I swear it's DANGEROUS. My heart cracked watching that shit unfold. I don't know what type of nigga Rashad is. I know he's a killer and he's in love them niggas went at it blow for blow. I know he's from the Eastside. I don't know too much about those Eastside niggas.

I've seen him with Slap and Wire everybody knows those two niggas ain't got no sense and they're reckless as fuck. I know Baine because he's from the Westside everybody knows him. He's from Grove Park. I used to see him around the way all the time. I didn't know him. I knew of him. He used to be a hoe back in the day. I didn't get that he was still a hoe now.

Sometimes we double date with each other and from my experience seeing the two of them interact with each other these past three years. I know everybody's confused. Shit I am. I just watched Baine dote and love on his wife. Shit went left real motherfuckin' quick. I noticed how he looked at Danielle all throughout the wedding. I swear I'm not going to anymore weddings. Journee's reception was a shit show too. Khadijah smacked the shit out of Dawn.

I don't think I've ever witnessed anything as intense. Maybe because me and Danielle are close. I didn't think they had problems. No relationship is perfect. Skeet and I have been together for years and we've never stepped out on each other. Our shit isn't perfect we argue, and we have plenty of disagreements. Skeet ain't crazy enough to fuck another bitch. I'm not saying I'm the baddest bitch walking because it's plenty of beautiful black women out here. I'll KILL Skeet before I ever let him be comfortable with another bitch.

I got four kids by this man and he wants another one. Danielle is bold as fuck. I don't know who's worse her or Alexis. I think Alexis got Danielle though. I swear I have the craziest friends.

I wouldn't trade my bitches for shit. I don't think she thought he would do that. She had to know that nigga was crazy. I would've never pulled that off. Ain't no MOTHERFUCKIN' WAY. Skeet would've murked something. Skeet looked at me and smiled. He whispered in my ear. I wish you motherfuckin' would. I didn't even look at him. I know how Skeet feels about marriage he doesn't believe in cheating and all that extra shit. Thank God I found me a real one early.

I just knew somebody was about to killed at the wedding reception. Baine had that look in his eyes he was hurt and ready to murk something. I swear those Eastside niggas ain't shit. She kept brushing me off and said he's flirting. I knew better. I looked at my phone and it's Journee calling. Damn what does she want.

I was hoping it was Danielle's sneaky ass calling me. I swear we got to fuckin' rap ASAP. I need the tea. She never told me her and Rashad had history that nigga said I ended your marriage for you. I damn near passed out. I felt that shit. Rashad didn't give a fuck. I shouldn't answer but that's my bitch. Shit I'm trying to get in touch with Danielle maybe she's heard from Crimson. I went ahead and answered anyway.

"What Journee Leigh!" I sighed. It's too early for her shit. I knew she would be calling me because Skeet, Juelz and Alonzo went to handle some business. I know that's the only reason why she's on my phone this morning.

The kids are on Fall break my mother has mine and Juelz's parents has hers. I need to get my ass up and head to the bar. We open at 11:00 a.m. and it'll be rolling around quick. We always have crowd before noon.

I wanted Skeet to open this spot for years and he's finally done it. I'm excited. It's a lot work of running a business. Our bar is booming we're thinking about opening another location off Hollywood Road. I wanted it; Skeet made it happen. I can't complain.

I love being a business owner. I needed to do something with Skeet's money besides spend it. It's time to start investing and buying back the block. We should've done it years ago, but we're doing it now.

"Damn! Excuse you! Who pissed in your fuckin' cheerios? Let me guess Skeet didn't buss that pussy wide open before he left? I'm just returning your phone call. I see you called me earlier I'll call you back later." I swear Journee makes me sick with her smart-ass mouth. She saw I called her, but she didn't answer the phone. I know she wasn't doing shit, but she expects me to answer and talk whenever she calls.

"Bitch don't do me. You know I sat all on Skeet's face before he left. It's a daily routine. Squat and ride HOE! I'm trying to get in touch with Danielle to make sure she's alive. Have you heard from Crimson because I'm this close to calling her motherfuckin' phone to see what's up?"

I mean that shit. "We need to know what's up and what's going on." Journee called herself laughing at me. I don't see what's funny. I swear Journee always think some shit funny. Yes, our home front is okay finally. It took us a while to get here, but it's some people that's not as fortunate as us.

We were taking hits left and right. I know Danielle needs us. Black women don't stick together but in our circle we do. We uplift inspire and encourage each other. I know Danielle needs us because if she didn't, she wouldn't be on my mind so heavy.

"Yeah that why I called you back. I just got finish talking to Crimson on Facetime. Danielle's good, shit she looked great to me. Them bitches are balling shit I should've ran right behind them. They're in Hawaii posted up at Danielle's momma's house. Kid fuckin' free something told me to run with them," she stated. Oh okay. Journee of all people should know motherfuckas can put on fronts for the public and still be going through it on the inside. She was with Kairo for years but knowing damn well her stubborn ass wanted Juelz's ass. Girl bye!

"For real bitch call Crimson on three way so I can speak to Danielle's motherfuckin' ass. Hell, yeah, we should've run too. I need a vacation and Hawaii doesn't sound too bad right now."

"Okay hold on." Journee placed me on hold. She merged Crimson in.

She answered on the first ring. “Crimson, girl I didn’t mean to call you back, but put Danielle’s ass on the phone Nikki wants to speak with her before she dies.” I wasn't even about to argue with Journee. I'm just concerned.

“Hey Nikki! I told Danielle to call you, hold on,” Crimson beamed. I know why Danielle hasn't called me. She probably thinks I'm judging her but I'm not. I'm Team HER. I'm riding for my girl before I ride with any nigga.

“Okay.” I fuck with Crimson tough too. She’s cool people.

“Hello who is this,” she sassed. I swear I’m going to hurt Danielle’s ass this bitch is out here living her best life and I’m worried sick about her.

“The BITCH you should’ve called a few days ago. What’s up? I thought we were better than that Danielle. We talk everyday Danielle come on NOW. We don’t text we talk. I’m trying to make sure you’re still breathing. I get it you’re going through some shit, but BITCH I’m going through it too. Ain't shit changed with us plenty of women find their selves in sticky situations. You ain't the first and you won't be the last. I'm here if you need me. I just wanted to check on you. I’m good.” I know Danielle's going through some shit, but now isn't the time to be shutting motherfuckas out.

“Nikki I’m sorry. Please don’t take offense to me not reaching out. We are better than that. I’ve been going through some shit. You saw what went down.

I'm in Hawaii but I'm not relaxing. I wish I could, but I can't. My husband is trying to strip me from every fuckin' thing. Her burned down my fuckin' clinic. You know my business is my baby. I'll protect my business at all cost. Thank God I got all my shit out of there. All the accounts that we had together. He cleaned all the money out of the accounts. I swear niggas ain't shit.

It's cool though because I always bounce back. I'm rebuilding. I need you to do something for me. It maybe overstepping my boundaries. I don't know how much you heard but. It's this bitch named Mya. She met my husband at your club. I don't know how long ago she used to fuck with Rashad. She was the one that sent him the pictures. I need to see that camera footage.

I want to know how long he's been having conversations with her. I didn't want to call you because I thought you might have known Baine was fuckin' around me." I know Danielle didn't say what the fuck I think she said. Any female that I'm close too and they're significant others know me. Those motherfuckas ain't crazy enough to let see me them with another female. I'll cut up on their nigga the same way I would cut up on mine.

"Danielle are you fuckin' serious? Bitch I would never watch your husband cheat or entertain a female in my presence and not tell you. We're better than that. I work the morning shift and Skeets works the night shift. I'll check the footage to see what I can find out.

Who is Mya and where did she come from? What's her name on social media? I need it so I can look her ass up. She needs her motherfuckin' ass whooped. Danielle don't give that bitch no pass she violated for real. I can't believe Baine. I would never expect that from him." I heard of females doing some low shit, but I ain't never ran with a bitch that got down like that.

How did she get those pictures? I love Skeet but damn I'm not doing all that. You caught a nigga you were fuckin'; fuckin' somebody else you take pictures and send it to her husband. Bitch you need you ass whooped.

The last bitch that sent me a picture of Skeet that bitch can't talk or use her brain she's a fuckin' vegetable. Rashad out here slanging good pipe for days he got this bitch going wild.

"I wish I was lying Nikki, but I'm not. He wants a divorce. I'll give him one. I talked to him a few days ago. Of course, he's still salty but, he's adamant about divorcing me and leaving me with nothing. Nikki to be honest I'm not even going to fight for my marriage. I've been keeping this together for as long as I can.

I don't have any more fight in me. I done gave this shit all I fuckin' got. Baine always had money I can't deny that, but since we've been together, he acquired a lot more by investing in legitimate businesses. I helped with that. I lawyered up.

If he wants to play ball, I'm the wrong BITCH to be on the court with. I don't even want anything from him. It's just the principle. I didn't marry him for his money. I married him because I loved him, and I thought what we had was real. My one fuck up could never weigh up to his numerous fuck ups.

I don't know shit about Mya. I just know how she looks. Trust me I'm going to beat her ass. I gave her a pass when she caught us but from here on out. It's on sight. Hopefully Crimson can call Rashad and get her last name." My heart goes out to Danielle.

My girl is going through it. In so many ways she said he cheated but she stayed down through it all. Baine got her fucked up. We all make mistakes. If she loved, you past yours why can't you do the same. I swear I don't get niggas. It's okay for you to fuck up, but if I fuck up, you're gone. What type of shit is that?

"I got your back. You don't have to go through this shit alone. I got you never question that. I'm down for whatever. I'm sorry you're going through this. I didn't think it was that deep to scream he wants a divorce. I need a last name and location on Mya. I don't know too many chicks from the Eastside.

I'll have Alexis to ask Leah. Danielle I'm about to head to the bar to get you this information.

On Mya's motherfuckin' MOMMA that BITCH should pray to the GOD you catch her before I do. Danielle I'm going to stomp that bitch out.

I'm just saying what if your husband was a fuckin' lunatic and killed you because of this bitch. It's levels to this shit. She violated you so that bitch violated me." I'm serious. I don't give a fuck. She could've gotten somebody killed. You don't do that shit because a man doesn't want you, he wants someone else. She doesn't even deserve to breathe the same air as Danielle. I hate to say it but they're going to find Mya somewhere stinking. Lame ass bitch.

"Nikki don't do that please. I got something special planned for Mya. I'll give it to her she shook my world up temporarily, but what I'm about to due to her is far worse than anything she could've ever done to me. Please don't take me beating her ass away from me. I appreciate you Pudd! I mean that. Thank you for always being a listening ear and confidant. I'm falling but thank you for picking me back up again. Thank you for always speaking life into me."

"No thanks needed. I'm only doing what I'm supposed to do. You're my PUDD and you're stuck with me. I can't promise you Danielle that I won't tap her ass. I'll never look a bitch in the face that's crossed one of MINE and not pass her these motherfuckin' HANDS. It's not who I am. She tried you which means she tried me. If you catch her than she deserves an extra ass whooping. She crossed the line and for her sake and not mine when I pull these tapes the conversation should is legit."

“I hope so too Nikki, but I know Baine. Whatever you find on those tapes I want to see them. I want to see everything. I won't be surprised. I've been with this man for seven years. I've seen it all and I've been through a lot. It's nothing he could do that would hurt me. I've been wearing my big girl panties for years.” Danielle and I ended our conversation. I can't believe my girl is going through all of this. To make matters worse this bitch pulled up on Baine at my place of business.

The late-night crowd is catered to a different type of people. It's $100.00 just to get in. If Mya paid $100.00 to get through the door that bitch was looking for something else besides exposing Danielle. Skeet didn't want me working at night because I need to be at home with the kids which is understandable.

I know he didn't want any niggas pushing up on me. All the dope boys and niggas with money post up at our spot at night. Basic bitches only pull up on the first of the month, when we host our first of the month event. Freaky Friday's and it's only $20.00 to get in and $8.00 drinks all night. We do that once a month. If you were a bitch looking for nigga with some money, it's going to cost you.

I swear I didn’t think Baine was out here doing my girl dirty. I guess it's true to never judge a book by its cover. Baine took Danielle through some shit. I swear she's better than me, because I can't. I get it though. Everybody isn't meant to walk away.

Some people stay and pray for better days. My phone started ringing Journee's calling me back. I shouldn't answer. I should do her how she does me. I'm different I want to hear what Journee thinks. If anybody can relate Journee for damn sure can.

"Hello." I pulled my covers back. It's time to get my day started. My clothes were already lying on the ironing board. I just need to get out the bed to take a shower.

"Why did you hang up," she asked? I rolled my eyes as if Journee could see me. She knew why I hung up. She didn't have to ask. I never drag me feet. I got shit to do.

"Because I need to get my day started. I need to get everything setup at the bar and grill because I'll be in my office checking out the tapes to see what's up. Are you dressed what time are you going in? Have you left your house yet?" Journee should've been gone by now.

"I'm not going in today. I'm coming to the bar to help you out. I feel so bad listening to Danielle man. I should've known better. Nikki we've been best friends forever.

I swear we may argue but we've never fought. We can agree to disagree that's just how we are.

I wouldn't trade our friendship for nothing in this world. I swear to God I'm so blessed to have you. You've never turned your back on me. I've never had to question your loyalty to me. I'm glad that someone else can experience what you are to me.

Danielle is lucky to have you in her corner," she explained. Hearing Journee reveal that brought tears to my eyes. I sniffled. I wiped my eyes with the back of my hands. I swear sometimes I think she takes me for granted. I'm glad she doesn't. I'm always there when she needs me.

"Thank you, Journee! I appreciate you. It's too early for you to be making me cry."

"I'm sorry I just don't want you to ever think I take you for granted. I swear I want to kill Baine. I want to know what he did Nikki. Me and Crimson are closer than me and Danielle because I met her first. I'm always open. Whenever we have our lady's night and we pick a topic to discuss none of us hold back. Bitch Danielle has been holding back. She's been suffering in silence and she didn't have too. I know what that feels like. I missed the fuckin' sign Nikki." I hear what Journee is saying and I know how she feels. The last thing I need is for her to beat herself up.

"Don't do that Journee don't beat yourself up. We missed the signs. We would've never known they had problems until the wedding. We can't dwell on that. The only thing we can focus on is the right now. I really don't want the details. I heard enough. If Baine's doing everything, she claims he is. I see what type of nigga he is. That's wrong I can't rock with that. Danielle ain't no gold digger. I've never been a fan of a fuck nigga. Hell, Kairo loved you and even though it didn't work out. He left you all that shit."

"True." Me and Journee finished rapping with each other. I looked at the clock it's 8:45 a.m. I jumped in the shower to handle my hygiene.

I finally made it to the restaurant. My employees were in their cars waiting on me to open. It's almost 10:00 a.m. I noticed Journee's car. She's sitting in her car waiting on me. I stepped out my car and headed toward her car. I knocked on her window. She was too busy on her phone she didn't even notice me walk up. She jumped. Oops I opened her car door.

"Damn Nikki you scared me! You look cute does Skeet know his wife comes to work dressed like this," she beamed. I threw up my middle finger. Skeet doesn't tell me what I can and can't wear to work.

"You should've been paying attention. Come on Journee let's go. We got shit to do. I hope you didn't tell Juelz what's going on. I don't need him telling Skeet what we're doing. Niggas stick together." Journee's looking at me like I'm crazy. Shit I'm telling the truth. I unlocked my office door. She took a seat behind my desk.

I'm glad she came to help me because I have a lot to do here. I won't be able to sit back here until about 2:00 p.m. I logged into my computer. I know she's tells Juelz everything because that's her husband. I tell Skeet everything too, but I'm not about to tell him I'm looking through these fuckin' tapes to see what Baine has been up too.

I brought up the cameras. It's so much footage to go through. I don't even know where to start but we need to start somewhere.

“Danicllc said Mya showed him the pictures a month ago. I'm going to start the footage back two months prior. Let me know what you see.” Journee nodded her head in agreement. I went out to help assist my employees with our workload. I know Journee she'll find everything we need. I went back in the kitchen to check out the menu. One of the local businesses in the community are having a party here this afternoon for lunch.

They wanted a specific menu. The cooks we have here are so dope. I know they can pull it off. It smells good. I know they're doing an amazing job. I tasted the spinach dip and the baby back ribs it tastes amazing. I left the kitchen and headed to the bar. I had to make sure our bar was fully stocked they paid $3000.00 for an open bar for their staff. I want their business again.

The liquor and beer were just delivered. I didn't want Skeet to run out of anything tonight. I made sure the place is extra clean. I checked the bathrooms. They were spotless. The tables where clean. Our guests just arrived. I greeted our guest. I made sure our DJ played contemporary music not just rap. I made the playlist last night.

My servers brought out the food. They started setting up everything to serve the guest. So far so good.

I gave my assistant manager the okay to take over. She knows to come and get me if she needs me.

I made my way back to my office to see what Journee came up on. I ordered us some food and something to drink. My assistant helped me bring it back. I know Journee would want some wings and a salad. I wanted a Caesar salad with chicken strips. I opened the door and Journee's head was buried behind the computer.

“Are you hungry,” I asked?

“Of course, what you got,” she asked?

“The only thing you order.” Journee had the biggest smile on her face. I slid Journee's food in front of her. She grabbed her drink. I took a seat beside her. I'm hungry too. I skipped out on breakfast.

“Did you find anything?” Journee wiped her mouth with her napkin.

“Did I find anything? Bitch I found a lot. You've been gone about two hours. I'm not even halfway through the month yet. I don't know if this is the Mya chic, but Baine meets a lot of women here. I done seen about three different bitches pull up on this nigga within a month. Nikki, Danielle must not come out with her husband at night. Baine's a real fuckin' hoe out here girl look at this shit. I'm glad she cheated on his friendly dick ass look at him.”

Journee hit rewind. I looked at the footage. Baine's so fuckin' disrespectful with his shit. Skeet dapped this nigga up while he had a bitch sitting on his lap that's not his fuckin' wife. I don't even want to show Danielle this shit, but we're trying to find Mya, so I don't know if this is her or not.

"Journee, I don't want to show Danielle this. I wish I wouldn't have agreed to it. I can't wait to see Skeet. I'm going to slap the shit out of him. How dare he smile up in Danielle's face knowing damn well her husband got some shit going on." Speak of the devil Skeet and Juelz just walked in. Skeet looked at me and ran his tongue across his lips Why are they here? I looked at Journee and rolled my eyes because they weren't supposed to be here. I know she told Juelz we were over here.

"What are you doing here," I asked? Skeet leaned in to kiss me and I curved him. I'm not feeling him right now. I can't get down with him seeing Baine cheat and he doesn't say anything.

"Damn I didn't think I needed a reason to pop up at our business or to see my wife?" I ignored Skeet. Juelz walked straight over to Journee. He picked her up and sat her in his lap. She started feeding him her food. Skeet stepped in my personal space. He sized me up. I smacked the shit out of his ass.

Journee and Juelz both looked at me. Skeet grabbed my waist roughly. I tried to remove his hands off me.

He had a tight hold on my waist. I don’t give a fuck. I don’t play that shit.

“Aye Nikki you better watch your motherfuckin' hands. What the fuck is wrong with you? What the fuck I do? I ain't did shit,” he argued. I don’t care about him having a fuckin’ attitude. I got a fuckin’ attitude too.

“You've done plenty. You knew Baine was cheating on my girl and you didn't say shit. Baine meets a different bitch here every fuckin' week. Looking at the cameras Skeet, you see all that shit and you don’t say shit.” Skeet cupped my chin roughly forcing me to look at him.

“Nikki, whatever the FUCK that man got going on with his wife ain't got a MOTHERFUCKIN' THING to do WITH ME AND YOU. I met that nigga through YOU. We only had a conversation because of YOU and his wife. You wanted to double date I did that shit for YOU. Baine ain't my nigga. You know my FUCKIN' NIGGAS. Juelz, Alonzo, and Smoke. My niggas ain’t out cheating on none of their wives. I don’t give a fuck about what the next man is doing because it’s not my fuckin’ business.

My NIGGAS ain't gone never cheat on their wives. Nikki we ain't got no MOTHERFUCKIN’ problems. So, don’t make us have none. Do you understand what the fuck I’m saying? Stay out them folk business.

You're doing too much. Why are you checking the FUCKIN' cameras to see what this nigga is up too? Don't use OUR MOTHERFUCKIN' club for no ID investigation type SHIT. It's bad for business.

We don't work for MOTHERFUCKIN' CHEATERS. Y'all are trying to catch this nigga cheating and scheming shit? It's not our business stay out of that shit. You know me and I know you. I understand Danielle's your girl and I know you're going to ride for your girl no matter what. I expect you too. Danielle's a smart girl. She's knows her husband better than you. She knew what type of nigga he was when she married him.

A man changes because he wants too. I always wanted to be faithful to you. I know what the fuck I got at home. It's not a bitch out here that's worth me losing YOU or our family. Nikki do you understand me," he asked. I nodded my head in agreement. Journee and Juelz left. Skeet's sitting at the desk mugging me.

"I understand where you're coming from Skeet but understand where the fuck I'm coming from. All money ain't good money and guess what I don't want that niggas fuckin' money. It's not good here. He can't stop a fuckin' bag. Danielle's my bitch. I'm in her corner forever. I don't give a fuck if Baine ain't your nigga.

You condoned that shit. You watched that man cheat on his wife a few times. See that's the problem with niggas now days.

Nobody wants to speak up and say that's wrong. You were the same nigga that was talking shit in my ear about what I better not do, but you knew this nigga was cheating. I can't rock with that."

"I'm sorry Nikki." Skeet cupped my chin and kissed me.

"I forgive you don't let it happen again," I moaned. I sent Danielle all the footage she can go through it herself.

Danielle

I've been busy as fuck these past few days. I wanted to enjoy Hawaii, but I couldn't. I've been working since I got here. If you don't grind you don't shine. If you don't work, you don't eat. Baine's working overtime to make me miserable. I'm picking up the pieces and putting my life back together one piece at a time. I made an offer on our new location the seller accepted. We're closing in two weeks. My mother paid the earns money. She wired the attorney the remaining balance. Now I got to find a house.

My parents insisted on buying it for me. I'm going to let them. My daddy said whatever I want. I'm moving back to the Eastside so I can be close to my Gigi if something happened. I've been looking on Zillow and Realtor all morning. I hated living way out in The Vining's. It's official I'm starting over. My email alerted me that I had an email message from Nikki. It's the video footage. I asked for at this point I'm not sure if I want to look at it. Nothing surprises me anymore. I'll let Crimson do it because I need to find a house and furniture.

"Crimson, Nikki sent the video footage. Can you look at it for me while I continue to look at houses," I asked? Crimson nodded her head in agreement. I gave her my computer to look at the footage. I used my iPad to look at houses. I found eight houses that I like.

I don't want something to big, because it's just me. I don't have any plans to start a family anytime soon. I sent my list to my mother and father's realtor. I'm waiting on a response from her so Madison can meet up to view the properties for me. Crimson tapped me on my shoulder. I looked up to see what she wanted.

"Danielle you know I love you, and I'll protect you at all cost. What's understood doesn't need to be explained or seen. I don't want you to see anything on here. He's hurt you enough and these videos only adds fire to the flame. Just forward it to your attorney and let her do what she does. He fuckin' disgusts me. What I will say is Baine and Mya have been pushing up on each other a few times. I swear I wouldn't think Baine is a as foul as he is, if you wouldn't have said anything. I've seen it with my own two eyes. You deserve so much more," she cried.

"Okay I trust you Crimson that's why I didn't want to look at it, because I knew it would trigger me. I know who he is and I'm trying move past him. If Mya wants him, she can have him and Rashad. I'm good. It's somebody for everybody. I'm sure it's somebody for me out here," I smiled.

A WEEK LATER

Chapter-13

Griff

Danielle sent me a text telling me to come and pick up my wife. I can have her back now. It's one stipulation with that. I can't tell Rashad where she is. I can promise her that I won't. I just want my wife at home with me and our kids that's it. She didn't have to tell me twice. I'm on my fuckin' way. I miss my wife so fuckin' much. A week without her has been crazy. I need her at home right now. I have access to private jet. It'll take us a few hours to get there. I need to get the kids from Crimson's father. He has the kids he got them last night because I had to make a few moves. I told him to have them dressed before I come. It's a lot of work handling three kids on your own. I pulled up and got the kids.

Me and Bone made our way to the airport. Since it's a long flight. I guess we can stay out there for two days and come back home Monday or Tuesday. The kids have never been to Hawaii. Bone said he's coming too because Cheree needs to bring her ass home.

He knows she's trying hide from him. I stay out of people's business but if he wants to bring her home, who am I to stop him. The flight's eleven hours. Damn that's a long flight, but I'll do it again just to bring Crimson home. It took us about an hour to get to the airstrip. I made sure Camina and Cariuna were fastened in their seats good before we took off.

The flight wasn't too bad. Camina whined the whole time and aggravated her brother. I'm convinced she's my damn problem child. It's my fault because I never discipline her. I'm about to start popping her ass. Mother Dear said she can't come back over there anymore. Since she called the police on Sherry. Cariuna's an angel.

We finally made it to Honolulu about an hour ago. I checked the time on my watch it's 12:42 p.m. Danielle's mothers house was an hour away from the landing strip. We just pulled up to her house. I grabbed Lil Griff out his car seat. Cariuna and Camina stood right beside me. Bone was behind me. I knocked on Danielle's mother door. An older nigga came to the door and sized me up.

"How can I help you? You seem lost," he asked? A small laugh escaped my lips.

"I'm here to get my wife Crimson," I chuckled. Bone made his way toward the front. I heard they use to run together back in the day, but they fell out.

I really didn't want Bone coming with me because if it was still drama between the two of them.

I didn't want any parts in it because I have my kids with me, and I don't want them exposed to that shit.

"Coop stop playing fuckin' games and tell Cheree and my daughter to bring their ass on." Bone argued. He folded his arms across his chest and bit down on his toothpick. Coop sized up Bone. I swear I don't have time for these two old niggas.

"OG Bone is that you, old ass nigga. I heard that nigga was still a TECHWOOD VET? It's been some years since I saw you," he chuckled. Coop folded his arms across his chest. Bone and Coop slapped hands with each other. They gave each other a hug. "I see Cheree still got you by the balls if you're on my doorstep. I told her to tell you I said what's up. I miss you, nigga. Come on in. I got something I want to give you anyway," he stated. Bone nodded his head in agreement. Coop allowed us into his home.

"Crimson and Cheree come here," he yelled. Bone followed Coop. Damn this shit is nice as fuck. I took a seat in the family room waiting on my wife. Crimson finally came downstairs. Her mother's right behind her. I missed the fuck out of Crimson. She's looking good as fuck too.

"Mommy!" Camina and Cariuna ran to their mother. They damn near tackled her to the floor. Crimson looked at me and smiled. She knows she's in trouble. She made her way over to us. Lil Griff reached for his mother with his hands. She scooped him up and placed kisses all on his face. Crimson had her ass facing me. I missed all that.

I grabbed the belt loop on the back of her shorts and pulled her onto my lap. She smelled so fuckin' good. I missed all this.

I wrapped my arms around her waist and bit the crook of her neck. I've never heard Lil Griff laugh until his mother got him. She bounced him on her lap, and he was laughing. I whispered in Crimson's ear.

"I love you Crimson Griffey. I missed you. Can I get some love too," I asked? Crimson leaned her head back on my chest. I ran my hands through her hair. I missed everything about this woman.

"I love you to Mr. Griffey. You know I missed you. I can't wait to love on you," she smiled. I leaned in and placed a kiss on her lips. Danielle made her way downstairs.

"What's up Griff? I see you made it," Danielle asked? Cariuna ran over to give her a hug. I don't know what Camina's problem is with Danielle. Camina marched over to Danielle and stood in front of her. I wanted to see what Camina was about to say.

"Good looking out. I appreciate that." My eyes were trained on Camina and Danielle.

"Don't be taking my mommy with you. She got kids and I'm telling my uncle Rashad where you at," she laughed. Crimson looked at me and laughed. Camina whipped out her iPad to call Rashad. Danielle snatched it out of her hand and ran. Camina chased Danielle.

Cariuna ran right behind her. Ms. Cheree grabbed Lil Griff out Crimson's hand giving us some alone time.

"You heard what your daughter said you got kids. You can't bc running off likc that. Wc got a family and a newborn who needs his mother. Our girls need you too. I'm not tripping I love you Crimson, and I let you pull this stunt because I love you. I want you to always have Danielle's back because that's your girl. I need my wife too. You know I'm lost in this world without you. Do you hear me," I asked? Crimson nodded her head in agreement. She placed a kiss on my lips.

"I'm sorry Griff Danielle needed me, and she still does. I know she called you and told you to come and get me. I was leaving tomorrow to come back home. I miss you and my babies. She's in good hands with her mother and father. They got her," she sighed.

"She'll be in good hands if she brings her ass home. Rashad got her too. I won't let Baine touch her. I'll kill him before I allow that. I figured we can stay out here for two days since the flight is long. We can do something with the kids. I booked us a suite on Waikiki Beach. Grab your phone and let's go." Crimson went to grab her stuff and the kids. Danielle came out. I dapped my girl up.

"I'm sorry for ruining your honeymoon and taking your wife with me," she sighed.

"You're good. You need to call Rashad and let him know you're okay. He's worried about you."

Danielle shook her head no. "Don't be liked that. He loves you stop playing with my niggas feelings."

"I thought about, but I'm not. He should've waited on me. Your wedding wasn't the time, now my life is a mess," she sighed.

"I know but let Rashad fixed what he messed up. I'm just saying Danielle y'all love each other. You can't hide from love shawty. Call him." Crimson came back with her stuff. The kids came trailing behind her. Camina had her hand out she wanted her iPad. Danielle wasn't trying to give her that.

Crimson

Imagine my surprised when I walked in Daniella's living room and my husband and my babies were waiting on me. Danielle could've told me she wanted me to take my ass home. I know she was just looking out. My father swooped in and got my mother quick. I haven't seen Griff since our wedding. I feel bad. I missed my husband and my babies so much. I hope Griff didn't think I was running out on him and our family because I wasn't. We talked everyday but it wasn't the same. I should've been gone home but I couldn't leave Danielle.

My best friend has been through a lot. I feel like a bad friend because I wasn't there to go through none of that with her. I'm out here living my life and my girl is suffering in silence. I fastened Lil Griff in his car seat. He started screaming he wanted me to hold him. I will as soon as we get to our destination. I fastened Cariuna in her car seat. She snatched my phone out of my hand.

I know she's calling Rashad. I know Griff's mad at me, but he didn't show it, but I could feel it. His words were short. I climbed inside the SUV and fastened my seatbelt. Griff pulled off and headed to our destination. No words were spoken between us. The tension is thick. He grabbed my hand and kissed it. We locked eyes with each other. I whispered.

“I'm sorry.” Griff nodded his head in agreement. God, I missed this man something serious. Cariuna finally got Lil Griff to stop crying. Camina was in her own world. I couldn't stop catching glances at my babies in the back. I caught Griff catching a few glances at me.

We finally made it to our condo on the beach. It's nice. I'll take in the scenery later. I had Griff to stop by the store. I haven't cooked my husband and my babies a home cooked meal in a week. It's long overdue. Cariuna and Camina wanted lasagna for dinner and a fudge brownie and ice cream for dessert. I made lasagna, corn on the cob, salad and garlic bread. Camina and Cariuna helped with the brownie. The food is almost done. Lil Griff he’s in my arms asleep. I went to lay him down beside his father. Griff looked so good while he was asleep. I can't wait to lay next to him tonight. I bit my bottom lip just thinking about it.

“Come lay with me,” he asked? If he only knew how bad I wanted to lay with him. It’s going down tonight. We haven’t been intimate, with each other in over a week, but tonight is the night,

“I want too, but I can't right now. Dinner's almost ready. Once I feed the girls and you. I need to give them bath and put them asleep. We can lay with each other all night. I know you have needs and I plan on fulfilling all of them.”

"Come here," he asked? He didn't have to tell me twice. I made my way over to Griff. He picked me up and laid me on his chest. I stroked the side of his face. His hands roamed every inch of my body. Our lips had there on conversation. "I missed you Crimson. I missed this." If he only knew how much I missed this. "I didn't want you to cook for us tonight. I wanted to order some food because I want some time alone with my wife." I know whenever we travel Griff never wants me to cook, but my babies wanted me too. I wasn't about to tell them no and I haven't seen them in over a week.

"I want some time alone with my husband too. I need to cook for my babies they missed me. When I cook for them it's our alone time. I've been gone for a week, so I need to catch up with them. Cariuna told me about dance and Camina told me Mother Dear said she can't come back over there without us. I miss this too Carius. I missed us." Griff cupped my face and kissed me. I needed him.

"Mommy can you stop kissing my daddy. I'm hungry," Camina pouted. I buried my head into Griff's chest. We both started laughing. I swear nobody can win with this child. I'll let Griff handle her.

"Camina, I told you about busting in our room. Knock first your brother is asleep. You're not grown you don't run nothing. Do you want me to pop you? If you don't want to listen. I'm taking your iPad and TV out of your room," he argued. I can't believe Griff got ahold of Camina like that. I wanted to laugh but I can't that's my baby.

"I'm sorry daddy. Mommy said she was coming right back. I'm hungry and we can't eat a snack," she cried. Camina was laying it on Griff real thick. Griff raised up. I got up off him. He made his way toward Camina and knelt in front of her. I swear she got him wrapped around her finger.

"I'm sorry Camina it's my fault. I missed your mommy. Come on so we can eat," he stated. We made our way into the kitchen.

"Mommy I told Camina not to go back there she wouldn't listen. She said I'm not her momma or daddy so don't tell her what to do," Cariuna explained. I looked at Griff and rolled my eyes. Griff pulled Camina to the side and had a private conversation with her. I started fixing our plates. Griff said grace.

We started eating our food. I missed this. Lil Griff didn't stay sleep for too long. Griff's done with his food, so he went to grab him. Camina and Cariuna finished eating their food and fixed their dessert. I started cleaning the kitchen and putting the food up. Cariuna ran her and Camina some bath water. Griff and I finally got the kids situated. He ran us a nice hot bubble bath. I filled the champagne flutes with some wine. Griff slid in behind me.

I started straddling him. He started massaging my shoulders. I rested my head on his chest. He washed my back Griff ran his tongue up the side of my neck giving me chills instantly.

"Griff," I moaned. His hands cupped my breasts. I want to feel him so bad.

"What's up," he asked? Griff's trying to squeeze his dick inside of me. I opened my legs giving him easy access. He finally made his way in. He started stroking me long, deep and hard.

"Go deeper," I moaned. Griff did as he was told. "Can I ask you a question and I want you to be honest with me?" Griff grew up with Baine. I want to know did he know he's a fuckin' monster and a whore.

"How come you never told me Baine was a whore. I would've told Danielle about him sooner. Did you know he was cheating on Danielle and had kids by multiple women?" I noticed Griff's body tensed up.

"Crimson I haven't seen you in a week. I don't want to talk about Danielle and Baine. I want to talk about us. I want to make love to you. I want you to sit on my dick and get this nut out." I know Griff wanted to have sex I do too.

"I want to do that too Griff. My intentions are to fulfill all your needs. I want to talk about us too. I want you to be honest with me. You're the only man I ever been with. I want to keep it that way. In my eyes your perfect you're all I want and need in a man. Nobody can compare to you. On the outside looking in Danielle's marriage to Baine was perfect in my eyes. I told her that. She married a fuckin' monster. I never recognized the signs.

My sister was suffering behind closed doors for years Griff and I didn't fuckin' know. I know you don't want to talk about it, but I do. I've been holding this in all week because I had to be strong for her. We fuckin' failed her. I can't say I because there's no I in team. We're a fuckin' team. I'm not in the streets so I wouldn't know him. I've never been in the streets. You fuckin' know him very well. Here we are living our life to fullest and my sister is suffering in silence by a fuck nigga. I know you know just tell me that's all I'm asking," I cried.

"Crimson stop crying. I know you're upset but let that shit go. I'm about to tell you some shit that you may not understand. I'm going to always be honest with you and I don't want you to ever look at me like I'm a fuck nigga because I'm not. I didn't tell you about Keondra because she was irrelevant. I divorced her. Juggling multiple women was never my thing. You're it for me. It's not a woman out here that can come between my family. I cherish what we have. It gets greater for us. I love Danielle she's my sister and sorry she went through whatever she went through behind him.

I can't say Danielle knew who hc was when she married him, because it's possibility he hid who he was from her. Sometimes men do everything to get a woman and once they do, they switch up. He's always been that way. I heard about him having children with other women, but I didn't know if it was true or not. I didn't know if the things I heard where true because you never told me.

You know I'm not the type of man that's in another man's business. It's not my thing.

Baine would never cheat on his wife in front of me because he's knows how close you and Danielle are. I don't fuck with him like that anymore. We grew apart and we severed our business relationship years ago. I may see him in passing but that's about it. I know Rashad loves her and she loves him. I don't agree with how they reconnected, but you can't help who you love.

Rashad was going to take his shot no matter what, if given the chance. He was going to tell Baine he had his wife no matter what. The beef Rashad and Baine have is deeper than Danielle. We're in the middle of it, but it is what it is. Baine and I had a few words after the reception. I'm not tripping off him. Don't worry about nothing you can't control Crimson.

At least we know what type of man he is NOW, so we can protect Danielle. I know how much you love her I'll never nobody take that away from you, but God. I can promise you that. Did she find a new clinic? Rashad wants to know where it's at so he can pay for the space," he asked? I leaned my head back on Griff's chest. He placed a kiss on my forehead. I turned around to face him.

I wrapped my arms around his neck. He picked me up and slammed me on his dick. I wrapped my legs around his waist. Griff started digging in my guts DEEP.

The only sounds you can hear is the water splashing mixed with my moans. I felt every stroke. I had no choice but to take it. My eyes rolled in the back of my head. He bit the crook of my neck intensifying the orgasm I'm building up.

"She found a place, her parent's paid for it. I don't know where it's at though," I moaned. Griff picked up the pace.

"Are you done asking questions Mrs. Griffey? I got a million and one questions I want to ask this pussy. I think she missed me. I want to show her how much I missed her," he asked? I nodded my head in agreement.

A WEEK LATER

Chapter-14

Danielle

My time in Hawaii is winding down. I swear it doesn't seem like I've been out here for two weeks. If I could stay longer I would but I can't. I'm dreading going back home. I'm going to miss it here. Hawaii's my second home. It's so beautiful and peaceful. Even though I've been working I've been relaxing too. Baine filed for divorce. I'm not surprised. He said he was going to do it. He should've done it years ago. He only did it because I cheated. He wouldn't let me file when he cheated. My attorney advised me that his attorney is looking for me so I can be served. Bitch please get the fuck out of here. He wants to have me served. It's cool but everything he's demanding he's not getting.

His demands were so fuckin' ridiculous. He can have our house I don't want it. Baine thinks I'm not entitled to anything. We didn't sign a prenup. The properties we acquired together I want it, or he can sell it and we can split the profits. Crimson left me about a week ago. I thought I wouldn't miss her, but I do.

I know her children and her husband need her. We talk everyday but it's not the same. She's been overseeing the clinic while I'm out here.

I want Crimson to be my business partner. I don't know why she's prolonging it. I'm going to have a talk with her once I get back home. It's finally time to go back home to face the music. I'm ready it's now or never. I've been giving myself pep talks all morning. My mother she's coming with me. She doesn't trust Baine. I tried to talk her out of it, but she wouldn't listen. I'm glad to have her in my corner. I need her now more than she would ever know. I guess the saying's true. Things don't come when you want it, but it's always right on time.

My Gigi she's been calling me every day to see when I'm coming back home. I'm going to surprise her tomorrow. My parents have been spoiling me like crazy especially my father. I think I'm going to miss him the most. Every morning he cooks me breakfast and we sit up and talk. He works a lot too. In the morning when I'm working on my stuff for my business.

I work in his office right beside him. It's safe to say we have the same work ethic. I've accumulated so much stuff since I've been here. I can't bring all these clothes with me. I'm going to leave majority of the stuff here so once I come back to visit, I won't have to pack a bag. My mom said she'll ship it but, I don't trust it somebody will steal all my shit.

"My baby's finally leaving me. You want to see your old man cry again? Are you sure you don't want me to come with you? Daniella, I want you back in a week. Danielle please, look after your mother. I don't trust her roaming my old streets alone. She likes trouble and it's never had a problem finding her," he explained. My daddy pulled me in for a hug. He squeezed me so tight I didn't want to leave him. My daddy placed a kiss on my forehead.

"Daddy I don't want to leave you, but I got to face my reality. Trust me I'll be back sooner than you think. I'll keep an eye on her. I'll make sure she's on her best behavior. We'll be together every day, so she won't be able to get in any trouble. My life is pretty boring, it's not that exciting," I beamed.

My father grabbed my bags and my mother's bags and placed them in the car. He drove us to the airport. Next Stop Atlanta. I'm going to miss Hawaii so much. We finally made it to the airstrip. It's about an hour away from their house which wasn't too bad.

My mother and father said their goodbyes. I want what they have one day. I can tell it's real. I love the way he looks at her. It's too bad It won't be anytime soon. I'm good on niggas. No matter how much I think about Rashad we can never be. My parents had there on private plane.

The moment my mother and I stepped foot on the plane my face lit up. It's decked out. I took a seat by mother.

I'm glad she's coming home with me to assist me on this journey. We fastened our seat belts and the plane took off. I swear eleven hours is a long time to be on a flight. I didn't mind because I got the chance to see my parents and I'm with my mother. I rested my head on my mother's shoulders.

" Get you some rest. I'm not going anywhere," she smiled. She didn't have to tell me twice. I know once I make it back home. I'll be ripping and running, and I won't have any time to catch up on sleep.

We finally made it back to Atlanta. Home sweet home. I can't wait to see my Gigi. The moment we stepped off the plane. I inhaled the air it doesn't smell the same as Hawaii, but It'll do. Crimson and Cheree were waiting on us. Crimson and I locked eyes with each other. She grabbed my bags and tossed them in the trunk. Cheree grabbed a few of my mother bags. I know they're up to no good Cheree's the driver as usual. My mother slid in the passenger seat. I slid in the back seat beside Crimson.

"You look good and refreshed. I missed you. What's the move," she asked?

"I just talked to you yesterday. I missed you too. I need to go buy my house to get my car if it's still there and what few things I still have left. After that I'm going home to relax and cook dinner for my momma and Gigi.

You're more than welcome, but under one condition Camina can't come. I don't want her telling Rashad where I live." I meant that shit.

Crimson looked at me and rolled her eyes. "I'm dead ass serious Crimson your child is out to get me." My momma and Cheree started laughing too.

"Danielle leave my child alone. She hasn't done anything to you physically. I believe you be pinching my baby on the low that's why she can't stand you," she laughed. I threw my middle finger up at Crimson yeah right.

"Danielle don't do my granddaughter please don't she's misunderstood. She goes hard for the people that she loves. Rashad just so happens to be one of them. I don't know why Camina doesn't like you," Cheree laughed. Fuck Cheree! I've been nothing but good to that demon spawn.

"Like is an understatement she hates me because I don't let her get away with shit. She can come but leave that damn iPad at home. She needs her little ass whooped CRIMSON." I mean that shit. She takes that iPad every damn where.

"Danielle and Crimson y'all wouldn't believe this if I told y'all, but Camina's behavior is genetic. She gets it from none other than her grandmother. Cheree was the same way growing up. She said whatever was on her mind and didn't care who had a problem with. I'm sorry Crimson but you're raising your mother. Ask Mrs. Cara she'll tell you," my mother laughed.

It makes sense now that's why Cheree's always taking up for her. We finished catching up with each other. Crimson stared a hole in me. I looked over my shoulders to see what she wanted.

"What Crimson, what did I do," I asked?

"You haven't done anything yet. I talked to Rashad a few days ago. He asked about you. I just want to know when you're going to sit down and talk to him. It's no reason why y'all can't be together and you're getting a divorce. He's sorry and he misses you. I started to let him use my phone to call you, but I decided not to," she smiled. I looked at Crimson and rolled my eyes. I laid my head on her shoulder.

"I wish the fuck you would. Crimson I don't know why you're pressing the issue. I love Rashad but I'm trying to figure out how to un love him. If that makes sense. What am I supposed to say Crimson? He's already said and done enough. I'm going to tell you like I told Griff I'll pass. Rashad and I could never be together. Somethings aren't meant to be and we're one of those things. We tried once. We were about to try again BUT he fucked it up before we could even get to that point. The next man I date he won't be a friend of Griff's. I'm cool on him. When you talk to him again tell him I said he can move on. Give up on us because it'll never happen thanks to him."

"Danielle I'm not telling him shit. How about you tell him. I swear you're stubborn as hell. You're not the only one to catch feelings. He has feelings too.

You said it yourself if two sides to every story. Your words not mine. I know how you feel, but how do you think he feels?

What's wrong with a conversation. If you love him why are you fighting being with him. Let me guess you just wanted to creep with him. You had no plans in to be in a relationship with him. You just wanted the dick that's it? Unlike you Rashad wasn't about to hide his feelings he didn't give a fuck about Baine and outing your secrets," she argued. I wasn't even about to argue with Crimson.

I'll see Rashad whenever I see him. I closed my eyes and enjoyed the ride. Crimson didn't like that, but it is what it is.

We finally made our way to my home. I swear it feels like we've been driving forever. I'm tired the flight was super long. I want to go home and relax and take a hot bubble and reminisce about Rashad. I can't be with him, but it won't hurt to think about us. Ms. Cheree pulled up to my house. My mother and Crimson stepped out behind me. My mother pulled a gun out from the nape of her back. I looked at her with wide eyes. My father said she was up to something.

"Don't look like that Danielle. If he acts stupid. I'll shoot his stupid ass without fuckin' blinking," she argued. The sign Baine's stupid ass painted in front of our house was still up. My mother and Cheree looked at the sign with disgust. Crimson cut the rope and took it down. It's early in the afternoon. I know Baine isn't here.

I entered my key code on the keypad to enter our home. I know Baine didn't change the code because I'm the one that set it up.

My house looked exactly how I left it, the day Baine and I left to go to Crimson's wedding. I checked the garage and my car's still inside the garage. I went upstairs to the room we once shared. My closet was empty. I shook my head. He cleaned out everything. I checked my drawers the only thing left is bras and panties. All my jewelry is gone. Baine brought me a lot of pieces, but I spoiled myself also. Tears slid down my face. My mother tapped me on my shoulder.

"Come on Danielle. Get your car if you want it. If you don't want it, I'll have Cheree take us to the lot. I'll buy you whatever you want. I don't want nann motherfucka taking anything from you. Whatever he took I'll replace it. I'll get your jewelry custom made. Leave that ring too if you want fuck him Danielle. I'll burn this fuckin' house down. I've never seen a man move like him. I swear he's petty as hell. Who raised him," she asked? Baine's mother she's quite a character.

I wouldn't dare let my mother and her cross paths. I took my ring off and sat it in Baine's jewelry box. He'll see it. This is the last time that I'll step foot in this house. I grabbed my keys off the counter. I sat my door keys on the island in the kitchen. I hit the garage button to open the garage. My mother slid in the passenger seat and we pulled off and headed to my new home.

It took us about an hour to get to my side of town. Traffic is heavy coming down I-20E. It felt good to have my mother riding in the passenger seat with me.

The neighborhood where I'm now residing in. It's nice I'm in Lithonia right off Browns Mill Road. It's a nice area. It's hardly any crime. It's not too far from my new location. I can come home and have lunch or take a nap if I want too. I can't wait to see the inside. The pictures and the view on Facetime were beautiful. The outside looked exactly like the pictures.

I stopped by Bath and Body works to get some candles and plug ins. I stopped by Bed Bath and Beyond to get a comforter set. I wanted the Ugg one because I know in the winter it'll be getting cold. I grabbed one for the summer too, but I can't wait to use the Ugg one for the winter. It's too bad I'll be sleeping by myself. I did the walk through in my new home. The appliances were stainless steel. The hard wood floors were smoke gray with a wet look. I love the smell of fresh paint. I need some pictures and a few new accent rugs.

"Thank you, mommy, for everything. I appreciate you," My momma had everything setup nice. My house is amazing. My mother did everything she said she would. I'm in love.

"You don't have to thank me Danielle I'm supposed to do this. I don't want you to ever feel alone in this world. As long, as I'm living, you'll forever be straight.

I just don't like how he went about things. He wanted to leave you assed out. He couldn't have known who your parents were," she explained. He couldn't have known because I didn't. They have money lots of it because she's been cashing out since I've been with them.

"I know mommy. I'm still thankful that you've done this for me. I had 2.5 million dollars stashed for a day like this because a man can switch up at any time and he's switched up. I'm thankful that I can keep this money and continue to save," I explained. Me and my mother took the tour of my house. I can't wait to see the master bedroom. I stepped foot inside and It's huge. I walked in the closet it's huge too. My closet is flooded with nothing but designer shit. The vanity is amazing it's fit for a queen. I looked around and smiled at my momma.

"Mommy you didn't. Why didn't you tell me you did this? How did you pull this off without me knowing," I asked? She looked at me and smiled.

"I have my ways and I know how much you wanted everything that was in your room at home. I wanted you to have it. Especially after he gave your stuff to the next person. Not my daughter she'll never go without," she beamed. I stepped in the bathroom. It's sick. I can't wait to swim in the garden tub.

"Mommy what do you to eat. I want to cook for you tonight if that's okay," I asked?

“Danielle let me cook tonight. I want you to relax. You have to work tomorrow get you some rest and I'll handle everything else.” I know she wouldn't let me cook. I should've done it any way without asking her. I want to cook for my mother she's been catering to me since we reconnected. Tomorrow I'm going to cater to her. My mother and I got situated.

We went to the grocery store to grab a few things to cook. She decided on a sea food boil. Crabs, lobsters, shrimp, red potatoes, corn on the cob, oysters and Andouille sausage. It smells so good I can't wait to eat. Gigi and Mother Dear came over. I've never had my mother and grandmother in the same room. We took plenty of pictures. Three generations. We had a great time. I grabbed a big bowl and fed my face. Gigi said she's going to spend the night. I know she missed her daughter. I can tell her face lit up the room. I cleaned up the kitchen and put everything away. I'm taking some for lunch tomorrow.

“Danielle I'm going to turn a few corners with Cheree. I'll be back in a few. If your father calls tell him I'm asleep,” she laughed.

“Mommy you want me to lie to my daddy. I hope he doesn’t Facetime me because if he does, you’re on your own,” I laughed.

“I know you got your car back Danielle and that's cool, but I don't trust it.

Tomorrow or Saturday we're going to the dealership to get you a new car. I don't want you driving shit that he brought," she explained.

"But momma," I pouted. She cut me off before I could say anything else.

"No buts he wants you to start over. I'm going to show that motherfucka how you start over. Sell that car because I don't want you driving it. I don't trust him it's mother's intuition. When you have a child of your own, you'll understand," she smiled. I went upstairs to my room. I got my work clothes out for tomorrow.

I haven't been to work in two weeks. I feel rusty. I ran me some bath water. When I'm alone my mind seems to roam. I stepped in the tub. The water was hot to my liking. I'll soak in the tub for about an hour.

I grabbed my phone. I'm thinking about texting Rashad, but I decided not to. I don't know why I can't shake Rashad like I want too, but I'm trying. I swear he has a hex on me. I stayed in the tub until the water turned cold. I dried off and grabbed my robe. I pulled the covers back.

This bed feels so good. I closed my eyes hoping sleep would take over me. I thought the moment I got comfortable in my bed I would fall asleep instantly, but that's the farthest from the truth.

When I was in Hawaii Rashad invaded my mind, but I was able to turn it off immediately.

Since I've been at home and he's only a few miles away I can't stop thinking about him. I missed the way he held me and touched me. It's too bad that he would never be able to do that again. Rashad will never know how much I miss. I did it once and I'm praying I can do it again. It's too much fuckin' drama.

I woke up bright and early. I can't sleep. Rashad invaded my mind all night. I couldn't wait to go to work. I felt like a kid going to bed before the first day of school. I took a shower and handled my hygiene. My work clothes were already laid out. I ordered some new scrubs too that I've been dying to wear.

I'm so anxious to see my new facility. It's only fifteen minutes away from my house. I picked out everything. It looked good on Facetime, but I need to see it in the flesh. I walked around the whole facility and I'm impressed.

The cleaning crew done a great job it smells good. The coffee bar is so dope. I went ahead and started brewing a fresh batch. We open in about an hour and forty-five minutes. My office is amazing. I setup everything to my liking. I beat Madison here. She walked in my office with the biggest smile on her face.

“Boss Lady it's good seeing you. I missed you. I'm glad you're back you look great.

Crimson's been a great help. I think you should bring her in full time,” she beamed. Crimson likes to work. I don't know why she doesn't want to work with me. I want her to be my partner.

“Madison did you tell Crimson that maybe she'll listen to you because she won't listen to me. I want her to be my business partner. I'm great despite the bullshit. How are you. I can't thank you enough for everything that you've been doing around here. I brought you something,” I beamed. Madison is so dope. I couldn't run this place without her.

She made shit happen. I grabbed the gift and the envelope I had under my desk for Madison. I brought her a Chanel bag. I gave her a $1500.00 bonus. Madison started crying. She's good people and I'll always look out for those that look out for me.

“Boss lady thank you! I can't accept this. I'm just doing my job and doing everything you asked me too,” she cried. Madison is so emotional. She's my little gangster. She got the job done.

“Madison you will accept this. You've done way more than your job requires. I pay you to oversee this facility and to assist me. I don't pay you to oversee my personal life and you've done that and more. I appreciate you. I just want to show you how much I appreciate you.”

I shoved the bag in Madison's hand. "Take it. Stop crying please! I've been crying enough and I'm not trying to cry anymore.

We'll be open in about an hour. You want to grab some breakfast before we open?

Madison nodded her head in agreement. Ihop isn't too far from here. We grabbed our stuff and headed to my car.

I swear time is flying by. It feels good to be back at work. My staff missed me, and I missed them too. It's time to get back to work. My new location it's bigger and better. I pulled in a few new clients from Conyers and Covington Georgia. Crimson came back today. I'm surprised to see her at work. I'm happy she came back. I didn't even realize it was lunch time. Griff pulled up for lunch with Lil Griff. He brought me and Crimson some food. I thought me and Crimson were going to pull off and grab something to eat. I guess that's wishful thinking. I swear my godson is so fair. He looks like Crimson and Griff they make the prettiest kids. I swear it feels like Deja Vu.

I remember when Crimson and Griff first started dating when we worked at Walgreens. He used to pull up on Crimson every day for lunch. I swear her husband is perfect. Thank God Griff didn't bring his boy up in here. The moment I saw him I rolled my eyes. When you saw Griff, Rashad wasn't too far.

I kissed Lil Griff on his cheeks and headed back to my office. I had two patients scheduled to come in within the next thirty minutes. I had to get ready for that. I just started a new book **Dope Love Karma** by **Dedra B.** this book is so damn good. Keyana Castillo she's that bitch. I think I can get a few pages in before my next client pulls up. I heard a knock at my door. I swear to God I hate to be bothered when I'm reading a good ass book.

"Come in!" Crimson and my insurance biller Taylor walked in. I didn't like the look that was plastered on their faces. I felt the tension immediately this is my first day back. I swear to God if Baine comes in here on some bullshit I'm going off. For real. I folded my arms across my chest. Crimson spoke up first.

"Danielle, we got a motherfuckin' problem. I'm so glad I'm here because it's better for me to NIKE check a bitch than you because you're the face of the company and not me," she argued. I haven't heard Crimson talk like this since she killed Keondra. Her tone and choice of words piqued my interest. I knew something bad was about to happen. I just didn't want it to happen here at my place of business.

"Crimson what's going on," I asked?

"The other baby momma you were telling me about Nova. I'm not for sure if it's her or not but I think it is. She made a fuckin' appointment to see you. Danielle she's your 2:00 p.m. appointment.

I brought Taylor in her with me since she bills the insurance. Taylor confirmed that it's her," she explained. Taylor gave me the file. I looked at it. I swear Baine ain't shit. How is she using his fuckin' insurance card and we're fuckin' married? I looked at the address.

I know this motherfucka don't have this bitch living in house that we fuckin' own. I thought I was having a fuckin' good day. I swear the devil has tried me so many fuckin' times but I'll never let that motherfucka win. I haven't even been in this location for three weeks, but this bitch shows up. I guess Baine told all his hoes we were a wrap and its free game to fuck with me. It's safe to say bitches were googling to see where I moved too. I had to count to ten.

I'm running a business. I got to keep it professional. I have patients watching me. I sent my attorney a copy of this file. I made sure it's encrypted. I need this for my divorce.

Baine keeps fuckin' up but he doesn't want me to get anything. I swear for a nigga to be so smart he's dumb, we're in the middle of a fuckin' divorce. If a bitch wanted to see me, they're about to wait. I'm grabbed my Fendi purse from my drawer. I checked myself out in the mirror.

I'm on point. I applied some lip gloss to lips. My shit is popping. I grabbed my lab coat. I stepped out in the waiting room. I looked around to see if I saw the bitch. She made her way to the counter.

Crimson came from the back and stood behind her. Nova looked at me and smiled. Nova stepped to the counter like she's motherfuckin' bad. Bitch Please! I haven't drug, a bitch in a long time. I swear if she gets slick at the mouth. I will spit in her face and not give a fuck. I don't give a damn how many patients are in here. I'll never let a bitch disrespect me. I don't give a fuck where I'm at.

"Crimson I'm good I know where we stand, she's not worth it. We got too much to fuckin' loose. It's difference between us and them. How can I help you Nova what brings you by my place of business? Baine let you lose," I asked? A small laugh escaped my lips.

"It's good to see you too Danielle It's been a long time. I've been seeing a lot of Baine maybe a little bit more than you. He did let me loose this morning and last night. I just wanted to let you know that we're expecting. I want you to be my nurse," she laughed. Nova rubbed her stomach and threw up two fingers. "I ain't never stopped fuckin' your husband. I got two kids by him and BITCH you ain't got NONE that speaks volumes.

I got the best pussy and you don't. I live in a fuckin' house that you own. Mortgage FREE Baine ain't never stopped fuckin' with me or taking care of me. Guess what bitch ain't shit you can motherfuckin' do about it." This bitch came in swinging today. Nova's loud she's putting on for these motherfuckas in here. I can already see people recording and shit.

I might as well give these folks what they want. I swear these bitches better ask about me. If she wants smoke I motherfuckin' got it.

"Congratulations NOVA and you can tell BAINE that too. I've been married to Baine for five years and let me school YOU, so I don't ever have to school you again. I ain't never came number two to NANN BITCH not even YOU. Baine ain't never had me on a fuckin' leash. I always did what I want and said whatever the fuck I WANT. He already knew to keep his HOES on a LEASH. All y'all HOES got FLEAS. I told Baine to keep his HOES the fuck away from me. Nova you're one of his hoes TOO! One of MANY might I add! Kudos to you BITCH.

As far as you claiming to have the best pussy that's your opinion and not mine. I have more to offer a NIGGA besides PUSSY. It's just a bonus. You're cute I'll give you that, but that's about it. I'm cute and I'm smart. I'm the whole fuckin' package. I bring a lot to the fuckin' table. My spot was never up for grabs. I gave my spot up. I haven't wanted it for a long time.

You're proud to be fuckin' a married man and having two kids by him? I WOULD NEVER! That's says a lot about you. You're not wifey material you're only good enough to FUCK and catch his NUT. I would never have his kids and he's fuckin' the world. I don't want my kids to admire that type of man. In the five years we've been married.

He ain't never left ME to MARRY YOU. Who's the fool ME or YOU? Your SON ain't never stepped foot in my HOUSE because the MOTHERFUCKA WASN'T ALLOWED. I made that rule not BAINE and he fuckin' abided by it. You're bragging about fuckin' him and having kids by him. Girl you're silly as fuck. Your son can't even spend the night at my house.

If I was to kill you right now and Baine and I were still together. He couldn't bring your child home with him. Who got the best pussy? I think it's me, because whatever I say goes. You should be worried about living in a house that I own, and your name isn't on the deed.

I can put you in your son out in the fuckin' streets. It ain't shit you or Baine can do about it because my name is on that fuckin' deed. I can be a HEARTLESS BITCH if I want too. Bitch you ain't worth these motherfuckin' hands. Tell that motherfucka to divorce me. I asked for one when you had your BABY. He begged me and threatened me not to leave. Guess what Nova you ain't the only baby momma that's still fuckin' him.

You can keep sharing him with her and whoever else. I'm free of him and all his bullshit. I'm happy I don't have to worry or stress myself out over who he's fuckin' that's your job and baby girl you can keep it. You came here for what bitch you disgust me," I chuckled. I coughed up some spit and spit in her face. She drew her arm back like she wanted to swing at me. Crimson grabbed her arm and pulled that bitch out of socket. I heard it crack.

"Nova or Not whatever the fuck your name is, bitch you better watch fuckin' yourself. You talked your shit and Danielle talked hers. The moment you drew your fist back to hit her. Is the moment I'll beat your ass in this motherfuckin' office. You can get these MOTHERFUCKIN' HANDS. I want to slide them to you, because in my eyes you're more than worth it. You came along way to fuck with my sister. Try your luck if you want too.

You won't live long enough to gloat about carrying baby number two. Try that shit if you MOTHERFUCKIN' want too. I can guarantee you won't like the fuckin' outcome. Danielle got too much to lose and I'll never let my sister lose shit when it comes to a BITCH like you!" Crimson argued. Damn Crimson read that bitch. Nova marched her stupid ass out of here. I swear to God this ain't what the fuck you want. I walked back to my office. Crimson and Madison came right behind me.

"Boss Lady you read the fuck out of that bitch. That bitch came to throw shade and you through the whole fuckin' tree," she beamed. I swear I don't even bother people. Me and Nova haven't had words in a minute. Baine always kept that bitch in line. "Crimson I'm a little surprised about you too. I thought you were innocent.

I forgot y'all were from Decatur. We finished talking with each other. I'm ready to go home. I'm tired of being a trending topic. I grabbed a Kiwi out my fruit basket. After two bites I started throwing up. I need some water.

Chapter-15

Crimson

Danielle's been sick for two days now. She claims she has food poison from the Kiwi she ate. I ate two Kiwi's and I didn't sick. I'm a little concerned because Danielle never gets sick. I know she's been stressed out. She's been throwing up and running a fever. I started to call the ambulance just for the hell of it. I know she's a registered nurse, but I still want her to get a second opinion. She's hardheaded. I swear I can't tell Danielle shit. She won't listen I started to bring Rashad over here. Thank God her mother's still here an able to look after her. Me and Daniella both placed a bet against Danielle that she's pregnant. I'm ready to cash out. I know she's pregnant. She's in denial and won't take a pregnancy test.

Our cycles always come around the same time. If I don't start mine first, she'll start hers. Normally whoever starts their cycle first we'll grab each other a box of scented tampons, wipes or whatever we want. I've brought two boxes of tampons. The past two months I have yet to buy Danielle any. Instead of going to work today I thought I would come by Danielle's and kick it and possibly try to get her to take a test. I have the code to her house so I'm able to let myself in.

Mrs. Daniella's in the kitchen whipping up some breakfast it smells so good.

The food aroma mixed with the coffee brewing. I'm in heaven. I walked over toward the stove to see what she has cooking. Bacon and turkey sausages. I grabbed one and she popped my hand.

"Ouch!" I swear Daniella reminds me of Ms. Gladys because she used to do that to me and Danielle whenever we would try to grab a piece of food while she was cooking.

"Good morning Crimson I thought that was you. Do you want some breakfast," she asked? I nodded my head in agreement. She fixed me a plate "She's upstairs still in her room. She ate a little bit last night. I brought a few pregnancy tests. She won't take them. She said she's on birth control. I told her it's not one hundred percent," she laughed. Me and Mrs. Daniella ate our breakfast and caught up a little bit.

I swear I remember when I got pregnant with Cariuna. Danielle shoved the pregnancy tests in my hand like it wasn't nothing. She's scared to take one because she knows it's positive. Fuck that she's taking one today rather she likes it or not.

"I'm glad you're here. I know she's glad too. I can see it. She needed this more than you would ever know," I explained. I didn't mean to make Daniella cry I'm just letting it be known. "Don't cry I didn't mean to upset you."

"I know but I needed this more than Danielle. Your mother and I made a lot of mistakes growing up. The mistakes we made caused us not to be around.

I look at Danielle and I regret that shit every day. Your children are, a reflection of you growing up.

I'm proud of the women that you and Danielle have become you two are nothing like us. I'm glad that she accepted me with open arms due to my absence. Yes, we have money but at what cost. Money doesn't mean anything. If you got to look over your shoulders every second and kill everybody that you feel is a threat. I wish I could've lived a normal life," she explained. Me and Daniella finished talking. I understand where she's coming from. I used to hate my momma for leaving me. It was more to her story and Daniella's. I made my way upstairs to Danielle's room. She's sitting up on her bed looking at TV.

"I thought that was you. I've been wondering when you were going to come upstairs to see me. I hate being sick. If you get sick. I don't want you to catch what I have. You know I won't be able to take care of you because I'm not coming to your house so Camina can set me up." I flipped Danielle off.

"I'm tired of you talking about my daughter. Leave my baby the fuck alone. She ain't got shit to do with your luck. I can't get what you have because you're pregnant and I'm not. Danielle you haven't had a period in two months. I haven't brought you any tampons and you haven't brought me any. If you're not pregnant just take the test so we can clear up any suspicions. If you don't take a pregnancy test. I'm going to call Rashad myself and tell him you're sick and pregnant with his baby."

Danielle looked me and rolled her eyes. The moment she turned her nose up. I knew she was about to say something smart. "Try me Danielle." I'm not budging I let her off the hook yesterday and I shouldn't have.

"Crimson I know you're motherfuckin' lying. You wouldn't do that. Bitch you play too much. You would do all that after everything I've been through creeping with this man. I know God wouldn't set me up like this?" I shoved the pregnancy test in her hand. Danielle acted like she wasn't budging. She threw the test on floor. We both know she's pregnant I don't understand why she doesn't want to confirm it.

I grabbed my phone and placed it on speaker phone to call Rashad. He answered on the first ring. Danielle gave me an evil glare. I stuck my tongue out at her. I don't know why she's surprised. I told her I wasn't fuckin' around. I knew if she wouldn't do for it me. She would do it If I threatened to call him. He's been asking about her too. It's tempting to give him her phone number and address. They need to talk. It seems like I'm going to have to force Danielle to talk to him.

"Rashad what's up. Where are you? I need you to meet me somewhere. I got somebody with me. I know you want to see," I beamed. I can hear Rashad smiling through the phone. I know he's with Griff. Danielle's pissed. I don't give a fuck. If she takes the test, I wouldn't even be doing this.

“Oh yeah what's the address Me and your husband are about to pull up.” Danielle snatched my phone out of my hand. She hung up in his face. Rashad called right back. She kept clearing him out. Danielle’s face is red. Rashad got her pregnant she’s stuck with him.

“Damn Crimson whose side are you on. Why would you fuckin' do that? You know he's the last person I want to see. Why would you get that man hopes up high? He isn't coming over here. Crimson I'm stick and I'm stressed out, did that ever occur to you. I'm on the shot I can't get pregnant,” she argued. I’m tired of arguing with Danielle.

“Prove it. Do you remember how you did me when I found out I was pregnant with Cariuna just take the test?”

“Crimson our situations aren't the same you weren't on birth control and I am. Let me prove you wrong since you think you're so fuckin' smart. I swear I'm about sick of you and your daughter fuckin' trying me. You should be glad that I need to pee or else I wouldn't even be doing this shit,” she argued. Danielle snatched the pregnancy test out my hand. She marched her ass in the bathroom. She slammed the door on the way in. I started to open the door, but I'll give her space. I'm sure she needs privacy.

I looked at my watch. Danielle's been in there for ten minutes. It doesn't take that long to find out if you're pregnant or not. I've gave Danielle enough privacy. I knocked on the door. I'm coming in rather she lets me in or not.

I opened the door and walked in the bathroom. Danielle's sitting on the toilet staring at the test. I cleared my throat and she looked at me. I snatched it out of her hand. I figured as much. I knelt in front of Danielle and cupped her cheeks forcing her to look at me.

"I told you! Congratulations I'm going to be an auntie. I'm going to need you to run me that $100.00 today Camina needs some new shoes. When are we telling Rashad you're pregnant? Is it Baine's," I asked? A small laugh escaped my lips. I didn't mean to do it, but I did. Danielle looked at me and rolled her eyes. Rashad done knocked my girl up. He made that creeping count for something.

"Go home Crimson! I'm not paying you or my momma shit. It's not Baine's, it's Rashad's. I don't want to be pregnant by him. I can't have his baby. I'm not excited about it. What am I going to do with a baby? I'm going through a nasty divorce. I'm not trying to deal with Rashad. I know I've done my dirt and Baine has done his. I got this divorce in the bag. I can't let anybody know I'm pregnant. I'm not even sure if I want to have this baby or not. My life is a mess and a baby will only complicate things. It's not the right time. I can't win for loosing. I'm tired Crimson. I'm falling," she cried. I wiped Danielle's tears with a few pieces of Kleenex.

"What doesn't kill you makes your stronger. If you fall, I'm always here to catch you. Danielle you're going to be a great mother. You're a great Godmother I think the baby you're carrying deserves that. Rashad he's a great father. Shit Camina listens more to him than she does Griff.

When she gets in trouble at school, they call Rashad first." Danielle started laughing.

"Y'all need to do something about Camina for real Crimson. She'll be really mad at me if I have Rashad's baby," she sighed. I looked at Danielle and rolled my eyes. I know how she feels. I was in her shoes once. I'm in her corner. I got her back regardless. I'm sure Rashad wants this baby more than anything. I want her to have the baby too. Danielle's a great Godmother. I don't even buy Cariuna clothes or shoes. She does it all. Now that I think about it, she ain't brought Camina shit in a long time. She brought Lil Griff so much stuff. Me and Griff didn't have to buy him anything.

"Girl come on and leave my child alone. Danielle, I know how you feel. Wipe yourself and come on." I stepped out the bathroom and took a seat on the bed waiting for Danielle to come out. She finally came out and climbed into the bed. She laid her head on my shoulder. I placed my hand on her forehead to see if she still had a fever. Danielle's fever broke. Thank God for that she needs some prenatal vitamins. I grabbed my phone and snapped a picture of us and posted it on my Instagram **#Mysisterskeeper #fever #sick.**

"Crimson I know you didn't post that picture of me? I look a mess," she argued. I heard Danielle suck her teeth. I looked at her and rolled my eyes. Bitch please. No wonder she's been so bitchy lately she's pregnant. I bet she's having a girl and she's going to be worse than Camina.

"Danielle be quiet. You're the only sick person I know that looks cute. Look don't start getting on my nerves because you're pregnant. You still haven't answered my question yet. When are you going to tell Rashad?" Danielle completely ignored me. She's not trying to answer that question.

"I'm not trying to talk about that Crimson. We can talk about anything but that. Let me see your phone. I want to see how I look. I forgot your Instagram is dry as fuck. I'm sure you have a few lurkers. Bitches will follow you just to see if you post some shit about me." I tossed Danielle my phone so she could see the picture. "Crimson this post hasn't even been up a good five minutes and we have fifty likes and twenty comments. Girl look at this comment from Rashad I didn't even know this nigga had a page." Danielle tossed me my phone back. She had the biggest smile on her face. I wish she would stop playing hard to get.

"Rashad asked, where are we? Drop the location and he'll come and take care of you and be your keeper. Drop it Danielle you know you want too. If he knew you were pregnant with his baby, he would really be tripping." Danielle tossed the pillow at me. She knows I'm not lying.

Rashad

Crimson called me earlier. I should've known she was fuckin' with me. I knew she had me on speaker phone. I knew Danielle's petty ass hung up in my face. She knows I hate that disrespectful as shit. Danielle's sick I wonder what's wrong with her. Crimson posted a picture of her on her Instagram. Danielle's still sexy as fuck. I can tell she's sick, but she still looked good though. I miss shawty something serious.

I commented under Crimson's picture. I know Crimson showed her what I said. I don't give a fuck. I'm tired of doing this shit with her. Danielle's too old to play these little games that she's playing. Motherfuckas wonder why I spas the fuck out. I tapped Griff on the shoulder.

"Aye call your wife I'm trying to see what's up with Danielle. Griff I'm going to fuck around and hurt her. Where does she live at? I know you know nigga and don't lie to me and say you don't. Where's her new building damn tell me something." Griff and Slap were laughing at me. They think shit is a game and it's not.

"Rashad you got my wife's number. Call Crimson back she's not going to tell me shit because she knows I'll tell you. Ask Ms. Gladys she might drop the dime on her. Give Danielle some time she'll come around."

“How much time does she need? I haven’t seen in her in about three weeks. Before her little secret came out, I didn’t have problem getting in touch with her or pulling up. I had access plenty of access.” I grabbed my phone to call Crimson. She answered on the third ring.

“What’s up Rashad,” she laughed. Everybody thinks this shit is a game and it isn’t. I’m too old to play fuckin’ games. On some real shit I’m not about keep doing this with Danielle. It’s stressing me the fuck out. I shouldn’t even have to call somebody else’s phone to speak with her.

“Put Danielle on the phone Crimson.”

“Rashad she’s asleep. She got food poison. She isn’t going to talk to you. Do you need me to relay a message,” she asked? Crimson knows I need her to relay a message.

“Yeah I need you to relay a message. Put me on speaker phone and put the phone by Danielle’s ear. I know she’s not asleep. Crimson quit covering for her. Danielle you know I’ve been trying to get up with you. I know you hear me. Don’t make me come find you. I need a conversation ASAP. You think this shit is over because you ain’t communicating. It ain’t. I’ll see you soon the lil fake ass dream you having over there. I’ll invade that shit.” I hung up the phone.

“Danielle got you gone Rashad you’re tripping hard,” he laughed. Fuck Griff and Slap.

THREE WEEKS LATER

Chapter-16

Nikki

It's been a minute since me and my girls linked up. Tonight's the tonight it's going down. It's Friday too. I'm letting my hair down. I slid into a pair of Abercrombie and Fitch distressed jeans. I threw on my Crenshaw t-shirt. I slid my feet in a fresh pair of Pumas. I want to be comfortable. We haven't saw each other in over a month. It's time for a link up.

Ladies Night is in a full effect! Danielle's back in the city. We've been talking here and there but we haven't been able to catch up like we need too. Crimson, Journee, Khadijah, Alexis, Leah and Malone are coming through too. We're kicking it at Alexis Honeycomb Hideout in the city.

It's my turn to host. I could've had it at my house, but I wanted to get away from the house. My mom has the kids. We couldn't talk at my house like I wanted too. Skeet, Juelz, Alonzo or Smoke would pop up. I didn't want that. I setup a taco and fajita bar.

I had the wine and liquor on chill. Khadijah came by early to make the hunch punch and frozen daiquiris. It’s safe to say that nobody’s going home tonight. Journee made us a bomb playlist. I’m hungry but I don’t want to start eating and sipping until everybody gets here.

Khadijah took a seat by me on the couch. I hate to say it, but I miss this brat. I hardly ever get to see her since she's married with two children. She looks good I can tell Mook's treating her right. I'm surprised to see her in the city. Khadijah and Mook moved to Miami because Mook's a real motherfuckin' BOSS. He's a MADEMAN. Mook was traveling back and forth to Miami at least three times a week after Khadijah got kidnapped.

Mook refused to let her be alone for any amount of time so they moved. Smoke didn't like it a first, but him and Mook had a sit down and came to an agreement. Khadijah looked at me and smiled. This is the first time that she's attended one of our Ladies Night events. Khadijah’s my baby and nothing will ever change that. She’s the little sister I wanted but never got.

“What's up with you. How you been? I miss you. You don't call nobody or text anybody anymore. You think you're grown now since you can properly fuck? How's life treating you. I miss you living here because I don't get to see Lil Smoke or Juleesa grow up. Smoke always brings him by to see me. I don't get to see Juleesa at all. She's not going to know me.

Sededra brings Khadira by all the time. I love her. She's still making Khadir sweat with her man Capone. I'm surprised he ain't dead yet. Where are my babies," I asked? Khadijah and I haven't been close since she got caught selling drugs. She knew I told on her.

I didn't want her selling drugs she didn't need too. Me telling on her landed her with Mook. I hated her and Smoke didn't work out but it's nothing I could do to change that. I don't like Dawn, but shit Smoke loves her. I'm cordial because of my husband but that's about it.

"I miss you too. I know how to fuck I been knowing how too! Life's good I can't complain. Smoke has Lil Smoke of course and Mrs. Kaisha has Juleesa. Mook is everything Nikki. He's everything I ever wanted and needed in a man. He's my soulmate. God, I love that man. Everybody's busy Nikki. You're running your business you have a family of four. Journee's busy.

I'm busy I'm finally opening a business. I'm trying to get that off the ground it's hard and I'm not from the city. I want to be known outside of being his wife. I love me some Jefe Santana. I have two small children so it's hard to catch up with you guys every day, but I'm good," she beamed. I know she's good and I'm so happy that she is.

Khadijah Santana. She doesn't even look the same. She looks different. She looks grown real fuckin' grown. She looks just like Julissa the older she gets. I can't believe she cut her hair into a shoulder length bob.

It compliments her face well. Mook has her iced the fuck out too. Khadijah walked in the door looking like money. I heard the doorbell ring.

"I'm so proud of you Khadijah. I really am. I'm happy that you found your soul mate. I'm glad you're here. I'll help you with your business as much I can. Just let me know what you need as far as marketing and promotion." Khadijah's growing up. She's no longer the little girl that used to run up behind me and Journee. Everything we wanted her to be she's finally becoming. Khadijah went to open the door.

Journee came in with the wings and fries. Alexis came in right behind her with the ice. I swear that's the only thing she's bringing to any thing is fuckin' ice. I wonder if Alonzo knows she still has this place. The doorbell rang again. Khadijah grabbed the door again. It's Leah, Malone, Danielle and Crimson. "Where's Layla?" Everybody pulled up at the same time. Crimson brought a bottle of liquor and Danielle brought red wine.

Malone and Leah brought the weed. They set the weed and cigars on the table. Yep tonight is going down tonight. Malone started breaking down the weed. I'm ready for her to roll up. Malone always has the best weed. It smells so good. I'm ready to smoke something.

"Malone what do you want to eat? I'll fix your plate since you're rolling up," I asked? I fuck with Malone. I met her through Alexis. She's cool as fuck. Her husband is crazy than a motherfucka. I don't see how she married him.

I heard he's changed though. Malone and I click because we both have twins. They're the same age so we have play dates.

"Everything! Layla couldn't come Shalani is sick. I'm hungry I need something to drink. Make it strong I've had a long week," she smiled. I fixed Malone's plate. Leah and Alexis were posted up in the corner. I can tell they're up to no good. Journee and Khadijah were fixing everybody a drink. Crimson pulled out her selfie stick so we can take our pictures before we got to fucked up. Malone finished rolling our blunts they were laid on the table.

"Khadijah come here I want you to meet Crimson and Danielle," I beamed. Khadijah made her way over to where we're standing. I introduced her to Crimson and Danielle. We all clicked instantly. Khadijah's big on vibes. I knew she would vibe with them because if she didn't, they wouldn't be here. Our husbands all know each other. I noticed Danielle's picked up a few pounds. Her ass and hips are spreading. Her breasts look a little fuller. No more tank tops for her. I'll be sure to ask her about that later.

"It's nice to meet y'all. What y'all doing hanging with Nikki? She's bossy and rude. I can't believe she's this cordial. Y'all cute where y'all from," Khadijah asked? I pinched Khadijah I don't appreciate her saying that shit. A small smile appeared on Khadijah's face. She's messy and still with the shit. I ain't never ran with no ugly bitches. All my bitches bad. All of them!

"We're the from East Atlanta! Wesley Chapel and Snapfinger Road. You cute too," Crimson and Danielle said in unison. We stood around and caught up with each other. Journee had everybody's drinks lined up on the Island with a shot right beside it. I'm ready to turn up. I'm kid free and I've been working all fuckin' week. Malone lit the blunt and passed it.

"Let's take a few flicks before we get fucked up," Crimson stated. Everybody grabbed their drinks! We made our way over to Alexis's wall. It's a stone brick stained wall. It's cute. Our pictures always turned out perfect. I love it. Crimson whipped out her selfie stick. We made a toast to tonight! All my bitches were bad. We took at least twenty pictures. I'll post them to my social media pages later.

"Crimson let me get one by myself. Can you post me to your Instagram please," she asked? Danielle had the biggest smile on her face. I know she's up to no good. Danielle had a glass of red wine in her hand. Her Mohawk is on a point as always. She looks cute. Danielle's getting thick. Rashad's nut does a body good. I heard Crimson suck her teeth. I wanted to hear what she had to say. I'm all ears! Crimson she's the queen of motherfuckin' shade bougie ass.

"Danielle why are we baiting Rashad if you won't talk to him? I'm trying to enjoy my night. I'm kid free and my husband hasn't started calling me yet. I'll do it because you're my bitch," Crimson stated. I see we have a lot to talk about! Everybody grabbed their shots and tossed them back. I noticed Danielle didn't take her shot.

We grabbed our food and took our seats on Alexis's sectional. We made small talk in between eating.

"Danielle, we haven't seen you since the wedding reception. How are you despite everything that's going on. I know we've been talking here and there but I haven't seen you. I'm glad you came out tonight to kick with us." I missed Danielle she went to Hawaii for a few weeks and bounced back on us. I heard about all the bull shit Baine's been doing. I swear I never knew he was a fuck nigga. I knew he was a hoe though.

"I'm doing okay Nikki! Thank you for always checking on me. I'm taking it one day at a time. My divorce is messy it's one for the books. My ex-husband is trying to take me for everything we acquired together. I'm rebuilding. I'm not drinking heavy because I'm expecting," she sighed. I looked at Danielle with wide eyes. No wonder she's glowing! I can't wait to plan her baby shower.

"Congratulations I noticed you picked up a few pounds. Girl fuck him! He ain't taking shit. I'm sick of his motherfuckin' ass. The million, dollar, question is why did you cheat and is the baby his?" I swear Baine is doing to fuckin' much. Damn nigga she cheated it ain't the end of the fuckin' world. Get over it or move on. He's acting worse than bitches that get cheated on. Women get cheated on every fuckin' day. Tuck ya dick nigga.

"Thank you! I appreciate y'all for not judging me.

It's been me and Crimson for years and over the past few years and months we've all became close. I feel like I can talk to y'all without any judgement because we're all human. I'm pregnant and I'm in denial as fuck. I don't want a baby now isn't the time. Leah and Malone please don't say shit. I'm pregnant by Rashad.

I haven't told him yet and I'm not sure if I want too. It was never my intentions to cheat on Baine. I wanted to leave him for years I just couldn't. Rashad and I just happened.

The night we thought Griff died it started there. One kiss led to all this. Rashad was my first love and I never stopped loving him. I stayed away from him for years. Rashad cheated on me when we first got together. I hate you Nikki because I swear, I don't want to relive none of this shit I'm about to say.

You're about to make me fuck up my make-up. Rashad disappeared for months because he fucked up and instead of owning up to his wrong doings. He broke my heart. It took me a minute to bounce back from that. I never stopped loving him. I hated him but I still loved him.

He forced himself on me, but I wanted it, even if it was only for one night. I wanted him. I couldn't shake him. I loved Baine, but he's never been perfect. He's cheated on me all through our marriage.

His two kids are a product of that. I wanted to leave him years ago, but he wouldn't allow me too.

I loved him through all his fucks ups. He made me stay down when I didn't want too. I fucked up one time and he won't even be cordial or love me past this one thing. I'm okay with getting the divorce. I swear to God y'all don't know what that nigga has took me through," she cried. I wrapped my arms around Danielle. I swear I hate dirty dick niggas. Two fuckin' babies oh hell no I would've killed Skeet. I wish the fuck he would. I swear that nigga wouldn't live to fuck another bitch.

"Danielle don't cry we've all been cheated on," Malone stated. I had to cut Malone off because I'm not a part of the WE! Bitch NIKKI ain't been cheated on. Since me and SKEET have been together, he ain't never fucked another BITCH. If he did, he might as well kill himself before I do.

"I don't mean to cut you off Malone, but I haven't been cheated on Skeet knows better." Everybody looked at me like I was crazy shit I'm being honest. Since we're laying out our truths. I'm blessed to have Skeet; shit we're blessed to have each other.

"I haven't been cheated on either," Crimson stated. Me and Crimson slapped hands with each other. Everybody is side giving us the side eye. I threw up my middle finger. Alexis rolled her eyes at me. She passed me the blunt so I could shut the fuck up.

"Correction most of us have been cheated on except Nikki and Crimson! I can't stand y'all lucky motherfuckas but anyways. I hate you went through that. Holding it in is the worse part. I can relate because I went through that with my baby daddy. He had two kids on me when we were together, and I didn't know until we broke up.

When I got pregnant by husband I was pissed because of his past reputation. I'm not gone lie he's not like that with me at all. Men do change. What doesn't kill you makes you stronger. We got your back no matter what. If you want to ride out and fuck Baine up let's go. I'm in the Escalade tonight," Malone explained. I kept staring at Journee because I wanted her to speak her truth she can relate too. I know she feels me staring at her. She looked at me and rolled her eyes. I don't give a fuck. Journee grabbed the blunt and hit it a few times.

"Danielle real women do real things. I don't blame you for cheating. If he took you through all that he deserved that shit. I wasn't going to say anything but since Nikki wants to pour into my soul tonight. I'll go ahead and get this shit off my chest. I know your situation to well. It's one of the reasons why I didn't want to say shit because it's opening old wounds. Juelz was my first love.

He cheated on me when we first started fuckin' around. I left his ass and ran right into the arms of Kairo Hussein. I loved Kairo but I was never in love with Kairo. Kairo did the same shit but worse. Juelz had my heart. When I left Juelz, I was pregnant with his baby.

I was selfish as fuck he cheated on me. I kept his daughter away from him. I'm saying this to say this I stayed away from Juelz for seven years. I missed the fuck out of him. I was miserable. Kairo had plenty of money I'm still spending it.

If it wasn't for Khadijah and Nikki, we probably would've never saw each other again. We saw each other one-time girl, that nigga stalked me. He found out I had his baby and kept her from him. He damn near killed me. I ran back into the arms of the man I was hiding from just to end up being his wife. I stayed away and shouldn't have because we could've been together sooner raising our daughter. We were both with someone miserable just to be with each other in the end.

Don't miss Rashad if you don't have too. I know how you feel, but don't keep the baby away from him. If you love Rashad, Danielle be with him fuck what anybody has to say motherfuckas are going to talk anyway. Niggas fuck up but they learn. It took me leaving Juelz for him to grow up. Rashad he's probably not the same person anymore. You won't know unless you find out for yourself.

If he told your husband about y'all. I don't see him fuckin' up. We got your back Danielle fuck that nigga." By the time everybody finished talking we were all full and drunk and teary eyed. I wanted Danielle to know that we're all here for her. She's not alone. Shit I'm ready to go home. I called Skeet to come and get me. I'm ready to fuck. We cleaned up Alexis's spot. I'm too drunk to drive.

A MONTH LATER

Chapter-17

Danielle

I've been through a lot the past few months. I know God wouldn't put more on me than I can bear. I'm going through a nasty divorce and I'm pregnant. I swear a child is the last thing I need. I haven't told Rashad I'm pregnant with his child and I don't plan too. My life is finally starting to make sense despite everything I'm going through. I'm three months pregnant and I've been in denial for a while now. I'm starting to show. I swear every week it seems like my stomach is getting bigger and bigger.

I'm starting to feel little things. I took three pregnancy tests. I checked my blood and submitted a urine sample and they both confirmed what I already knew. I can handle my prenatal care myself, but I decided to seek outside help from another OBGYN and support some other nurses that do what I do.

I have so much going on. It's easy for me to forget the things I'm supposed to pertaining to the child I'm carrying.

I have an appointment today to see my OBGYN. My clothes were already laid out. I did my hair last night. My hair has grown out so much. I needed a touch up bad. I had no choice but to color my hair. My mohawk is on point. I can't wait to see how it turned out once I take my curl rods out.

I wanted to look cute at my first doctor's appointment. I thumbed through my closet. I grabbed my oatmeal Fendi logo sweater dress. I paired it with the matching Fendi logo booties. After my appointment I'm going to work.

I have my work clothes packed in my duffel bag. I jumped in the shower to handle my hygiene. I haven't lived alone in years. The moment Crimson and I got our first apartment we couldn't enjoy it together. Crimson moved out because she got pregnant with Cariuna and a few months after that Baine and I made it official and we moved in with each other. I'm enjoying my alone time. Majority of the time I was alone anyway.

☆

I finally made it to the OBGYN. I maneuvered my way through the parking lot trying to find a parking spot. It's the beginning of the fall. The weather is perfect. I saw a car that looked familiar. I didn't pay it any mind.

A lot of people have the same cars. I grabbed my Fendi tote off my passenger seat. I threw my Fendi aviator sunglasses on. I looked in the mirror to make sure I'm on point. I am. I made my way inside of the OBGYN. The moment I stepped in all eyes were on me. It's mixed crowd I could tell when I walked in.

I stepped up toward the counter to sign in. The receptionist asked for my driver's license and insurance card. She made copies. I took a seat in the waiting area until they called my name. I grabbed my phone out my purse. I need to check my emails and to see if I have any missed calls from my assistant and office manager.

I felt someone staring a hole in me. I looked around to see if I know anybody in here. It's Rashad and Mya. Me and Rashad locked eyes with each other. I gave him an evil scowl. I can't believe out of all places I chose to come. I see him here with this bitch. I quickly turned my head. It's a reminder why I'm not fuckin' with him.

I haven't saw or heard from Rashad in months. I had no plans too. I swear to God if Mya's pregnant by him too. I'm going to trip. I know God wouldn't do this to me. I still haven't served that bitch with a dose of her own medicine. It's coming though when she least expects it. The receptionist called a name.

"Mya Truitt." Truitt's her last name. I keyed that into my phone. It's time for the games to begin. Mya and Rashad got up from their seats. They walked past me.

Oh, she's fuckin' pregnant too. I shook my head in disgust. No wonder that bitch was doing the most. The receptionist called my name. "Danielle MAHONE."

Mya looked around to see if she saw me. Her eyes landed on me. I had the biggest smile on my face. She's breaking her neck to see me.

I'm glad I'm dressed to the nines today. I walked past them. I could feel Mya and Rashad both burning a hole in me. Worry about her and not me. My doctor greeted me. Lala went to nursing school with me. We graduated together. Lala gave me a hug. I hate Rashad and Mya are still out here too. It's so much tension between us it crazy. I want to smack the shit out of him and shoot her in her chest.

"It's been a minute Danielle it's good seeing you! You look great as always. Your baby bump is so cute. Let's check your weight. Since you're pregnant you're going to have to let the heels go." I rolled my eyes at Lala she knows how I feel about my shoes. "Danielle I'm serious."

"Thank you! I know," I sighed. Lala checked my weight. Rashad is starring a hole in me. I refused to acknowledge him. Mya's getting her weight checked too. She's being loud so I can acknowledge her. She wants my attention. Bitch I will never acknowledge you. Lala escorted me in her station. She checked all my vitals and got a brief history of my health.

"Danielle you're eleven weeks. You're due on or around February 26th.

Your date of conception occurred on or around May 26th. Everything looks good despite you being in denial. Your baby is healthy. I'll schedule you another appointment in thirty days. You can find out what you're having," she beamed. Rashad got me pregnant the night before Crimson's wedding. I want a girl. I'm glad to hear everything looks great. Lala gave me a prescription for some prenatal vitamins. When you're pregnant it's supposed to be one of the happiest times of your live. I need to get in the spirit. I always wanted my pregnancy to be dope. I sent my mom a picture of the ultrasound. She sent me a text back. Lala and I finished catching up. I hope Rashad and Mya are gone. I said my goodbyes to Lala and exited out the clinic.

Mommy-Congratulations! I told you. I'm moving in to smother you and my grandchild. I'll be there Thursday to spend the week with you.

Me- I'm waiting

I grabbed my sunglasses out my purse. I know he's somewhere lurking around. I can feel it. I'm drawn to him and I can't change it. I miss my mommy. I can't wait until she comes back. I can't wait to get out of here. I got to call the girls to let them know who I seen at the fuckin' doctor. My baby daddy. Rashad looked so fuckin' good.

He knew he did too that's why I hated his ass. Fine ass parading another bitch around. Why is he trying to look good for her? Why does she have to be pregnant by him? I need to stop thinking about his ass.

Rashad

I haven't seen Danielle since the wedding. I've seen the little pictures Crimson has been posting of her on Instagram. Imagine my surprise when she walked in the OBGYN pregnant. Griff didn't tell me she was pregnant. She's been fuckin' hiding from me, now I know why. I knew she was back in the city because Griff confirmed that. She blocked my number and everything. It's safe to say she's not trying to fuck with me, but it's not going down like that.

I heard Baine burned down her clinic. I heard she setup shop somewhere else, but I don't know where. Crimson's not fuckin' with me so she won't relay any of my fuckin' messages. I fell back, but I haven't fell all the way back. Damn my luck got to be bad. Mya's pregnant and Danielle is too. I know the baby Danielle's carrying is mine. She wouldn't even look at me. I know she could feel me starring at her.

I ain't did shit to Danielle but let her husband know she's mine. When was she going to tell me she's fuckin' pregnant? I'm glad I didn't fuckin' drive. My car's in the shop and Slap dropped me off. I had him scan the parking lot for Danielle's car. I wanted him to block it in so she couldn't fuckin' move.

Mya's being nosey as shit too. The moment they called Danielle's name she was on some bullshit.

She wanted Danielle to see her, but Danielle wasn't thinking about her ass and neither am I. She wanted me to take her to lunch. I gave her some lunch money I'm not fuckin' with her ass. I walked Mya to her car so I can send her on her way.

"Are you waiting on her," she asked? I knew Mya had a fuckin' attitude, but that ain't my problem. I'm not your man and the only thing I'm promising is taking care of our child. I looked at Mya like she was crazy. Stay in your fuckin' lane.

"Am I waiting on who?" Mya knows I'm irritated. My business doesn't fuckin' concern her. If I am waiting on Danielle, why is she worried about it. We ain't together and we'll never be together.

"Danielle." I stepped in Mya's personal space. I cupped her chin roughly. She looked at me with wide eyes. I'm tired of fuckin' telling her.

"Aye I'm only going to tell you one time and one time only. You can run back and tell Baine this shit if you want too. Stop worrying about a motherfucka that ain't worried about you. Danielle ain't your issue. Whatever me and you got going on is between us not her. I'm not your issue because we'll never be together.

I can never commit to female I don't trust. If I am waiting on her why are you worried about it. I came here with you not her. You wanted me to come to the doctor's appointments. I'm here and on time.

Don't make this shit harder than what it is." Mya had tears in her eyes. What the fuck is she crying for? She asked a question. I gave her a fuckin' answer.

"Rashad you're hurting me. Why does it have to be like this," she cried. I know she didn't just ask me a question. I just gave her the answer too.

"You made it like this Mya. You're sneaky as fuck. I know more than you think I know. Get the fuck out of here and take your ass home," I argued. Mya climbed inside of her car. She slammed the door and pulled off. I had Wire following her ass. I know she's been fuckin' with Baine on the low. He can have her I'm not tripping.

If she wants to fuck Baine to get back at me do that shit. I just hope it doesn't backfire on her. If I find out she's crossed me for that nigga. It's going to be some problems that her and Baine ain't ready for. I didn't even want to handle her like that, but she made it like this.

I walked back toward the entrance. Mya looked at me with wide eyes as she exited the parking lot. Her sad face doesn't move me anymore. The last thing I need is Mya lurking around here while I'm trying to talk to Danielle. Slap sent me a text that Danielle just made it to her car. I called him to see what direction I need to head toward. I scanned the parking lot look for his car. I found it.

I jogged my way over there. Danielle was knocking on Slap's window telling him to move. I wanted to laugh but I couldn't.

“Move your fuckin’ car so I can move before I call the fuckin’ police,” she argued. I walked up behind Danielle. She didn’t even notice me. I wrapped my arms around her waist. I bit the crook of her neck. She tried to pry my arms from around her waist. I had a death grip on her hips. “Get the fuck off me. I should’ve known this had something to do with you. Leave me alone.” I felt Danielle’s body tense up. She knows I’m not letting her go.

“I miss you too! Calm down! I got you. If you wouldn’t have put me on the block list. I wouldn’t even be doing this. Give me your keys. I’m riding with you.” Danielle pushed me off her. She folded her arms across her chest. She looked good as fuck pregnant too. I placed my hands on her stomach.

“I’m not going anywhere with you Rashad. The same bitch you were in there with. Ride with her. Our days of riding with each other or over. Leave me the fuck alone. I’m not fuckin’ with you. We’re done in case you didn’t get the memo,” she argued. I swear I’m not trying to put on a show for these folks.

I stepped in Danielle’s personal space closing the gap between us. I leaned in and placed my lips on Danielle’s. I grabbed her face and shoved my tongue down her throat. She didn’t stop me. She knew what it was between us.

“I’m riding with you because I don’t want to make a fuckin’ scene. You know I don’t give a fuck about making a scene.” I snatched Danielle’s keys from her.

No wonder I couldn't find her she's driving something I didn't know she had. Danielle climb in the passenger seat. I don't know why she has an attitude. She can get over that shit. "Are you hungry?"

"I'm not hungry Rashad I got to get work. I don't have time to talk."

"I don't give a fuck about you having to go to work Danielle. You're your own boss. You can miss a day of work. The way you're dressed. I know you're not going to work. Today Danielle you're going to make fuckin' time." I heard her mumble some shit under breath. "Danielle when were you going to tell me that you're pregnant with my child," I asked? Danielle refused to answer my question. I grabbed her leg and applied pressure to it. She scratched my hand. "I know you hear me fuckin' talking to you."

"Keep your hands to yourself? Is she pregnant by you Rashad? If she is that's the only baby, you need to worry about. Mya being pregnant by you says a lot. More of the reason why we don't need to have a conversation. That says enough. Where can I drop you off at, because we're done here." Damn I can't believe I got two women pregnant at the same time.

"She's pregnant with my child Danielle. I'm not going to lie and say that she's not. Me and Mya ain't got shit going on. I'm not a dead beat. I'm going to take care of my child regardless of who their mother is. I want to know if the child you're carrying is mine."

I can tell by Danielle's body language that she's pissed. At least I'm honest shit I fucked up.

"I don't think it is Rashad. It's my EX husband's that's why I didn't say anything," she lied. I didn't miss the smirk on her face. I gripped the steering wheel. I swear Danielle wants me to hurt her. I pulled over at Trap Eats on Lavista Road. I through Danielle's car in park. I turned around to face her. She looked at everything but me. I tapped her on her shoulder. She finally looked at me. "What Rashad?" She folded her arms across her chest.

"It's your husbands? When are you due? You look about two or three months? As long as you've been fuckin' with him you ain't never had that niggas baby. You knew better. All a sudden now it's his baby you're carrying. You lied to me you were still fuckin' him too? I figured you was. I watched him play with that pussy at the wedding. I'm going to fuck you up.

I still want a DNA test. I want to see if it's mine. I think you're lying. Danielle, I swear to God if you're pregnant with my baby and you're lying to me. I'm going to fuckin' hurt you. I love you but don't play with my kids. I'm going to fall back because that's what you want. Is that what you want? You want me to fall back. You don't want me to love you?"

"Why do you want to hurt me? You've done enough. Sometimes shit ain't meant. We ain't meant. Just let it go Rashad. Be glad my child isn't yours.

You were fuckin' her unprotected and still fuckin' on me too. She's pregnant BE GLAD YOU AIN'T GOT TWO babies on the way at the same time. She RUINED US. Ain't no way in hell I'm dealing with her or you? She can have you. Stay out of my face enjoy your life Rashad and stop fuckin' up mine.

Congratulations on your new addition. Do you have somewhere I can drop you off? I need to get to work. I don't want to stress my child out arguing with you." I had Danielle to drop me off at the trap. The whole ride was awkward. She stayed on her phone the whole time. She hopped out and walked toward the driver's door. I sized her up. It was a lot of niggas on the block peeping Danielle. They knew she was fuckin' mine.

"D. Elle what's up?" I didn't even know Griff was over here. Danielle threw her hand up at Griff. She stepped in her car. She attempted to close the door. I held her door open. Danielle looked at me and I looked at her. I stepped in her personal space.

"I love you and incase I never see you again. I want you know." I cupped Danielle's face and shoved my tongue down her throat. I could feel her heartbeat. She didn't break the kiss. My eyes were trained on Danielle as we exchanged the kiss. She refuses to look at me.

"You don't love me you just like ruining me," she argued. Danielle's eyes pierced through mine. She slammed the door and pulled off. I can win for losing with her.

I swear I can't. Griff walked up behind me and smacked me on the back of my head.

"She's pregnant? Damn Rashad you need to start strapping up. How far along is Danielle," he asked?

"Yep! I thought you knew she was pregnant. I was about to hit you up and go in. Mya just happened. I wanted to get Danielle pregnant. She said it's not mine. I know she's lying."

"Crimson didn't tell me because she know I would tell you. You got a lot of ass kissing to do," he laughed. Me and Griff headed into the trap to discuss business. I need a real conversation with Danielle.

Mya

I swear to God I hate that bitch. Why her? I can never have my moment because of her. It never fuckin' fails. Out of all places why did we have to share the same fuckin' OBGYN facility. I'm finding another facility. I don't want to see her at every fuckin' appointment. I don't want tension between me and Rashad. Whenever she's in the room she brings tension. Make no mistake he will be at every appointment. Where's Baine why wasn't he with his wife at her doctor's appointment? If Danielle's baby is Rashad's we got a motherfuckin' problem. He couldn't even focus on me at our appointment because he was so fuckin' focused on her. I knew he was waiting on her to come out. I know he didn't want to have lunch with me because of her.

He could've had lunch with me and then ran up behind her later. Something told me to ride back through there. I did. I just wanted to see for myself what he was too. Rashad's really sweating this bitch in broad daylight. He didn't even dote on me and

I'm carrying his child. She knows she wants him. I don't even know why she's fronting. I zoomed in on my phone to take a picture of them. I'm sure Baine would love to see this. He needs to keep his wife on a fuckin' leash. I swear this bitch is like a troll that won't go away.

Baine didn't tell me he had a baby on the way. It's only right I congratulate him. I grabbed my phone to call him. He didn't answer. I sent him a message. I saw your baby momma. I thought that would get his attention. He called my phone back. I answered on the first ring.

"I didn't want anything. I saw your baby momma at the OBGYN clinic. She was dressed in Fendi from head to toe. It must be nice! Baby daddy tricking," I beamed. I'm lying it on thick. I knew Baine and Danielle were still having problems he's been sucking on me every chance he gets. I don't care. I want him to keep her away from us.

"Baby momma? What the fuck are you talking about?" Baine's stupid ass didn't even look at the pictures. He must not know Danielle's pregnant. I swear if her baby is Rashad's it's going to be some fuckin' problems. I'm not sharing him with her. I don't care.

"You didn't look at the pictures I sent you Baine? I saw Danielle I didn't know the two of you were expecting. She's pregnant," I beamed.

"I haven't seen Danielle in a few months. Let me look at the pictures." The phone line went quiet for a minute as Baine looked at the pictures. "Where they at," he asked? I had his attention now. I gave Baine the rundown of our day. "She hasn't told me we're expecting. I wonder why?"

"Maybe you should find out. Inside the clinic they acted as if they didn't know each other. I'm sure Rashad wants the baby to be his. Clearly the pictures state something else. Congratulations I hope the baby is yours.

Keep your troll in her place." I hung up the phone with Baine. If Danielle didn't tell her husband she's pregnant, it's not his.

Chapter-18

Baine

Danielle's pregnant? She didn't tell me because she knows the baby, she's carrying isn't mine. I haven't killed a bitch in a long time. It's nothing for me to add Danielle to my hit list. I told that bitch a few months ago to tread fuckin' lightly. I swear to God I'm going to fuckin' hurt her. I didn't even look at the pictures Mya sent. Mya's a freak I thought she was sending me some pictures of her playing with her pussy.

I knew Mya was pregnant, but she didn't say Rashad was her baby daddy. I haven't seen Danielle in a few months. She knew not to show her fuckin' face. Danielle really wants to make a fuckin' fool out of me. She has me looking bad out here in these streets. I know where she's lives.

She didn't know I knew but I did. I'm about to pay her a visit, I want her to see how real shit is about to get. She can't seem to stay away from that nigga. I'll make her stay away from him. I know it's his baby the picture speaks volumes.

I want Danielle to tell me to my face the baby she's carrying isn't mine. She'll fuck around and lose her baby today. I need to switch cars. I can't pull up on her in none of my cars.

I sent Ike a text and told him to meet me at the Trap with the 2018 Honda Accord. I'm sure it'll blend in with the cars on her block. Ike came through with the Honda. He told me not to do anything crazy. I can't and I won't promise that.

Danielle's had a house out in Lithonia near StoneCrest. She thinks she's being discreet about her moves. I still get the credit notifications anytime something gets open in her name or mine. I wrote the address down, because I knew I would need it.

I wonder where Danielle got the money from to move. She didn't have access to anything. I made sure of that. She couldn't fuck my enemy and spend my money. She couldn't fuck anything. It's not going down like that. Rashad must be footing the bill. I swear this nigga wants to be me so fuckin' bad. I got to touch him. It's time. He fucked my wife.

It took me about an hour to get to her house. I've been posted at the corner of her house for about an hour. I can see Danielle's house from here. A cocaine white Mercedes Benz stopped at the stop sign. Custom plates. D. COOP. I know that's Danielle. I pulled up right behind her. Danielle killed her engine. She stepped out the car looking good as fuck too. I had to adjust my dick. She's picked up a few pounds. Danielle wasn't even paying attention to her surroundings. She's all on her phone smiling and shit without a care in the world. Not knowing her life could end in a matter of minutes.

"Crimson, he was at the clinic with that bitch! It took everything in me not spas the fuck out. I kept my composure," she laughed. Danielle thinks this shit is funny. I walked up behind her. She was trying to open the door. I grabbed my gun from behind my waist. I shoved it in her back.

"Danielle open the fuckin' door. If you move wrong. I swear to God I'll shoot your dumb ass." I felt Danielle's body tense up. I hope she knows I'm not fuckin' around. I'm doing what I made plans to do after the wedding. She's bragging about fuckin' with this nigga and she's still married to me.

"Baine why are you here? Leave me alone! Am I fuckin' bothering you? I'm not, so what's the motherfuckin' problem. When I tried to go home you weren't there. You gave all my shit away to your baby momma. You wanted to embarrass me in front of the whole subdivision. You wanted the world to know I cheated.

The difference between you and me. I didn't want anybody to know my EX HUSBAND cheated. I got my own shit now Baine. You're trespassing," she argued. I grabbed Danielle's phone and smashed that motherfucka. "Why would you do that? Have I broken any of your stuff? You're buying me another one. I don't have money to keep replacing everything you fuckin' took from me. You're making shit hard and it shouldn't be."

"You're feeling yourself. You can either let me in or I'll let myself in," I argued. I didn't come here to argue with Danielle. She wanted to flaunt in my face about her leaving and having her own spot. I did give Bre'Elle her shit, she didn't need it. I brought her that shit anyway. It was my fuckin' money.

"I'm always feeling myself. I'm not letting you in Baine for what. What do we have to talk about? You've done enough talking. I've listened. You want a divorce okay." I pushed Danielle inside of her house. I pushed her back up against the wall. Danielle's eyes were trained on me. She knelt and slid her shoes off. I stepped in her personal space closing the gap between us. I can feel her heart beating. She's scared and she should be. I placed my hand on her stomach.

"Let's talk Danielle. You know why I'm fuckin' here. This isn't a friendly fuckin' visit. You're pregnant Danielle? When were you going to tell me that we're expecting," I asked? Danielle didn't respond because she knows I'm telling the truth. "I'm not done talking though. You didn't tell me because it's not mine, right? Tell me it's not mine Danielle. I want to hear it from you that It's his. I've wanted a child with MY EX WIFE for a while, BUT she would NEVER give me one. As soon as she starts fuckin' this nigga. She gets pregnant by him. You're keeping it too?

How does that even look Danielle and we're still married and you're carrying a baby for someone else. You had this shit all figured out right? You made plans to leave me for him.

You wanted OUT the only way you're getting out is in a fuckin' body bag." I banged Danielle's head up against the wall.

"Move Baine! We don't have to do this. We really don't, you've done plenty already. You hate me and we're done REMEMBER? What's understood doesn't need to be explained. It's not yours there I said it. Are you happy? You wanted me to have your child? I can't FUCKIN' tell. Baine we've been married for five years. In the five years we've been married you've had two children on me. Your baby mommas they weren't the best bitches to deal with. But I dealt with them bitches because of you? How do you think I felt my husband had two babies during our marriage? The only thing I got was an I'm sorry that wasn't fuckin' good enough.

Oh yeah, I saw Nova a few weeks ago. She came to my NEW office on some bullshit. She wanted me to know that she's carrying ANOTHER child for you. I knew you were still FUCKIN' her you never stopped. Baine you could've been with her years ago. You were too selfish to let me be happy with someone else. She caught me on a FUCKIN' good day. I swear I'm not the bitch I used to be.

I'm no longer Danielle Mahone. I'm DANIELLE COOPER. I'm MOTHERFUCKIN D. ELLE HOE. I'm done giving these bitches PASSES because of you. I don't give a fuck what a motherfucka thinks about me. They're going to talk anyway. Let them motherfuckas talk.

You know what's funny Mr. MAHONE the house she lives in WE OWN IT. The medical insurance card she's using to provide for her child's medical expenses your name is on the fuckin' card.

Baine you don't give a fuck about me. I wanted to fight for my marriage, but what am I fighting for? You never stopped cheating. I'm surprised I can even have FUCKIN' kids. You gave me so many FUCKIN' diseases from the different bitches you were fuckin'. I'm surprised your dick didn't fall off.

Thank God I'm a NURSE. I'm sure motherfuckas would've been laughing at me if they saw my medical records. Thank God you didn't give me anything I couldn't get rid of. I've been nothing, but loyal to you. I didn't think it would turn out like this, but it did. You made your bed a long time ago, now you can lay in it peacefully. You don't have to sneak around to fuck. You can do it openly.

I had your FUCKIN' back when I shouldn't have. You ain't never had my FUCKIN' back. I don't want anything from you. You can keep it all. Let’s be realistic you ain't never gave me SHIT. Anything you ever gave me; you've always thrown it up in my fuckin' face. You NEVER FUCKIN' MADE ME. I always had a fuckin' BAG. I always had clothes and shoes. You got shit confused Baine the bitches you fuck with on the side you made them.

The only reason why they're with you is because you're wealthy. I never wanted you for that. I wanted you for YOU. Just admit it Baine I was never enough for you," she argued. I clapped my hands. Danielle wanted a standing ovation for her little speech she gave. I stepped back in Danielle's fuckin' personal space. I cupped her chin roughly.

"I fuckin' made you Danielle. I'm going to be the nigga that breaks you. You can't talk to me or do shit to me without any repercussions. You could've left a long time ago, but you wanted to play the same game I'm playing. You wanted to sneak behind my back and fuck him. I can't let you walk around my city carrying his baby. I'm going to kill your first then I'm going to kill him." I wrapped my hands around Danielle's neck. I applied so much fuckin' pressure. She started clawing my arms with her nails. I picked her up by neck and banged her head against the wall.

"Baine are you really doing this," she cried. She wants to cry now.

"What the fuck are you crying for? You said what you had to say, and I said what I had to say. You tried to fuck me over so I'm killing you. It's a wrap Danielle. I'll let Rashad know I killed my bitch and his baby. If that nigga loved, you Danielle. He should've never been able to let me get this close to you and take your lying cheating scheming ass out." I choked Danielle until I couldn't choke that bitch no more. Her body slid to the ground. I checked her pulse it's faint.

I grabbed Danielle's hair and pulled her head toward my face. I coughed up some spit and spit in her face. “Bitch you ain't fuckin' worth it. I should stomp that baby up out of you. Killing you is too fuckin' easy. I rather kill that baby inside of you and watch you suffer.” I pulled Danielle's panties down. I might as well beat this pussy up. Danielle started squirming and trying to stop me. I pried her legs open. I shoved my dick inside of her. Her pussy was wet as fuck too. “You wanted to be a hoe anyway. I’m going to fuck you like one. Stop acting like you don't want this shit because you do. Your body is still responding to me. That pussy still gets wet for a nigga.” Danielle started mumbling some shit under her breath. “Say it Danielle so I can bust your motherfuckin’ head open.”

I put my hand over her mouth and squeezed her cheeks so fuckin' hard. I could feel her teeth. I stroked Danielle long deep and hard. It's been a minute since I've been able to feel her. I'm almost at my peak. I'm sure she could tell. I pulled out and busted my nut on Danielle's face. I wiped my dick with her panties and tossed them motherfuckas in her face. “You think that nigga is so much fuckin' better than me, but you and another bitch is pregnant by him too.” I made my way through Danielle's house. I left out the back door.

Crimson

I've been trying to reach Danielle since Baine pulled up on her. My heart dropped instantly when I heard his voice. Me and Danielle were both taken by surprise. I know something bad happened to her. I can feel it. My heart hurts. He hung up the phone and I haven't been able to reach her since. I've been calling her since the call ended. I had to get to her house quick. Griff knew I was upset so he wouldn't let me come alone. Tears poured down my face instantly. I swear to God if he did something to her I'm going to kill him myself. Griff grabbed my hand. I looked at him with sad eyes.

"Crimson baby please calm down. Think positive everything is going to be okay. For Baine's sake I pray he didn't do anything to Danielle. Rashad got a bullet with his name on it. Shoot Rashad Danielle's address so he can meet us over there." I sent Rashad Danielle's address like Griff told me too. It's funny once Mya saw Danielle at the clinic, Baine pulled up on her with this bull shit. I swear it's nothing coincidental about it. Mya needs her ass beat. I don't put shit past this bitch. If something happened to Danielle. I'm kicking Mya's ass.

☆

We finally made our way to Danielle's house. Rashad beat us there. He's sitting on the hood of his car. I jumped out the car before Griff could throw the car in park.

I banged on the door and it was open. Danielle would never leave her door open. I walked in and she's lying on the hardwood floor unconscious. I let out a loud piercing scream. Baine beat Danielle's ass and left her unconscious. I can't let them see her like this. Griff and Rashad both ran in. I checked Danielle's pulse she still had one. It's not strong though. He tried to kill her. He violated her. He's sick as fuck. He left his semen all on her face. I swear to God I hate him.

"Call an ambulance," I screamed. "Get out of here. I can't let y'all see her like this." Rashad pushed past me. He gave me an evil scowl. Rashad looked at Danielle. He's pissed. His eyes turned dark as coal. I noticed the stress lines appear on his forehead. Baine took shit too far.

"What the fuck happened to her Crimson what the fuck is going on," he asked? I gave Rashad the rundown of what happened earlier. He started pacing the floors back and forth. He scooped Danielle up off the floor. He carried Danielle upstairs to her room. "I know Baine did this I'm going to fuckin' kill him. He fuckin' violated her. Where's the bathroom?" I pointed upstairs. Rashad went upstairs to run Danielle some bath water. I know he's concerned about his child. Danielle's needs to tell this man she's carrying his baby.

"Crimson call Auntie Kay please. We can't call the ambulance. GRIFF, I swear to God I'm going to kill that pussy ass nigga tonight. Why did he fuckin' handle her like that? Don't fuckin' touch her because you're mad at me.

Get at me nigga I ain't hard to fuckin' find. I'm posted up in my fuckin' hood all fuckin' day. When I approached that nigga, I was fuckin' DIRECT. Griff do me a solid. Call the moving crew and tell them I need them motherfuckas here ASAP. She can't fuckin' stay here anymore. I want all this shit packed up. It's hunting season," he argued. I swear my girl can't catch a break. Griff called the moving crew. Rashad slammed the bathroom door. I called Auntie Kay like he asked me too. She advised that she's on her way. I knocked on the door. Rashad opened it.

"What's up," he asked? Rashad was on one. I wish Danielle would stop playing with him and just be with him. It's not that fuckin' hard. I've never met a person that fights love so hard. I did it with Griff, but finally I caved in. She's pregnant with his baby. I want to tell Rashad so bad that her baby is his, but it's not my place. I promised Danielle I wouldn't. I think he needs to know, because if something would've happened to his baby. He probably wouldn't even be this calm.

"I know you're concerned but I don't think Danielle would be comfortable with you packing up her stuff without her knowing," I explained. I know she would never agree to this. Rashad looked at me and smiled. I see what Rashad's doing. He's capitalizing off this moment. I hate it happened.

"Crimson you know you're my sister. I love Danielle and she loves me. Nobody can change that, not even her. Danielle can't stay here anymore it's not safe. We wouldn't even be here if she wasn't so stubborn.

I know that's my baby she's carrying. I'm going to protect mine at all cost. I want Baine the worst fuckin' way. If he wants Danielle, he got to come through me, and I can guarantee you that motherfucka doesn't want to go toe to toe with me. The baby she's carrying Crimson is it mine," he asked? I was hoping that he wouldn't ask me that.

"I don't know Rashad. I didn't ask who's it was. It doesn't matter to me. I'm hoping it's yours though. If Baine's the father, her child will be fatherless courtesy of ME." I've never been a good liar. I hope Rashad believes me. Auntie Kay finally made her over to Danielle's house. I gave her a hug when I opened the door.

"Is she okay," she asked? I gave her a faint smile. Auntie Kay followed me upstairs.

"I don't know! She was lying unconscious when I found her. Her pulse was faint when I found her. I more concerned for the baby she's carrying. Rashad's up here with her. I'm praying she's okay." Auntie Kay's cool I trust her. I'm praying she doesn't ask who did this because she's fond of Baine. I can't believe he done this. You think you really know person until you don't. I escorted Auntie Kay upstairs to the bathroom where Rashad was with Danielle.

Rashad carried Danielle out the bathroom and into her room. He wrapped a towel around her body. Auntie Kay followed Rashad into Danielle's room. She setup her medical equipment so she could look at her. I laid beside Danielle I grabbed her hand. Baine fucked Danielle up bad.

I noticed a tear slid down Auntie Kay's cheek. Danielle's still out of it. I whispered in her ear.

"I'm sorry I wasn't here with you. I came as fast as I can. I knew something happened. I need you. I'm trying to keep it together, but I can't. I love you. Your baby needs you. Bitch you got to fight we've been fighting all our life and we're not giving up now." Danielle squeezed my hand. I brushed her hair into a ponytail. Auntie Kay checked Danielle's vitals.

"She's breathing good and the baby is too. Crimson and Rashad, she'll be just fine. The baby's a fighter like her mother. I want to put her on bedrest for two or three weeks. Her blood pressure is high. She suffered a lot of trauma to her head. It's a little fluid on her brain. It'll a drain on it's on. I know she's in a lot of pain. I'll call her prescription in. I brought some Tylenol 3's with me. She only needs a half. I can't give her anything stronger because she's pregnant.

Who's going to look after her. I mean it. I want her on bedrest for two weeks because of the trauma," she explained. A girl? I wonder how Auntie Kay knows Danielle's pregnant with a girl that's what she wants. I bet her daughter ends up looking like Rashad. He spoke up before I had the chance to say anything.

"I got her Auntie Kay she'll be staying with me." Auntie Kay looked at me with wide eyes.

"Oh, really is that true Crimson? What happened to Danielle if you don't mind me asking," she asked?

I was hoping she wouldn't ask but that's too much like right. Rashad spoke up.

“Your nephew did this. I didn't get to kill him behind Griff, but I am going to kill him behind these two,” he argued. Rashad pointed at Danielle and her stomach. He knows that baby is his. Auntie Kay broke down and started crying. I know she always considered Baine as her nephew, but he's not who she thinks he is. Shit he had me fooled too. He's done so much to Danielle. I was shocked after she told us all the shit, he done her. My best friend has been through a lot. Rashad pulled Auntie Kay in for a hug.

Auntie Kay finally got herself together. She gave Danielle a shot to sedate her. Rashad carried Danielle to his car. The movers had Danielle's entire house packed up. I looked at Griff and shook my head. He smiled at me. I swear I can't stand him and Rashad. Danielle's going to go crazy when she wakes up.

I rode with Rashad. Danielle's lying in my arms. I won’t be there when she wakes up. She's going to go crazy. She's already mad about Mya being pregnant by him. I don't know how she's going to take it living with him.

Chapter-19

Rashad

My mind is in a million FUCKIN' places. My mind won't stop FUCKIN' roaming until I'm able to touch that nigga. Ain't no way around it. I'm his issue not her. Baine knows how I give it up. I don't even know why he fuckin' tried me. I swear to God if he would've killed her. I would've killed his fuckin' momma. Griff wouldn't have a choice but to take me to her house. I may be a lot of things, but I ain't never had to take pussy from a female. He violated the fuck out her. Why would he do that shit? She's not your issue I am. Bainc knows I'm going to fuckin' kill him behind her.

He raped her and busted a nut on her face. I swear to God I want to kill his ass tonight. I can't though because I got to make sure she's straight. Pulling up on Baine would have to wait. This shit wouldn't even happened if she wouldn't be so fuckin stubborn. I wanted to take her to lunch. I deserve a real conversation. I want to spoil the baby she's carrying. I know it's mine. I heard a knock at my door. I'm sure it's my mother or my son. The door opened and It's my mother.

"Rashad what's going on what happened to her? You didn't tell me that she's pregnant?

How did you manage to get two women pregnant at the same time? I told you If you want to be with Danielle. I want you to do right by her. Part of you doing right by her is protecting her. None of this shit should've happened. Who did this," she asked? Damn my mother's treating me like I'm the fuckin' bad guy. I didn't do this shit. I want to protect Danielle that's the only thing I want to do.

"Ma, I didn't do it. Her EX did it. I'm trying to protect her she won't fuckin' let me. If she would've none of this would've happened. I didn't find out she was pregnant until today. She said it wasn't mine, but I don't believe that." I'm still tripping of that because I don't believe it.

"Rashad get you're shit together. I mean it. She doesn't need the extra stress coming from you and him. Her body isn't the same anymore. She's feeding for two. What stresses her out will stress the baby out. I don't want that even if it's your child or not." She explained. Damn who's side is my mother on?

"I know it's mine she's just fuckin' with me."

"I hope so. Has she eaten? I fried some chicken. I made some mash potatoes and gravy and baked macaroni and cheese and some yeast rolls. I put her a plate in the oven warmer."

"I don't know she's not fuckin' with me. I wanted to take her to lunch when I saw her at her appointment, but she saw Mya and assumed the worst of me. Did you fix me a plate too?" My mother gave me uneasy look.

"I haven't seen Danielle since the wedding she's been hiding from me. This is our first time seeing each other. I had no clue Mya and her where going to the same doctor's practice."

"Of course, I fixed you a plate. Rashad you got to do better. I try so hard to stay out of your business. I never wanted to be one of those mothers that meddles in her kid's business. Stop having sex with Mya if you haven't already. I haven't met her, but I don't trust her. God doesn't like ugly. All the little thing she's doing will come back on her. I wouldn't put it past her that she sent her EX some more pictures of you two that triggered him to do this." My mother left out the room. She did have a point. I don't put shit past Mya. I swear if she did that bullshit. I'll put my foot on her neck myself. She probably did that shit because she's mad. She kept asking about Danielle. I never took Mya as the jealous type. I'll ask Wire where did she go after the clinic? Mya's going to fuck around and get herself hurt.

Danielle's still asleep in my bed. I notice she kept tossing and turning. Auntie Kay gave her a shot to sedate her until we made it to my house. I didn't want her to be uncomfortable on the ride over here. I'm sure the shot is wearing off by now. I called my mother to come over here to help with Danielle. My son and Danielle haven't officially met, but I want her to be a part of our life.

"Where am I," she asked? Danielle looked around my room. She finally locked eyes with me. She wasn't beat up to bad, but he fucked her up.

I want to know what made him get at her. I didn't even know where she lived. Crimson said he didn't either. You never know that nigga could've been watching her. Danielle wasn't paying attention to her surroundings but it's not her fault. If she's not fuckin' with him, he shouldn't be fuckin' with her.

"At home." Danielle looked at me with wide eyes. She's at home. She's not leaving this motherfucka unless I got eyes on her. I don't trust her roaming the streets alone. Not until I touch Baine anyway. The streets aren't safe I don't know what he's capable of. I know what I'm capable of. I want his blood on my fuckin' hands and Ike's too. I know if I kill Baine. I got to take out Ike too.

"I'm not at home Rashad. What am I doing here where are my clothes," she asked? It's a small gap between us. I scooted closer to Danielle to close the gap between us. She tried to move away from me "What the fuck happened to me? What am I doing here? This is the last place I need to be is in your bed. I don't want to lay in your bed Rashad. I'm sure she's been here. I got to go Rashad I can't do this with you." She cried. Danielle's worried about the wrong shit. She tried to raise up, but she couldn't.

"Stop crying! Be still you can't be moving around. You're worried about the wrong shit. She hasn't been here Danielle. I don't fuck with Mya. She's never been here. You're the only woman that's been in my home and in this bed. I maybe a lot of things but I wouldn't do that to you. She's pregnant but I can't change that.

We made that child before you. I had no clue she was pregnant until after the wedding. I got you. If you would allow me too. I don't want you to upset your baby. You've been through enough today.

Crimson called me and said something happened to you. We met at your house and you were lying on the floor unconscious. Danielle, I know you ain't gone tell me what happened. I swear to God I'm going to kill that fuckin' nigga before Sunday. You can forget about going home. It's not safe. He fucked up that nigga knows where to find me at. He wants smoke he brought that shit to you and he could've brought it to me. What happened," I asked?

"Rashad I'm tired. I don't want to talk about it. I'm all cried out. I can't stay here with you. I'm over every fuckin' thing. I just want to live my life how I see fit without you and him. I can't even be seen with you. Every time we're around each other I keep getting hurt because of you. I'm so fuckin' tired of being hurt. I done gave this shit all I fuckin' got. I don't have anything else to give.

I can take the mental abuse, the name calling and all the other shit. I refuse to take the physical abuse. I'm not even fuckin' bothering him. I haven't asked him for one fuckin' thing Rashad, but he wants every fuckin' thing. I'm okay with that. I just want him and you to leave me the fuck alone," she cried. I picked Danielle up and laid her on chest. She kept punching her fist in my chest. I swear Danielle's words hurt a nigga soul. I didn't know I was the cause of her pain.

“Danielle I'm sorry. I understand how you feel, but I can't let you leave here. I put it on my fuckin’ life. I’ll never let him touch you again. Damn shawty I just want to love you that's it. Am I wrong for still loving you? Why are you making it so hard for me to love you? You know I'll protect you. I’ll give my life to save yours any day. He's a fuckin’ coward. Come on Danielle do you want me to kill him tonight? Come on let’s go It’s nothing you can ride with me if you want too.

The only reason why I'm still lying here next to you is because I need to make sure you’re straight. Danielle if you're one hundred percent let me know because I can leave now and I'm not coming back until I kill him. I can guarantee that. Whatever he took from you I'll replace it.” Danielle raised her head from my chest. I wiped her tears with my hands. I cupped her chin forcing her to look at me. I can tell Danielle's trying to get her words together. “Stop crying because I got you.” I mean that shit.

“I wish it was that simple,” she cried. What's so simple about listening and being submissive to your partner. I know Danielle's pulling back because of our past, but it's too late. I'm not that same nigga. I can't show her that if she won't let me. She keeps holding our past against me.

“I’ve caused this can you allow me to make this right? I told you months ago that I would buy you a new building. I told you to get your realtor on the phone so I can cut the check. It’s two types of niggas in this world. It’s niggas that do and niggas that don’t.

You wouldn’t be going through this if you would listen to me. I’m not trying to steer you down the wrong path. I want to be with you. I fucked up once Danielle, but I’m not trying to do that again. If I give you anything, I want you to have it.” I knew Baine was a bitch, but he's acting like a real bitch.

“Rashad he's not worth it. I don't want you to go to jail behind him,” she sniffled.

“Stop protecting him. It's a difference between me and him. He's worth it he's more than worth it. Danielle, I don't know everything he's done to you, but he won't get away with it. He can't breathe the same air as you. If I get caught in the process, it's worth it because I wanted to touch that nigga years ago. It has nothing to do with you. Griff was that niggas lifeline, but he isn't anymore. I see what the fuck he done to you. He shouldn't have handled you like that. I'm his fuckin' issue not YOU.

Auntie Kay said she wants you on bedrest for two weeks, so you're not leaving here until she clears you. If you're good. I'll get you some food and I'm out to go handle my business. Find you somewhere else to live because I had your shit packed up.” I picked Danielle up and laid her beside me. I stood up from the bed. Danielle placed her hands on my back. I looked over my shoulders to see what she wanted. If she doesn't want me here. I'll leave.

“Don't leave Rashad. Please don't leave,” she cried. She needs to come better than that. One minute she wants me here and the next minute she wants me gone. What's it going to be. I did a lot of shit for us to get to this moment. Was it worth it, that's what I'm trying to figure out? What more do I have to do to show her how much I love her?

“What do I need to stay for Danielle? You don't want me around. I'll kill him tonight and you can live your life shawty. I love you Danielle and you know that. I'm not trying to hurt you. I don't want you crying because of me. I don't want your life ruined because of ME. I'm sorry for showing you how much I LOVE YOU.” I grabbed my shirt and pants off the floor. Me and Danielle have been in a weird place for a minute. I’m going to respect her wishes. I think it’s time for me to bow out gracefully. I can’t be the only fighting for us. She’s not even willing to meet me halfway.

“I don't want to lose you Rashad please don’t leave me,” she sniffled. My back is still turned towards Danielle. I continued to put my clothes on. Baine had to go. I'm done fuckin' around. I felt her hands on mine. I turned around to look at Danielle.

“Why don't you want me to leave Danielle? You don't need me you've said that on a numerous of occasions. You want me and him gone. I'll kill him so you don't have to worry about him. I'll stay out your way shawty and let you be.” Danielle didn't like what I said, but I'm trying to make shit easy for her. This is what she wants. This isn't what I want.

"Rashad you have too much to lose. Your son needs you and the baby that you and Mya share needs you. As bad as I would like for him to disappear. I'll never wish bad on a nigga even though they're wishing bad on me. He'll get his it may not be today, but it'll be one day," she explained.

"My kids are going to be straight rather I'm here or not. Going to jail isn't an option. I'm going to see my son grow up. If I die at the hands of a pussy ass nigga it's his fate and it's my time, but I'm rolling the dice. It's going to happen and ain't shit you can do to change that. Your child will be fatherless is that why you don't want him to die? I got plenty of reasons to kill him. You're just the second reason why.

You said you need me. I know my son and my nephew are depending on me. I'm all they have. Why do you need me Danielle?" Danielle looked at me with wide eyes. Now isn't the time to hold back on how you fuckin' feel because since we've been fuckin' around. I haven't held back anything. I've put myself out there more than once. I'm tired of being in the background. I don't have to do none of this shit I'm doing. I'm doing it because I love her.

"I love you Rashad that's why. I may not like you right now, but I still love you. I'm scared and I don't want to be hurt again. I don't like what hurt feels like. It's hard to trust you, but I know I don't want to lose you. I don't want to know what losing you feels like. Life is gamble but I'll always bet on you. I'll never put you in a position to be away from your family." She keeps mentioning my family.

I want her to be a part of my family. Why doesn’t she understand that?

“If you love me Danielle? Why can't we be together? Why are we playing this game it's dangerous fuckin' with a nigga like me? I'll go to war for your HEART. You got a hex on my SOUL. I don't know what you've done to me but Danielle you're in control. I told you I loved you earlier and you didn't tell me you loved me back. You know you got my heart and I don't ever want it back.

Danielle I just want to love you and only you. Can we stop playing these fuckin' games and be what we're supposed to be? I know you're scared but shawty I'm not trying to hurt you. Damn can I show you?” What more can I fuckin’ do? My eyes were trained on Danielle waiting for her answer. What's it going to be.

“Do I have a choice,” she asked? Danielle had a small smile on her face.

“I’m tired of playing these games. You can play them by yourself. You always have a choice just make sure you make the right fuckin' one.” Danielle motioned with her hand for me to come here. I stepped in her personal space. I leaned in to see what she wanted. Our lips were damn near touching. I can feel her heart beating. She cupped my face with her hands.

“Yes, Rashad we can be together. Please don't make me regret it. Promise me you won't hurt me. I'm taking the safety off my heart.”

I dropped my tongue in Danielle's mouth. We exchanged a kiss. I swear I've been paying for hurting her.

"I'm not going to hurt you. I can promise you that. I want this too bad. The baby you're carrying is it mine Danielle or is it his?" She looked at me and rolled her eyes. "Don't do that. I want you to be honest with me because I'm honest with you. I got some things I want to tell you. Since we're making it official. I don't want any lies or secrets between us." Danielle thinks this shit is a game. If the baby isn't mine, I'll be hurt but I'll still take care of it. We can practice on making another one.

"It's yours," she sighed. Danielle held her down. I cupped her chin forcing her to look at me. It's nothing to be ashamed of. I got my work cut out for me. I wanted her to bear my child. I know Mya's about to be salty, but I don't give a fuck. I want Danielle to be my wife and she has no choice but to accept that.

"Don't do that Danielle please don't. I'm going to really kill his motherfuckin' ass because he touched you while you're pregnant and carrying my child. It's light off. Mya won't cause you any problems because I'll kill that bitch and raise my child myself. She's not a problem. I know you were carrying my child. I should fuck you up for lying to me, but I can't. Are you hungry my mom cooked for us and she wants to meet you?" My mother has been dying to meet Danielle. It's important that they hit off. I love Danielle and I want my mother to love her too. Danielle let out a long yawn. She stretched her arms.

"I'm hungry Rashad. If she's up, I'll meet her, she yawned." I know my mother is up. She loves Danielle and she hasn't even met her. I think she likes Danielle because she has me out here looking crazy. I don't care because Danielle she's my weakness.

"Okay cool I'm about to go downstairs to get your food and I'll be back." I went downstairs to grab Danielle's plate. I stopped by my mom's room and she's asleep. I guess she's tired. She can meet Danielle tomorrow. I'm sure Danielle's tired but she needs to eat first and then she can relax. I brought Danielle her plate and fed it to her.

"I can feed myself," she sighed.

"I know but I want too."

Chapter-20

Danielle

It's been a long day. I can't believe Baine done that to me. I'm afraid to even look in the mirror. He raped me. I swear I don't know who the fuck he is anymore. He's always been this way. I can't be on bed rest. I need to check myself for STD's fuckin' with him. I know he's been fuckin' around. He's showing his true colors. He laid hands on me because I'm not carrying his child. God doesn't make any mistakes. I wanted to give him a child, but it just didn't happen. Maybe God didn't think I needed a child with him.

I want to be with Rashad. I just hope I don't regret it. I know Mya told Bainc about mc and Rashad. Nobody that knows Baine knew I was pregnant. It makes perfect sense. I'm telling Rashad. I've been living there for two months no problems until I run into her stupid ass today. I heard what Rashad said. I know he's going to end up killing Mya. She needs to go.

I was a little hesitant about telling him how I feel. I'm at the point in my life where I don't care what people say about me. They're going to talk anyway so I'll let them talk. I'm not going to let anyone stop me from being happy. I'll be the first to admit, it feels good lying is his arms without any consequences. I just want Rashad to hold me. I hope Crimson didn't tell my parents because they'll go crazy.

It's crazy to wish bad on someone, but I can only imagine how Mya's going to act when she finds out that Rashad and I are together, and I'm carrying his child too. I don't give a fuck. I always had his heart and he's always had mine. He's told her that. I trust Rashad. I feel like things are about to be different. Rashad's head lying on my stomach. My hands were tracing the waves that adorned his head. I heard a knock at the door.

"Daddy can we come in," he asked? Rashad looked at me and smiled. I knew Rashad's son lived with him. It's late so I'm surprised he's still up. It's time we met since I'm going to be around and I'm carrying his sister or brother. I want a girl so bad. It'll be my luck I get a boy.

"Come in," Rashad yelled. Lil Rashad and his friend walked in and sized us up. I swear Rashad son looks just like him. He's so handsome. I want our child to be a combination of the both us. His friend is handsome too.

"Rashad and BJ, I want you to meet Danielle my lady," he smiled. I swear I can't stand Rashad. He has me blushing in front of these kids. I waived at them. It's something about BJ that looks familiar. I can't stop looking at him. It's like I know him from somewhere.

"Daddy can we chill in here with y'all. I know y'all ain't doing nothing because I see she's pregnant with a baby. Is that our baby," he asked? Umm excuse me, he's a little too grown. He snatched the remote control off the bed and started flipping the channels.

I wanted to laugh but I can't because my back hurts. Rashad looked at me and smiled. I swear his son's a mess.

"Yes, it's our baby. What do you want her to have? I want a daughter, but I'll take another son," Rashad smiled. Lil Rashad looked between me and his father. He had the biggest smile on his face with his little snag a tooth self.

"I don't care I'm the still the oldest. Ms. Danielle can you cook? My daddy needs a lady that can cook," he asked? Lil Rashad is a mess for real. What am I going to do with him? Crimson didn't tell me he was this motherfuckin' bad shit. I see where Camina gets this shit from.

"I can cook. What do you like to eat? Do you ask all your father's girlfriends this?" Rashad grabbed my leg. I popped him. I wanted to know. Rashad stared a hole in me. I don't care. I don't know what the future holds for us. If we're exclusive, I'll be around. I need to know what type of food he likes.

"I'm not picky. I like junk food, pizza, cheeseburgers. My daddy hasn't let me meet any of his ladies. He's met mine though," he laughed. I looked at Rashad and shook my head. His friend BJ didn't say much. I can see now Rashad's going to be a grandfather early dealing with him. We watched a movie Lil Rashad and BJ fell asleep. Rashad picked them up and carried them into their room. It's way past my bedtime. I need a new phone and I need my computer. Bedrest for two weeks I don't know how that's going to work.

Rashad walked back into the room. He stood in front of me and took his night pants off. We locked eyes with each other. I turned my head. His dick touches the middle of his thigh. If Baine didn't violate me tonight would've been perfect. Rashad climbed in the bed with me. I had my back turned toward him. I wanted him so bad, but I couldn't have him do to what happened earlier. Rashad picked me up and laid me on his chest. He placed a kissed on my forehead. Rashad ran his hands through my hair. His hands felt so good massaging my scalp.

"I love you," he stated.

"I love you too Rashad. I think Mya told Baine about the baby that's why he came over." Rashad cupped my chin forcing me to look at him. "I'm serious I know it was her. Baine didn't know I was pregnant somebody had to tell him. She's the only person that saw me that had something to gain from it." I can't read Rashad, but I know it was her.

"Oh yeah? She caused this. I wouldn't be surprised. I can't touch her now, but after she haves her baby I will. I'm sorry Danielle I'm going to be honest with you.

Mya's a problem and I don't like motherfuckas causing me problems. I want to be with you. I don't want you just to be my lady. I want us to be more than that. I'm an observer I sit back and watch shit. After you left the wedding Mya pulled up and told me she was pregnant. She gave me a list of demands. I didn't have a problem with it because I take care of all my kids.

Her demands came with one stipulation. Me and her being together and continuing to pay for her living expenses. She threatened not to let me see my kid.

I'm asking you if I kill Mya can you step up and be my child's mother? I know once she finds out we're together she won't let me see my child. I don't give a fuck about raising my kids by myself. I've had my son since he was four months old," he explained. Why would Rashad put me in this? I do have a problem with him taking care of her. He can't do that while we're together.

"Yes, I'll step up, but how do I know you won't kill me? Killing her is too easy she needs to suffer. I never overstepped my boundaries when she caught us. Rashad you're crazy if we're together in a relationship you're not paying her living expenses. I'm not even about to pretend like I'm okay with that because I'm not. I'll never stop you from being there for your child, but you're not taking care of her. If we don't work out, I won't expect you to take care of me." I'm just being honest my Gigi always told me to never depend on a man always have your own. She ain't never fuckin' lied. Rashad gripped my ass tight.

"Stop fuckin' playing with me. We will work you know it. I love you and you're different. I'm not about to let anybody come in between my happiness. She's needs to stay in her fuckin' place. I'm not with the crazy shit. I told her that. I want to be with you, and she needs to except that.

I made Mya a few promises, but the moment we started back fuckin' around. I cut her off. I knew I didn't want to risk losing you. I'm going to let her know that we're together and I'm not going to be able to cover her living expenses. I respect your wishes. I got something I need to tell you." Rashad looked at me with wide eyes. What did he have to tell me? I gave his beard a light tug.

"Are you going to look at me or you're going to tell me what you need to tell me," I asked? I'm glad me and Rashad are being open and honest with each other. I rather know now than later.

"Listen Danielle what I'm about to tell you is way before your time," he explained. I raised up off him because I need to hear this. I don't like the way he said that. I got in Rashad's face. My eyes were trained on him. Rashad lifted me up and sat me on his lap. Rashad's head is lying back against the headboard. I leaned my head back on his chest. He started massaging my shoulders. I'm trying to relax but I'm not sure if I should or not.

"I'm not an emotional nigga, but with you Danielle I'm comfortable enough to expose my feelings and thoughts with you. What I'm about to tell you nobody knows this but Griff. Come here I want you to see something," Rashad grabbed his phone. He showed me a picture of his son and BJ. I swear BJ and Rashad are so handsome.

“BJ and Lil Rashad, they're best friends huh? His parents do they let him stay over a lot,” I asked? I saw BJ at the wedding with Lil Rashad they looked so cute in their tuxedos. I wanted to compliment them, but Rashad was acting a fool. I don’t want him to snap on me.

“BJ's my nephew they’re cousins that’s why they’re always together. He lives with me too. His mother, she's my sister may she rest in peace.” I knew Rashad's sister was a touchy subject for him. I didn’t know that’s her son. I remember when we first started dating, she passed away. I grabbed his hand and held it. Rashad placed a kiss on my hand. “Rasheeda she's my younger sister.

We're eleven months apart. Damn I miss her so fuckin’ much. It’s not a day that goes by that I don’t think about her. I'm her big brother. It's always been my job to protect her. I'm her older brother. I never wanted to see my sister fuck with a nigga that's no good for her. She wouldn't listen to me. Let me get straight to the point Danielle. Rasheeda was fuckin' with a nigga she knew I wouldn't fuckin' approve of so she kept that shit away from me.

She’s my younger sister but I raised her as if she was my daughter. I never wanted one of these pussy ass niggas to take advantage of my sister. Rasheeda got pregnant with BJ when she was twenty-one. I did everything for my nephew. I'll do it until the day I fuckin' DIE. I live by and die by that shit. Rasheeda would never tell me who her child's father was. I always wondered why.

My mother knew who he was because they were close, but she wouldn't tell me because she knew I would have an issue with that. I didn't know him.

I wanted to meet the nigga that got my sister pregnant and didn't take care of his child. I had a fuckin' problem with that shit. My sister she was a good girl, the wrong nigga ruined her. Rasheeda was still fuckin' with him and he wasn't taking care of her son. I despised her for that shit. My mother said you can't help who you love. I agree but don't ever protect a motherfucka you love if they're not worthy of your protecting. I didn't have a problem with taking care of my nephew because as long as I'm living, he'll never want for anything.

One-night Rasheeda she went out she still lived with my mother and even though she's grown she had a curfew. My momma called me, and she said Rashad, Rasheeda hasn't made it home. I'm worried about her. It's after 1:00 a.m. I'm just leaving the trap. I called Rasheeda's phone and she didn't answer. I kept calling and she finally answered. My sister didn't drink or smoke she was out of it. She was like brother I'm at party on the Westside with my baby daddy. I asked Rasheeda for the address and she wouldn't tell me. She kept brushing me off telling me she's cool. She had a few drinks. I knew better Rasheeda didn't drink.

I didn't want her drinking in a hood that wasn't mine. I swear I had a bad feeling about that shit. I always trust my instincts. I didn't understand why she was still dealing with him and he didn't care of his kid?

Rasheeda never made it home that night. Me and Griff combed the Westside until we found we fuckin' found her. She was at party in Grove Park at an abandoned Trap house. I found my sister dead Danielle. She was drugged and raped, but she was with her baby daddy.

She didn't fuckin' deserve that shit. My sister would give you her fuckin' last. They were so fuckin' sloppy with that shit they left her phone. Her passcode is my birthday. I went through Rasheeda's phone you wouldn't believe who BJ's father is? I would never let a fuck nigga raise anything that my bloods flows through," he explained. I can't stop the tears from falling if I wanted too. I don't want to know who BJ's father is. I already know when he said Grove Park. Rashad put the phone in my hand forcing me to look at the text messages. I handed it back to him. He forced it back in my hand and scrolled through the messages. The only thing I could do was shake my head.

"Don't cry Danielle I'm not trying to upset you. BJ never got the chance to know his mother. She died when he was only a month old. I'm not saying he did it, because I wasn't there. She was over there because of him. He didn't give a fuck about my sister he didn't even show his face at her funeral. BJ's his because after she died. Me and Griff had to meet up with those niggas. I grabbed the beer that Baine was drinking out of.

I had it swabbed for his DNA. BJ's 99.999 percent his. You see this shit is deeper than you. He's the reason why my fuckin' sister isn't here. He took that away from me.

He touched you and you're carrying my child. I won't be satisfied until he's dead." I laid my head back on Rashad's chest. His eyes were blood shot red.

"I'm sorry. I didn't know I wish you would've told me sooner." Rashad leaned in and gave me a kiss.

"I tried too, but you wouldn't listen. I didn't want what happened to my sister to happen you." I snuggled up by Rashad I can't sleep, I swear if it's not one thing it's something else. It makes sense now BJ looks like Baine. I swear I don't know who this nigga is anymore. I've never known Baine to rape anyone.

He takes care of all his kids. He never mentioned dating Rashad sister ever. I wonder why? I don't know what to think anymore. Baine can never escape his past. Damn I can't believe Rashad's been holding that in. I can only imagine what BJ's going through he doesn't know his mother or father. Rashad will never let Baine be a part of his life.

Linda

Rashad stepped out for a few hours this morning. He went to take BJ and Lil Rashad to school. He mentioned something about he had to handle some business. I hope he's not out in the streets doing something crazy. I don't want my son to get killed or lost in the system. He gave me strict instructions on making sure Danielle didn't leave the house. If she hasn't left already, I don't think she will. I didn't get to meet Danielle last night, but I get to meet her today. I stopped Rashad from killing Baine years ago because I didn't believe that he would do that to my daughter, but he did.

Rashad didn't go into details about what happened to Danielle, but I know it had something to do with him. It's still early it's not even 8:00 a.m. yet. Every morning I cook BJ and Lil Rashad breakfast. This morning wasn't any different. I cooked sausage, grits, eggs and French toast. I made some extra for Danielle she needs to eat. I grabbed the eating tray and made my way upstairs to see if she's up and ready to eat. I knocked on the door. I wanted to make sure she had her clothes on.

"Come in." I made my way inside of the room. Danielle was sitting up looking at TV she's so beautiful. I hope Rashad does right by her she's been through a lot. "Good morning." I made my way over toward the bed. I can tell she's uncomfortable.

"Good morning Danielle. I'm Rashad's mother Linda it's nice to finally meet you. I've heard a lot about you. I don't know if you're hungry or not, but I cooked us some breakfast. I brought you a plate with everything. I don't know if you drink apple juice or orange juice, so I brought you both. I have coffee too, but my son told me don't give you any coffee. You look uncomfortable. Let me sit you up properly." I fixed the pillows in the bed, so Danielle can sit up properly.

"Thank you it's nice to meet you too. I hope the things that you heard about me where good? I'm hungry I've been smelling your food for a minute, but I can't get up. My back hurts. I'm not picky. I like both juices," she smiled. I sat Danielle's eating tray in front of her and the juice on the nightstand. Danielle started eating her food.

"I've heard nothing but good things about you. I'm sorry for the things my son has took you through. I always raised him to be a man. He's a good man. He loves hard. Nobody's perfect we all have made a few mistakes. It's up to you if you learn from your mistakes. Rashad loves you Danielle. Baby I got to give it you. You've been making him sweat and it's been a sight to see. He can't sleep at night because of you. I hope y'all work through your issues. He wants this more than anything," I explained.

Danielle started crying. "Baby don't cry. Please stop crying before Rashad comes back. I should've kept my mouth shut. I don't want you to upset the baby. Finish eating your food. I'll give you a bath when you finish."

I grabbed a Kleenex so she could wipe her tears. Rashad is going to kill me.

"Rashad's a grown man so you don't have to apologize for his actions. He knows right from wrong. I appreciate that you care. I'm glad that you don't want your son out here treating women wrong that alone speaks volumes. I'm sorry Ms. Linda. I love him too. I love him so much. I can't sleep either. Last night is the first night I've had a good sleep in months. I've been hurt a few times. I don't want to be hurt again.

I'm scared but at the end of the day what do I have to lose. I've lost so much. I'm going to take it one day at a time. I'm praying he didn't do all of this to get me just to hurt me in the end," she explained. I like Danielle because we're on the same page. She started back eating her food. Don't get me wrong Rashad is my son, but I'm a woman first a BLACK WOMAN. It's important that black women have each other's back society lacks a lot of that.

We're so quick to tear each other down and laugh at each other's short comings and make excuses for men. My mother didn't raise me that way. I understand where she's coming from. I've been in her shoes before with Rashad's father his mother wasn't the best deal with.

"Rashad and I had this same conversation after the wedding. I told him the exact same things. He asked me whose side am I on. I told him yours.

I don't know what your life was like with your husband, but if he came in between that. He better come correct and be everything that you need him to be and more. He got it bad Danielle it looks good on him," I laughed. I heard someone clear their throat. I looked toward the door and it's Rashad. He was standing there with the biggest smile on his face. He made his way toward the bed. I looked at Danielle and she's smiling too. She's loves him poor girl can't even hide it. I don't know how long he's been standing there but I said what I said.

"Momma dang that's how you do me when my back is turned? You're supposed to be on my side. I'm your only son. I love Danielle and she knows that. I don't want to hurt her. I just want to love her. I'm trying to come correct if she allows me too. I want to love the hurt that I put there out of her. I don't want nobody but HER. She's it for me," he explained. I ain't never heard my son talk like this about any female. She got to be the one.

"Rashad, I don't know how much you've heard, nor do I care. I'm not telling Danielle anything that I haven't told you. I like Danielle and this is my first time meeting her. You're not getting any younger. Everything that you messed up you need to fix it. She loves you too. I want you to make an honest woman of her. Actions speak louder than words show her that's all I'm saying. Danielle I'll let you enjoy your breakfast. It feels good to have another woman in the house. I want a grand-daughter thank you in advance."

A FEW WEEKS LATER

Chapter-21

Rashad

These past few weeks have been everything to a nigga. I had the woman I wanted. I love coming home to Danielle and pulling up on her at work to make sure she's good. I got to protect mine at all cost. I still got a bullet with Baine's name on it. I'm not letting the little stunt he pulled go. I've been wanting to leave the streets for a minute. I think now is the time. I want to spend more time with my son and nephew for a while now. Since we have a new baby on the way it's time. My son and my nephew are feeling Danielle. My mother loves her what more I could I want.

Danielle she's having my daughter. We found out a few weeks ago it's a girl. I wanted a girl too. I have someone else to spoil besides Camina and Cariuna. I haven't told Camina that her God-mommy Danielle is carrying my baby.

When she came to the house the other day, she wanted to know why Danielle was over here. Lil shawty bad as hell. Danielle terrorizes her too. I caught on to that. Crimson and Griff has the kids. My mom went out of town this weekend to go play Bingo. I wasn't feeling that shit but she's grown so I'll let her live. I wanted to do something special for Danielle since we were kid free. I told Danielle to be ready. I had to make her stop wearing heels. Danielle was standing in the mirror getting dressed. My daughter has put that pound game to her mother. I walked up behind her and wrapped my arms around her waist. Every time I touched her. I felt my daughter kick. Danielle looked at me through the mirror.

"We look good don't we Danielle. Just say it you don't got to stare at nigga. You love when I'm behind you and my dick is resting on your ass. I'm all yours though. Can't nobody get this dick but you. You're the only woman I want to give it too." Danielle had the biggest smile on her face. "Freaky ass you better be glad you're pregnant or else I'll dive in between those legs and knock your ass up again."

"Whatever Rashad you swear! Where are we going? I hope I'm not getting dressed for nothing. I'm tired your baby takes all of my energy," she sighed. My daughter she's kicking Danielle's ass.

"If I tell you it wouldn't be a surprise. I want to take you out. You know I'm trying to court you shawty. I got to flaunt you. I want the world to see us."

I can't wait to make Danielle my wife. She said she's not ready, but she is. Baine's prolonging the divorce since he knows we're together. His pussy ass wasn't stopping shit.

"Whatever Rashad you swear," she laughed. Danielle playfully pushed me. She coated her lips with lip stick. My phone started ringing. It's Mya! I had plans to ignore. I'm tired of that bitch always nagging me. Danielle's looking at me. "You can answer that and put that shit on speaker." I did as I was told. I'm not trying to be at odds with Danielle. Happy wife, happy life.

"Hello," I yelled. I swear I'm not beat for Mya's shit. Lately she's been calling me out the blue if it's not about my son. I don't want to hear that shit.

"Rashad where are you. I need you to meet me at Dekalb Medical. I fell at work and I'm bleeding. I think it might be something wrong with the baby," she cried. Damn if it ain't one thing it's something else. Me and Mya don't see eye to eye, but I don't want anything to happen to my son. I'm looking forward to meeting him in a few months.

"Aiight I'm on my way." Danielle tried to move away from me. I know she's mad. I can see it. "What did I do Danielle? I ain't did shit. Why are you mad at me?" I wrapped my arms around her waist holding her in place.

"Just leave Rashad. I'll see you when you get back," she sighed. I grabbed Danielle's hand and led her downstairs. I grabbed her coat and put it on. "Where are we going? You need to get to the hospital."

"I'm going to the hospital but you're coming with me. We're together and wherever I go you go. You're my support system and I'm yours. It ain't no secrets between us. I love you and I'm not about to spare nobody's fuckin' feelings when it comes to you. We're together it's just some shit she got to deal with it. After we leave the hospital, we'll go to dinner later and catch a movie. I don't like Mya's energy. I don't want to be confined in her space no matter the circumstances." Danielle didn't fight me on it. I made sure the house was locked up. I opened the door for Danielle she slid in the passenger seat. I backed out of the garage. I grabbed Danielle's hand and placed a kiss on it.

"I love you Rashad."

"I love you too." I know Mya wasn't the easiest bitch to deal with. She's carrying my son and I'm looking forward to him making his arrival. I'm praying nothing is wrong with him. I love Danielle and I didn't want to her to think that me and Mya had anything going on. I'm not about to spare Mya's feelings she needs to get used to seeing us together.

Mya

I'm praying I don't lose my baby. I don't know what happened I was at work. I had a few more patients to assist before my shift was up. I walked in room 246 I was about to help a patient. The patient was just brought in a few hours ago. I checked the chart to see exactly what the doctor wanted me to do. My clipboard fell. I knelt to pick it up. As soon as I came back up. Someone pushed me inside of the room. I fell to the floor. I tried to look and see who it was, but the moment. I turned around the punched me in my eye. I fell and they hit me in the head with a metal man. I fell hard so hard. I felt a sharp pain in my stomach instantly. I looked on the floor and blood's coming from my head and in between my legs.

Thank God the patient was awake and alert. They called security and help came immediately. The doctors and nurses rushed me to the emergency room immediately. I called my momma and Rashad. They said they were on the way. I called Rashad I need him here with me since our son's life might be in danger. The doctors haven't come in and told me anything. They advised me they got to do emergency surgery to stop the bleeding. I wanted him to be here before they prepped me for surgery. My momma made it. She ran to me and took a seat beside my bed. She held my hand. I'm so glad she's here. She cupped my face forcing me to look at her.

“Mya what happened to your face? Who did this baby,” she asked? My mother started crying. I didn’t want her to get upset. She had high blood pressure.

“I don’t know momma. It happened while I was at work about to check on my last patient before my shift was up,” I explained. My momma looked at me with wide eyes.

“Mya this happened at work this is a fuckin’ personal attack. Ever since you got pregnant by that guy your life has been going downhill. You need to leave him alone. I want whoever done this to pay.” The door opened. My mother and I looked toward the door to see who it was. It’s Rashad. He walked in with Danielle. I damn near grew an extra neck. I know he didn't bring this bitch with him.

My blood pressure is already high. Why would he do that? My momma looked between me and Rashad and rolled her eyes. My momma didn't know that me and Rashad weren't together, now she does. My eyes were trained on Danielle she wouldn't even look at me. She better not.

“Mya you should check him and her before I do,” she argued. Rashad looked between me and my momma and laughed. My momma didn't have to tell me twice. I noticed since he's been with Danielle, he hasn't been acting himself. He agreed to pay all my living expenses and he stopped doing that. He has brought our son everything he needs.

“Rashad, I told you to come and see about our child. Why is she here. She can fuckin' leave because I don't want her here.

Shouldn't she be with her husband instead of with you," I argued. Danielle looked at me and rolled her eyes. Rashad had that bitch trained she knew not to say shit to me.

"Mya you told me something might be wrong with my son, so I came. Me and Danielle were on a date, so we came to see about you and my son. Danielle isn't going any fuckin' where. We're together and she's about to be my wife. You don't have to accept it but you're going to respect her. Stop worried about a motherfucka that ain't worried about you.

Trust me she doesn't want to be here. I want her here. Maybe you should worry about her EX-HUSBAND you fuckin' him ain't you? Don't speak on some shit that you ain't ready to discuss," he argued. How dare he talk to me like I didn't mean shit to him. As soon as Rashad and I got finished arguing. The monitors started going off. My chest started hurting. My bed is soaked with blood. The doctors came in and rushed me to surgery. The bleeding wouldn't stop and my blood pressure's too high. They had to put me to sleep. I know Rashad's the reason my blood pressure went up. How did he know that Baine and I were fuckin' around? They hooked me up to all type of machines and everything went black.

☆

I looked at the time on the TV. It's a little after 8:00 p.m. I was in surgery for three hours. I remember they took me in a little after 5:00. I didn't even feel them bring me back to my room. I felt sluggish. I looked around my room.

My mother was still sitting beside me. Danielle and Rashad were sitting in the corner. She was sitting on his lap. His hands were wrapped around her stomach. I can tell he was whispering sweet nothings in her ear. She had the biggest smile on her face. I wish I had my phone to send it to Baine. The doctor came in. "Ms. Truitt! I have some good news and bad news. Do you want me to speak with you and private or is it okay discuss what happened in front of the people in the room," he asked? I instantly felt my stomach when he said bad news. I started crying because I didn't feel my baby anymore.

"Go ahead doctor it's okay," I cried, I know I lost my baby, but I didn't want to hear it. Who would do this to me? I don't have any enemies. I don't bother anyone.

"Ms. Truitt we were able to stop the bleeding, but we couldn't save the baby. Your bleeding and your high blood pressure cause the baby's heart to stop bleeding. I'm so sorry we did everything that we could to save him. What would you like to do with his remains? Ms. Truitt you lost a lot of blood. Even though you're not pregnant anymore. I recommend you stay on bedrest for seven days. You have stitches they'll dissolve within a few days. We have two prescriptions for you. Is this the father of your son," he asked?

"Yes," I sniffled.

"Ms. Truitt, we ran a few tests on you.

Your son was covered with gonorrhea. I think it's the reason your son didn't make it and you had a miscarriage also. It's because it wasn't treated. You tested positive for gonorrhea. We have a prescription to get it cleared up. Dad I suggest that you see a doctor too so you can get treated," he explained.

My heart dropped. I can feel Rashad starring a hole in me. The only person I've been having sex with is Baine. I shook my head I can't believe his fine as burned me. I had a yellowish discharge, but I didn't think anything of it.

"I'm good doctor. I haven't slept with Ms. Truitt in over five months. She didn't get that from she got it from someone else," Rashad argued. I feel so fuckin' embarrassed. Danielle had the biggest smile on her face. That bitch is glad I lost my fuckin' baby. This shit ain't over. The doctor sat my prescription on the table. He left a few pills for me to start taking. Rashad walked up toward my bed. My momma stood up.

"You need to fuckin' leave because you're the reason why she lost her fuckin' baby. You're so fuckin' disrespectful you brought another woman in here while my daughter is going through this with your son," she argued. Rashad stroked his beard. Danielle grabbed his free hand. A soft laugh escaped his lips.

"I don't know what you told your mother about me Mya but tell the truth. Ms. Truitt the shit me and Mya has going on has nothing to do with you.

I didn't make your daughter lose our baby. The doctor confirmed that so don't put that shit on me. My wife ain't got shit to do with Mya she's going to be here rather you two motherfuckas like it or not. She's not going anywhere. Y'all got so much to say to her and she hasn't addressed y'all one fuckin' time. Watch your fuckin' mouth. I don't give a fuck about bodying a bitch or nigga behind her. TRY ME I'm begging you too," he argued. Rashad pulled out a burner from behind his back. He cocked it back and pointed it at my momma.

"Stop Rashad please don't do that my momma doesn't have anything to do with us."

"Exactly so tell that bitch to stay in her fuckin' place and speak only when she's fuckin' spoken too. I'm not for the disrespect. I want to put my hands on you so fuckin' bad MYA but I'm not because shawty you ain't fuckin' worth it. You wanted to get back at me so bad you fucked that nigga and he got your pussy on fire. Your stupid ass done fucked around and gave my son some shit.

I hate I lost my son but bitch I ain't got to deal with you no more. God don't like ugly all the slick shit you've been doing that shit is coming back on you. Lose my fuckin' number and keep my name and my wife's name out your fuckin' mouth," he argued. Rashad slammed the door on his way out. I swear I hate him. I hope he dies.

A MONTH LATER

Chapter-22

Jermesha

I really didn't want to come over Mother Dear's house this year for Thanksgiving. I swear I didn't. I don't feel like dealing with these motherfuckas today, but I didn't have a choice. I wasn't invited anywhere else. Me and Ike were still fuckin' around but we weren't together. Ike's eating at his family's house, but me and my kids weren't invited. I never had my kids during the holiday's anyway they were always with their father. Ike and I weren't that serious anymore. We don't live together anymore. He put me out a few weeks after Keondra found out about us. Something told me don't give my place up. I'm glad I didn't. I knew I couldn't go back to Mother Dear's house.

Me and Ike we were still fuckin'. He still gives me money here and there. Ike used me to get to Keondra. I feel so fuckin' dumb. I haven't seen or heard from Keondra since she left the house that me and Ike shared.

I've been sitting out front of Mother Dear's house for about ten minutes now. My mother's in there. I don't even know why I'm tripping. She told me a month ago about Camina calling the police on her because she stinks. I swear I wish I would've been there. I would've pinched the fuck out of her. My momma came outside and knocked on my car window. I looked in the mirror to make sure I'm popping. I raised my window down to see what my mother wanted. My momma's so fine they ain't got shit on Sherry Tristan.

"Jermesha come on you look fine. Fuck these bitches. I wish they would fuck with you and I'm here," she argued. I love my momma. I wasn't tripping off them. I just didn't want to be bothered with them. I look cute. Before I made it over here, I had two dates. Both of my niggas told me I'm killing it. I had an oversized Tommy Hilfiger sweatshirt on. It's the one with the Tommy Jeans Logo. I paired it with a pair of Tommy Jeans distressed shorts.

It's a little cold outside. I paired it with a pair of white fishnet tights and a pair of red Ugg boots. I got my sew in tightened. My hair's flat ironed bone straight. I grabbed my Chanel bag off the seat. My momma looked at me and smiled. "You look good snatch up one of these niggas from their boring ass wives." Me and my momma slapped hands with each other. We made our way inside of Mother Dear's house it smells so good. My stomach started growling instantly. It's a lot of people here.

I saw Cheree and Crimson daddy hugged up in the corner. I elbowed my momma. We both rolled are eyes. I swear I can't stand her. Crimson and Griff were sitting on the couch. Crimson's lying on Griff. Take your motherfuckin' ass home don't nobody want to see that shit. Everybody knows y'all together. Ugh I still can't believe she married him. I wasn't fuckin' with Crimson like that because she didn't drop the charges and we're family. I don't know if I was staring at the them too long or what, but Griff grilled me. I guess Crimson caught on because she cupped his face and kissed him. Ugh. I made my way into the kitchen to fix my plate.

Mother Dear and Ms. Gladys is sitting at the table holding Lil Griff. Rashad and Danielle were talking to Ms. Gladys. Rashad's arms were wrapped around Danielle's waist. I heard she's pregnant by him. Danielle ain't nothing but a hoe. Tuna fish pussy smelling ass bitch. My laugh of the month is when Bre'Elle posted all of Danielle's clothes on Facebook and tagged her in it. Danielle thought she was better than everybody. I would've never married Baine that nigga is a hoe and she is too. Bre'Elle told me all about Baine burning her. He told her he got it from his wife.

"Jermesha I know you didn't come in here and not speak. You didn't even wash your motherfuckin' hands you know I don't play that shit? Why don't you have any clothes on. It's nice outside but it's pneumonia weather. If you get sick don't bring your ass over here," she argued.

I swear my grand momma does the most. I sat my plate down and I went to wash my hands.

"Hi Mother, Dear! I didn't speak because you were talking and I didn't want to interrupt you," I smiled. I continued to fix my plate. Camina and Cariuna ran in the kitchen. Camina looked at me and smiled. She came over here and got a piece of cake. She didn't wash her hands and Mother Dear didn't say shit. "Hey little girl you need to wash your hands." Camina ignored me and continued to eat her cake. I tapped her on her shoulder. She turned around and looked at me. "You need to wash your hands before you eat this cake." Everybody's attention is focused on us.

"Don't talk to me doo-doo breath. Ugh your breath stink," she laughed. Camina fanned her nose. Camina's laughing so hard she spit the cake out. It landed on my brand new Ugg boots. I started to yank her little ass up. I stepped forward I was about to grab her. Danielle cleared her throat.

"I wish the fuck you would. I think you should find something else to do because I would hate to drag you in this kitchen," Danielle argued. Rashad stood right behind her. I'll kick that baby out her stomach. Therefore, I didn't want to come over here because I knew something would pop of.

"Danielle you're a joke. You're the same bitch whose husband gave all your shit to his baby momma or should I say mistress, but you'll drag me. Bre'Elle dragged you on Facebook and you had no clap back. Girl sit the fuck down.

Rashad you might want to get your dick checked because Bre'Elle told me Baine burned her and he got it from his WIFE. Bitch you got that shit you're walking around here like your pussy don't stink and it DO," I laughed. A small laugh escaped Danielle's lips. Rashad held her back. "Let that bitch go Rashad. If she wants to keep her baby, she'll stay in her fuckin' place."

"Bre'Elle dragged me? Jermesha you're sillier than I thought. Every action doesn't need a reaction. I'm a CEO all eyes are always on me. I run a very profitable business. I'll never step off my throne to argue with a HOE on Facebook who's bragging about a nigga giving her my hand me downs. I'll never do that I don't need the clout. I burned BAINE. Excuse my language Gigi and Mother Dear. I've only been with one person besides him.

Ain't no way he got shit from me. The same way you gain them is how you lose them. Jermesha you're dumb as fuck. She's a mistress and guess what she ain't the only one that's fuckin' him. She's one of many. I got a clean bill of health. She can keep him. I don't want him. I'll drag you behind Camina, you know why because she used hand sanitizer to wash her hands.

You're so mad because Mother Dear checked you as she should. You wanted to take it out somebody. Leave her alone. I'm pregnant but I'm sure her momma won't hesitate to whoop your ass because it's evident that you don't like her."

"Her momma ain't gone whoop shit. Her momma needs to whoop her ass. Danielle stay in your fuckin' lane. I'll stomp that baby right out of your stomach." Rashad came from behind Danielle. He needs to stay in his place before I call Ike and Baine to set it off over here.

"Mother Dear I'm not trying to disrespect your house because I didn't come over here for that. I got to roll because I'll never put my child in danger. I don't take threats lightly. Jermesha watch yourself be careful shawty," he argued. Crimson and Griff came in the kitchen.

"What's going on," Crimson asked? Griff's right behind her.

"Mommy doo-doo breath messing with me," Camina whined. She pointed at me. Crimson and Griff both started laughing.

"Camina that's not nice. Her name is Jermesha."

"I know mommy, but her breath always smells like Doo-Doo she said I need to wash my hands and I did, God mommy Danielle saw me, but she keeps picking with me. I just want to eat my dessert." Camina pouted. Crimson sized me up. I swear I'll beat her ass.

"Jermesha leave my daughter alone. Treat my child the same way I treat yours. I'm sorry Mother Dear. Come on Camina let's go before I touch somebody," Crimson argued.

"You know what fuck this. I'm sick of y'all. I got something for all y'all pussy ass motherfuckas," I argued. Thank God I had my phone on silent. I snapped a picture of everybody and sent it to Ike. One of these motherfuckas are going to die tonight. Just watch. Hopefully all of them.

Me-They just jumped me I'm on the way to the hospital. I knew Ike cared about me a little. I know sending this picture to him. He'll send it to Baine.

Ike-Oh yeah where the fuck you at? Baine got a bullet with Rashad name on it. Did he fuckin' touch you because if that nigga did. He's dead. Checkmate I'm sick of them. I'll show Danielle how much power this pussy is packing.

Me- At my granny's house. They fucked me up bad. I wish you would've come with me. Yes, Ike he punched me a few times. I can't wait until Ike pulls up.

Ike-He's a dead man. When you leave the hospital. Come to the crib. What that nigga driving so I can send him a message. That's what the fuck I'm talking about. My nigga will go to war behind me.

Me- I don't know let me ask my momma. I went to go ass my momma. She came over here before I did. They're still here Thank God.

Ike-Find out I was about to do just that.

Me- Black Escalade

Ike- Take you ass home it's about to get ugly. He didn't have to tell me twice. I'll be in his bed waiting for him to come home. I continued to fix my plate. I don't give a damn about Mother Dear and Ms. Gladys staring at me. Not one time did Mother Dear correct any of them. I fixed me two plates to go. I left out of Mother Dear's house all eyes were on me.

Chapter-23

Danielle

Thanksgiving dinner was nice at Mother Dear's house as always. Ms. Linda and I cooked dinner at our house also. Rashad and I didn't make plans to stay out to long. I'm six months pregnant. I just want to lay in my bed and sleep. I'm almost seven months. I get tired fast. Rashad and I were about to leave anyway after we talked with my grandmother and Mother Dear. Lil Rashad and BJ were ready to go. I grabbed their coats and zipped them up. Me and Rashad said our goodbyes to everybody. Making plans to see them this weekend hopefully. We made our way into the truck. Lil Rashad and BJ fastened their seat belts. I fastened mine.

Rashad pulled off. BJ and Lil Rashad put a movie in. They grabbed the headphones and put them on. I love the way the Escalade is setup. It's perfect for a family. It's nice outside but BJ just overcame a cold. I didn't want him to get sick again. I can't believe he's Baine's son.

He looks just like him. I don't blame Rashad for not letting Baine raise him. I wouldn't either especially if he killed his mother. I don't see how he could deny him, and he looks more like him than any of his kids. He's a great kid. My mind is in a million places.

I can't wait to get home to call Crimson. I can't believe Jermesha's ass. I swear if I wasn't pregnant, I would've dragged that bitch. I swear these hoes are so fuckin' silly. I would never give Bre'Elle any clout. She's bragging about my hand me downs. Make that nigga buy you some shit. I know Camina's bad as hell, but I saw her use the hand sanitizer. Jermesha was fuckin' with her for no reason. Rashad grabbed my hand. I looked at him and smiled. I can't wait to get home. It's a lot of shit that I want to do to him. He's so fine.

"What's up why are you looking at me like that? What I do," I asked? I had the biggest smile plastered on my face. Every time he touches me, I get weak.

"You haven't done anything. I love you Danielle and I don't think I tell you enough. I had to get up out of Mother Dear's house because I didn't want to disrespect your grandmother or Mother Dear. Danielle, I don't hit women. I don't take threats lightly. It took everything in me not to slap the fuck out of Jermesha. I wasn't even trying to handle her like that. I don't get in between female drama because that's not my thing, but when it comes to my baby you're carrying.

I have to say something. I knew Jermesha was hater but damn. I owe that bitch one anyway since she was in on the shit with Keondra with Griff's funeral and trying to put Crimson out her house. I haven't forgot about that shit. If she disappears, you'll know why.

I love how you kept your composure and never stepped off your throne or lower your standards when she called herself trying to diss you. Why didn't you tell me he did that shit," he asked? I didn't want to explain this to him.

"When it happened, we weren't talking. You know I was mad at you. I was in Hawaii. I was hurt at first but that's who he is. I don't know why I was surprised." Baine is a thing of the past. I'll be so glad when are divorced is finalized. I've already moved on. I'm happy and I won't let him come in between that. He's still running around burning people. I know Mya felt stupid. She couldn't wait to fuck his nasty ass and he burned her. I'm so glad I don't have to worry about that anymore. After he raped me, I know Auntie Maria tested me, but I tested myself. I couldn't take any chances with him. I've been spared one to many times. Thank God he didn't give me anything.

"You were hiding from me and you shouldn't have. You know I would've replaced anything he took. Fuck him I don't want to talk about him." I'm glad Rashad said that because I didn't want to talk about him either. I just want to enjoy our night before we were interrupted with negativity. I'll be sure to burn some Sage when we get back home. "Baby call Griff and Crimson to see where they're at? Don't panic because I'm not going to let anything happen to you. It's car that's been following us since we left Mother Dear's house. Don't look over your shoulder either. I don't want them to know that I'm on to them," he explained. I looked at Rashad with wide eyes. He wanted me not to panic.

I can't promise that. I grabbed my phone to call Crimson she answered on the first ring.

“Crimson where are you,” I asked? I'm sure us being followed has everything to do with Baine. I don't put anything past him. Leave me the fuck alone. He can't accept the fact the I moved on. I don't understand why and he's fuckin' everybody. I just want to be happy that's it.

“We're about to leave Mother Dears and go home. Are you okay,” she asked? I wanted to say no, but I'm going to do what Rashad told me too. I don't want to panic. I'm from the hood but I ain't never been involved in this type of shit.

“Yeah I'm okay where's Griff put him on the phone. Rashad wants to speak to him,” I sighed. Rashad cupped my chin forcing me to look at him. He whispered. “I got you trust me.” At this point that's the only thing I can do. Crimson put Griff on the phone. Rashad tossed me his phone.

“What's up,” Griff asked?

“A lot! Get Slap and Wire on the fuckin' phone. Call them niggas on three way. Somebody's been following me since I left Mother Dear's house. I ain't got beef with nobody but one nigga out here in the streets. Griff, I put it on my sister if these pussy ass niggas attempt to get at me while my family is in the car them motherfuckas won't live to see DAY LIGHT and that's a fuckin' promise,” he argued. I know Rashad's hot because I can hear it and feel it.

"Aiight take them niggas through the old Trap. I'll meet you over there. Your bullet proof right," Griff asked?

"Of course," he chuckled. Griff and Rashad ended the call. Rashad had a devilish grin on his face. I pulled down the sun visor. Lil Rashad and BJ were asleep. Thank God. I felt someone bump us. Rashad kept driving and didn't pay it any mind. They bumped us again. Rashad ignored it.

"Baby what's going on," I asked? Rashad looked at me and smiled. I need more than a smile.

"Nothing you need to worry about. I need you to trust me. I got you." As soon as Rashad said that bullets started flying from every fuckin' direction. He kept driving. He pushed his foot down on the gas. He started driving fast. I jumped because the bullets started hitting the window. I ducked down instantly. I don't want to die or get hit.

"Baby I'm sorry! I didn't mean to get you in this mess. I didn't know loving you would be so dangerous," I cried. Baine's so fuckin' stupid. Why would he do this just because I left him. Rashad cupped my chin forcing me to look at him. He placed a kiss on my lips. He broke the kiss. I grabbed his face with both of my hands. I kissed him with so much passion. "I love you."

"I love you too! Stop crying before you upset my daughter. I need you to trust me. Danielle if I wasn't for sure that I couldn't get us out of this. I wouldn't tell you to trust me." Rashad threw the truck in park.

Bullets were still hitting the car. “Come here Danielle.” Rashad patted his lap. Telling me to come here. He slid the seat back.

“I can't because I'm too big,” I sighed. Rashad motioned with his hands for me to come join him.

“Come on you're not too big you're perfect.” I unfastened my seatbelt. I went to sit in Rashad's lap. He held me. I laid my head on his chest. Rashad cupped my chin forcing me to look at him. He placed a kiss on my lips. “Danielle, everything that we ride in is bullet proof. I'm going to protect you and my kids at all cost. This love thing that we got going on. I'll never let him come in between it. Once the bullets stop.

You're going to get in the car with Griff. I want you to stay at Crimson's with her and the kids. I promise you that I'm going to kill that pussy ass nigga and Ike tonight. I've been waiting on him to make a move. I'm playing chess tonight. Once I say check mate to the two of those niggas will be dead. I'll be back to get you.” I heard everything Rashad said but that still didn't soothe me or ease my feelings. I don't want anything to happen to him because of me.

“Rashad, I don't want to lose you. I swear I don't. We need you. I need you,” I cried. Rashad wiped my tears with his thumbs.

“I need you too. I'm not trying to lose you Danielle. It's my job to keep you safe and protect you.

I can't do that with him lurking around. This nigga got to go Danielle. I'm not waiting another day to handle my business. I'm not worried about this truck. I promise I'm going to make it back home to you." The bullets finally ceased. I felt at ease since I'm in Rashad's lap knowing that the truck is bullet proof. Now that the bullets have stopped, and they sped off. I know it's a matter of minutes before Rashad kills Baine. I don't want him to leave because Baine doesn't play fair. Griff pulled up like Rashad said he would. Rashad got me and the kids out the car and into Griff's car safely. He pulled me in for a hug. I can't stop the tears from falling if I wanted too. God, I don't want him to leave. Be careful who you love.

"Danielle stop crying! I swear I'll be back before you know it. Trust me you don't know how bad I want to kill this nigga and get it over with."

"I trust you hurry up. I'm not going to sleep until you come back." Me and Griff pulled off! Rashad followed us to the house. He walked us inside. He escorted us to the guest room. He stripped out of his clothes. I followed him into the bathroom. He suited up. He kissed me on the forehead. I'm not going to sleep until he makes it back home. Lil Rashad and BJ laid in the bed with me.

Rashad

Tonight's the fuckin' night. I didn't want to see Danielle cry, but I got to dead this shit. I don't want her crying or stressing over that pussy ass nigga anymore. I want Ike first though because I know Jermesha fuck with the nigga and she told him some bull shit. I want to kill the two of them at the same fuckin' time. She threatened my daughter's life so that bitch got to go. I owe the bitch one anyway. I'm not letting the hoe slide. I changed my clothes at Griff's house. Danielle stood in the bathroom and watched me like a hawk. I know Crimson's mad because Griff's coming. I just need my nigga to drive that's it. This is my mission. Everything's on me We hopped in Griff's low-key Toyota Camry and pulled off.

Crimson stood in the door and watched us like a hawk. Griff wouldn't even look at her. I know why because he'll end up going back in the house. I told him that he didn't have to come but he insisted on coming with me.

"Kiss your wife goodbye Griff. I don't want her mad at me," I chuckled. Griff waived me off I'm serious. Camina already got this shit popping. I got to kill Jermesha for fuckin' with my God daughter.

"I did that already she's tripping. I told her I wasn't going in, but I'll never send you on a dummy mission fuck that. If it's my time, it's my time. Crimson and my kids will forever be straight."

I understand where Griff's coming from, but I can't let him put his life on the line because of me. I'm not trying to have those problems with Crimson!

"Griff I can't let you do that. I just want you to drive. I don't want Crimson to get mad at me. Life is a gamble. I'll bet on me. I don't want to take you from your kids. I want to raise mine too, but I got to kill these niggas tonight. I'm not fuckin' waiting. You know I've been wanting to do this for years." Griff nodded his head in agreement. I had eyes on Baine and Ike. I knew it was them. Me and Griff had a little chick working for us Jessica. She's a hacker. Shorty could hack anything. I sent her to their spot a few weeks ago to bait those niggas.

They fell for it. She slid their wallet from them and got their home address. She put a tracker on their phone. I knew their locations without them knowing. I checked the app instantly. It confirmed what I already knew they were behind it. I'm going to get at Ike first he's already made it home. Ike stayed about forty minutes from Griff. It's closer to get him first. I knew he had a security system. We've been watching him for a minute. I'm cutting the electricity on the breaker. I'm going in that motherfucka to kill his ass and Jermesha too. If she's there she's going with that nigga.

We finally made it to Ike's house. Jermesha's car was parked in the driveway.

I put my blunt out and felt the hood. It's cold which means she's been here for a minute. I got to do this quick because I got to make it back home to baby.

She's already texted me a few times. Ike's breaker was in the back of his house. I cut the breaker. Me and Slap were going through the back door. I kicked that bitch open. Jessica told me Ike's room was upstairs on the left. I had the AK rested on my shoulder. I put the infrared beam on. Me and Slap took the stairs. I heard Ike and Jermesha talking. This shit was going to be easier than I thought.

"Jermesha let me go flip the breaker to see what happened," he stated. Ike made his way down the stairs. He's using his phone as a flashlight. He didn't have a gun on him. The moment he touched the bottom step. I pointed my AK in his face and cocked that motherfucka back. He put his hands up. He's about to say something. I shoved my gun in his fuckin mouth.

"Slap put that fuckin' light on me. So, this nigga can see who the fuck his killer is," I chuckled. Slap flashed his light on me. "You like shooting motherfuckas shit up huh? See the difference between me and you. I'm a real fuckin' killer and you ain't. I live by and die by that shit. Check mate motherfucka." I let my fuckin' clip loose. Ike's body dropped instantly one down and three more to go. Slap ran upstairs to find Jermesha that bitch had to go too. I ran right behind my nigga.

“Ike baby hurry up it's too dark in here,” she whined. Slap looked at me. He motioned with his fingers for me to go in. I had the flashlight on my phone. I wanted this bitch to see my face. I don't play with hoes.

“What's up Jermesha. I told you I don't take threats lightly. I'm the wrong nigga you want to fuckin' cross,” I argued. I could hear Jermesha's breathing pick up.

“Please don't do this Rashad I got kids. I didn't know they were going to shoot up your truck,” she cried.

“I don't give a fuck about what you didn't know. You made the wrong decision. You weren’t thinking about your kids when you threatened mine. I love the fuck out of Danielle. I'll never let a bitch, or a nigga threaten her. You've been doing a lot of foul shit lately and you've had one to many fuckin' passes. I can't give you another one.” I pointed the AK in the middle of Jermesha's head. I let that bitch loose. Jermesha's body dropped to the ground. Slap looked at me and shook his head.

“Aye nigga you're crazy that bitch should've been gone. She told on herself.”

“Hell, yeah that hoe told on herself. Let’s get the fuck up out of here.” Me and Slap left out the same way we came in. I slid in the passenger seat with Griff. Slap hopped in the back. Griff pulled off Wire still had eyes on Baine.

“Damn it took you a long time to kill Ike. He must have beat your ass,” he chuckled. I wasn't even about to go there with Griff.

“Shut up nigga and drive.” Baine's somewhere he's going to wish he fuckin' wasn't it. He's in my neck of the woods at Mya's house. After Mya lost our baby, she's been telling this nigga she hates me, and she wish I would die. I'll never wish bad on her no matter what fucked up shit she did. The worst thing she could've done is crossed a nigga like me. Me and Danielle don't sit up and talk about our exes because they’re irrelevant. We really want to be together. We finally made it to Mya’s house. Traffic’s heavy as fuck tonight. I forgot it’s Black Friday and motherfuckas are out shopping. Baine’s car was sitting in the driveway. Griff parked down the street. Me and Slap hopped out and met with Wire.

“Aye Rashad Baine’s in there bragging about killing y’all in that truck tonight. Make a fuckin’ mess. Don’t go back through the Trap the police are hot. They have your truck surrounded. Here’s her key let yourself in.” I slapped hands with Wire. Me and Slap made our way inside of Mya’s house. I swear to God that bitch is going to regret ever becoming an enemy of mine. Me and Slap headed upstairs toward Mya’s bedroom. Mya lived alone the door was wide open. She’s fuckin’ this nigga after he gave her that shit.

“Baby I’m so glad you killed them thank you,” she beamed. Mya was riding Baine. I don’t care about them fuckin’ around. Take that fuckin’ loss and move the fuck on.

"I'll do anything for you shawty and you know that fuck that bitch and that nigga. I need less talking and more fuckin," he chuckled. Slap looked me and pointed his fingers. It's time. I stood in Mya's door. Baine and Mya didn't see us. I had the AK pointed at Mya's head. I cocked back making sure one bullet was in the chamber.

"I never thought killing you would be so fuckin' easy Baine I'm done playing chess! Check mate" I laughed. Mya jumped up and Baine tried to grab his piece. I shot Baine in his fuckin' head one shot one Motherfuckin kill. I'll never let that pussy ass nigga get one up on me. Mya started crying She can save her fuckin' tears.

"Don't cry bitch keep riding that dick. You wish I was dead right? I told you to stop fuckin' worrying about me. You wished death on me now your about to die."

"Please Rashad don't do this," she cried.

"Bitch you got to go. It's too late for that. I heard you thank that nigga for killing me. Now you can thank him for getting you killed." I shot Mya two times in her fuckin' chest. Her eyes were wide open. Mya couldn't live in the same world with me. She's to jealous. I shot her again to make sure she was dead and Baine too. I don't need nann motherfucka coming back to kill me. Me and Slap left out Mya's house. Slap grabbed the recording equipment that's in Mya's house. We left out the back door and made our way back to Griff. We hopped in the car and Griff pulled off.

"Damn it's like that you finally killed Baine and ain't got shit to say," he chuckled. I waived Griff off. "Shut up nigga. Take me to house to get my car, so I can get my wife and kids." I can't wait to see Danielle. I know she's up stressing. I can't have that and she's pregnant.

"She's your wife," he chuckled. I swear Griff's with the shit. "Danielle made you want to settle down and wife her. That's a good look for you."

"You know she's my wife. I haven't asked her yet, but she is. I told her she would be a widow fuckin' with me. Baine's been giving her hard time with the divorce she doesn't have to worry about him anymore. Pussy ass nigga. I caught his ass slipping. Pussy was his downfall it'll never be mine." Me and Griff finished talking. He dropped me off at my house to get my car. Fuck letting my shit warm up. I had to get my kids and Danielle. It took me about forty minutes to make it to Griff's house. We pulled up at the same time. I jogged upstairs to the guest room. The moment the door opened. Danielle jumped up and ran to me. I wrapped my arms around her. She started crying.

"I told you I was coming back. You ain't got to worry about him no more. Stop crying. Let's go. I told you to stop upsetting my baby. I need you to have faith in me."

"I'm sorry. I do trust you. I have faith in you. It's dangerous out here. I just want you to be safe," she sniffled. I placed a kiss on Danielle's lips. I woke my son and my nephew. I locked up Griff's house.

We made our way to the car. I made sure everybody was locked in with their seatbelts before I pulled off.

EPILOGUE THREE MONTHS LATER

Danielle

My life's been crazy these past few months. I'm no longer existing I'm living my best life. The police found Baine and Mya dead a few days after Rashad killed them. He didn't tell me he killed Mya too. We were lying in the bed and they flashed her face along with Baine's on the news. He looked at me and smiled. I don't feel bad that girl came for me every chance she got. They found Jermesha and Ike dead too. I don't feel bad for Jermesha either she threatened my child's life. I felt bad for Mother Dear she had to bury her grandchild.

Crimson said Mother Dear is taking it pretty good, but Jermesha's momma is taking it hard. Fuck them hoes. Since Baine's dead everything's rightfully mine.

Baine's so slick. He had Nova and Bre'Elle both living in houses that we own. I transferred everything into my name and took his name off. I'm sitting out front of the house that Nova lived in. I'm getting her evicted. She was served over a month ago and she hasn't moved yet, but today is the motherfuckin' day. Crimson couldn't come with me. I had Nikki with me. She drove her car.

"Bitch I can't believe you're doing this shit," she laughed. I can't believe Nikki has a heart.

"Why are you surprised? Don't feel sorry for these bitches. They bragged so much about Baine and how they had him. Guess what he didn't have a will. I got access to all his money. I'm generous. I setup all his kids trust funds they can't touch them until they're eighteen on top of what he had setup. If their mothers don't have any money saved up that's a fuckin' personal problem. I shouldn't even do that after all the shit they took me through. Fuck it I want now."

"I feel you it's not your fault." The Sheriff pulled up right behind us. The Sheriff stepped out the car. He knocked on the door. Nova came out the house.

"Ms. you've been ordered to leave the premises. Get all of your personal belongings you can no longer occupy this property," he stated. The sheriff shoved the eviction paper in Nova's hand. I stepped out right behind him. I hired a new lock smith to change the locks. I'm selling this house. Nova looked at me and cried.

"Danielle you can't do this I'm pregnant," she cried.

“That’s not my Motherfuckin problem. I’m selling this house. You knew this months ago you should’ve moved. You thought I was playing, but I’m not.” Nova wanted to go back and forth. I refused to do it.

“It’s Nova, right? You’re the same bitch that was bragging about having two kids by a married man? Why would you expect for her to let you stay here and you’re the side bitch? Pack your shit and go. We ain’t making no fuckin’ deals. Baine didn’t have a will. He didn’t leave you shit but two fuckin’ babies,” Nikki argued. Nova started to say something else. Nikki put her hand up. “Bitch did you fuckin’ hear me we ain’t making no fuckin’ deals. The only deal you should’ve made was to stop fuckin’ and catching feelings for a nigga that would never be yours.” The lock smith changed the locks. The sheriff and movers started putting all of Nova’s stuff out. Me and Nikki had one more destination Bre’Elle’s house.

Bre’Elle’s house wasn’t that far from the house Baine and I shared. I can’t wait to see the look on her face when she gets put out. It took us about thirty minutes to get to her house. I knew Bre’Elle was home she didn’t work either. The Sheriff pulled up at her house. He stepped out the car and knocked on her door. The movers pulled up right behind him. Bre’Elle’s door swung open. Me and Nikki stepped out the car. We made our way toward the door. It smelled just like weed. Nikki looked at me and laughed. This bitch is going to jail.

"Ms. you've been ordered to leave the premises. Get all your personal belongings. You can no longer occupy this property," he stated. The sheriff shoved the eviction paper in Bre'Elle's hand. He started calling for backup on his radio. "Ms. your home smells like marijuana. I need to check the premises for drugs." Two more sheriff cars pulled up.

"You're not checking anything. You don't have a warrant," she argued. Bre'Elle looked at me and rolled her eyes. I hope she doesn't have anything in there.

"I don't need one you're being evicted, and this isn't your property." The sheriff stepped inside of Bre'Elle's house. He wasn't even in there two minutes. He brought out a big bag of weed. He slapped the hand cuffs on Bre'Elle. I shook my head. The sheriffs came out with pounds of weed and dope. Tears ran down her face. It's time to go. Dumb ass got caught with all this shit at her house. Me and Nikki hopped in the car and pulled off.

"Bitch It's time for me to take you home. I don't like being a part of drug busts," she laughed. I swear Nikki's so fuckin stupid. I couldn't stop laughing. I didn't even get to say all the shit I wanted to stay. I laughed so hard I pissed on myself.

"Nikki girl shut the fuck up. I done pissed on myself. I can't stop pissing." Nikki looked at me with wide eyes. I don't know why she was looking at me like that and she's the one that made me laugh crazy ass. I can't wait to tell Crimson this shit.

“Bitch are you sure your water didn’t fuckin’ break,” she asked?

“I don’t think so I’m not due until Friday.” Damn I know my baby wouldn’t make her appearance in the world today. I’m not ready. I don’t want to hear Rashad’s mouth. He didn’t want me doing this because it’s so close to my due date.

“Bitch if you’re due Friday you’re due any day now. You’re a nurse you know that stop being in denial. I got to hurry up and get your pissy ass out my car. Danielle, I think your water broke. Call Rashad and tell him to meet us at the hospital,” she argued. I looked at Nikki and rolled my eyes. Damn I didn’t want to call Rashad. The first thing he’s going to ask is where I’m at. I’m supposed to be at home. I grabbed my phone to call Rashad. He answered on the first ring.

“What’s up baby is everything okay? I’m about ten minutes from the house. Do you need anything,” he asked?

“Hey baby I’m good. My water broke. Can you meet me at the hospital? Grab the diaper bag and my overnight bag. It’s in the closet,” I sighed.

“Where are you Danielle,” he asked?

“I’m with Nikki we went to have lunch. She made me laugh and my water ended up breaking.” Technically I’m not lying it’s the truth. I wouldn't dare tell Rashad I put them bitches out today, but I did. He knew I was doing it.

He just didn't want me doing it today. I gave those bitches to many passes.

“Hey Rashad,” she beamed. Nikki was doing the most now. I'm sure Rashad could tell we were up to no good. Nikki looked at me and stuck her tongue out. I swear she plays too much.

“What’s up Nikki? Alright I’ll meet you there don’t have my baby until. I get there. I know you done some other shit too. You ain’t slick I’ll see you in a few minutes. I love you.”

“I love you.” I swear I can't get shit past Rashad. He knows everything. Oh well it is what it is. It's not my fault his nosey ass little girl wanted to come today when I'm having fun.

“I love you too.” Nikki drove me to the hospital. I can't believe today might be the day I get to meet my little one. Raishea Dior' Johnson. I called Crimson to meet me at the hospital. Damn Rashad is going to kill me once he sees the shoes on my feet. Damn I miss wearing heels.

“Nikki bitch we got a motherfuckin' problem. I need to wear your shoes. Rashad's going to trip if he sees me with these heels on.” Nikki thinks this is the funniest shit.

“I'm not giving you my shoes Danielle. Check my damn back seat. I got some Uggs and some Chuck Taylors you can throw on. Don't say I ain't never gave you shit sneaky ass.”

I reached in the back seat and grabbed the Uggs. Rashad knows I'm not wearing any Chuck Taylors. I fuck with Nikki the long way. We finally made it to the hospital. As soon as Nikki pulled up to the emergency room. I could see Rashad pacing back and forth. Nikki looked at me and shook her head.

“Girl that nigga pussy whipped. I ain't never seen no shit like this before. Get your pissy ass out my truck. I'm about to find a park.” Rashad grabbed my hand and escorted me out the truck. He had wheelchair and everything.

“About time you made it. What did you eat,” he asked? I swear Rashad won't let me be great.

“Something healthy vegetable soup with beef tips,” I beamed. Hopefully he bought it. Rashad didn't ask any more questions. Thank God! He escorted me up to the counter. I told the front desk lady my water broke. She called for help. Two nurses and a transporting assistant escorted us up to labor and delivery. I called my doctor in the car she's on her way. I need to change immediately. My panties are soaked. Rashad helped me into the bathroom.

“If you're ass would've been at home you would have on some dry clothes,” he chuckled.

“Whatever Rashad. I went to get some lunch,” I beamed. I changed into a gown. I'm so glad to take these panties off. Rashad snatched them and put them in my bag. Where's Crimson? I called my momma, and Gigi they said they're on the way.

My daddy would probably be here first. Rashad helped me into my bed. The nurses and doctors started setting up the equipment. I could hear my baby's heart beating. It's good and strong too. A nurse finally came into check me.

“Mrs. Mahone you're definitely in labor you're at six centimeters. Your princess should be here in a minute. Do you want an epidural if so, we need to go ahead and do it now? Your baby will be here soon.”

“I'm okay it doesn't hurt,” I explained. The nurse left. Nikki, Crimson and Griff walked in. My mother, father and my Gigi walked in. Ms. Linda walked in too. This is the first time that Rashad would be meeting them I'm nervous. Rashad whispered in my ear.

“I can't wait to change your last name. I wonder what made you go into labor early,” he chuckled. Rashad bit my ear. I didn't want my parents to see me blushing.

“Stop before my daddy sees us. I don't want them to think the worse of me.” I whispered.

“Make me! Your father knows this pussy belongs to me. I want to make a few more babies this is one of many.” My mother and father walked over to us. I introduced them to Rashad. I noticed my father sized Rashad up before he shook his hand. Crimson came and sat beside me.

“My niece is about to make her entrance are you ready,” she asked? I nodded my head no.

"You should get ready. Rashad said you're six centimeters. Let me take a few pictures before Raishea' bust that pussy open." I pushed Crimson. I can't wait to see my baby. Everybody cleared out of our room. Crimson and Nikki went to go get some food. Rashad's lying next to me. My mother and father are in the corner. Griff and Mrs. Linda went to get the kids. The contractions started to speed up. I grabbed Rashad's hand. He raised up to see what's wrong with me.

"What's wrong are you okay," he asked? I nodded my head no.

"The contractions hurt can you get a nurse please. I think it's time Rashad," I whined. Rashad left to go get the nurse. They came back in to check. The nurse smiled at me. I gave her a faint smile.

"Mrs. Mahone it's time. She's crowning. I feel her head. We'll go ahead and get you prepped for delivery. She's ready I'm thinking one maybe two pushes and she'll be out." Thank you, Jesus. My doctor came in they started setting up. Rashad sat next to me and held my hand. I squeezed his hand. His lips traced kisses on my hand. I appreciate the gesture by I want this baby out.

"Okay Mrs. Mahone on the count of three start pushing. I need you to push. Give me one big strong push. 1,2,3." I mustered up some strength and pushed. I looked between my legs and I didn't see anything. Damn.

"Okay Mrs. Mahone her head is poking out one more push. Dad do you want to come and see your princess," she asked?

"No," I yelled. "Rashad ain't going no fuckin' where but right here." Rashad looked at me and laughed.

"Okay Mrs. Mahone I get it, let's try again on the count of three 1,2,3 push." I'm sure this one is it. I looked between my legs and nothing. "Come on Mrs. Mahone one more." I pushed again and still nothing. I'm frustrated rated now. "One more this one is it." I pushed again and she finally came out screaming. I started screaming too. I see now little Ms. Raishea' Dior she's a hell raiser.

I pushed too many damn times. Hell, no I'm not doing this shit no more. Rashad went to cut the umbilical cord. I need a fuckin' nap. Who told this baby to come today any fuckin' way? I need a drink. The nurses cleaned and stitched me up. Raishea' Dior Johnson weighed in 7 pounds 7 ounces. Her bald, headed ass didn't have a lick of hair. She's cute though. I can't deny that. I can't wait to get her ears pierced and dress her up.

She needs lots of bows since she doesn't have any hair. Rashad was already doting on her. She's going to be spoiled rotten. "Danielle do you want to hold my daughter," he asked? I swear I can't stand him sometimes. I nodded my head yes. Of course, I want to hold my baby. "Look I know this is your first child and all, but it's certain way I want you to hold my daughter.

Make sure you hold her head. Don't let it wobble. Make sure her pamper ain't never wet. Make sure you always wash your hands before you hold her. Don't be kissing her in her face. Don't be posting my baby on the internet. Thank you for giving birth to my daughter. I appreciate you." I looked at Rashad like he was fuckin' crazy.

"Give me my daughter and stop playing." Raishea' Dior she's so beautiful. I can't stop looking at her. She had big brown hazel eyes like her father. I can't wait to dress her up. "Give me her baby bag, so I can dress her up."

"You got plenty of time to do that Danielle let her be a baby."

A FEW MONTHS LATER

Rashad

I've been planning this proposal for months. I've never asked a woman to marry me. Danielle would be the one and only one. I wasn't scared to propose to Danielle, but I wanted it to be perfect. I asked her father for permission to marry his daughter. Coop was cool with after her mother told her the shit that between her and Baine. Fuck that nigga he can watch me from hell. Every day I pull up on Danielle for lunch. Today I had all the kids with me. Danielle's mother and father were up at her clinic visiting. I wanted them to be there when I proposed. We didn't stay too far from her clinic. It took me about thirty minutes to get there.

"You really love Danielle Rashad. I hope she say yes," my mother smiled. I swear my mother be tripping.

"I hope she does too." I'm about to do some shit that I've never done before. I hope she doesn't shut it down.

My mother got Raishea' out her car seat. Lil Rashad and BJ hopped out. We made our way inside of Danielle's clinic. All eyes were on us. I walked back toward Danielle's office. She looked at us with wide eyes. She had the biggest smile on her face. Lil Rashad and BJ ran straight to Danielle and gave her a hug. They're crazy about her. I told them about hugging my woman.

"What are y'all doing here," she asked? Danielle grabbed Raishea out of my mother's hands.

"We came to see you. Sit down I brought you some food." Danielle took a seat at her desk. I sat the food in front of her. I'm glad Danielle wore heels today it's perfect for when I get on one knee. I knelt on my knee. I slid Danielle's shoes off. I started massaging her feet. I took my jacket off. She didn't notice my shirt. It said will you marry me. My mother took the lead.

"Danielle will you marry my son," she asked?

"Danielle will you marry my uncle," BJ asked?

"Danielle will you marry my daddy," my son asked? My mother went to take off Raishea's jacket so she could see her shirt. My mother pointed to Raishea's shirt. It read Mommy will you marry my daddy. Danielle started crying.

"Don't cry Danielle. You know I hate to see your tears. Shawty or should I say D. Elle. I've been loving you for a long time. It's nothing in this world that could stop you from being mine but YOU.

We've been through a lot these past few months. I'm sorry for all that. I'm still making up from that. I love you Danielle and I don't want to ever stop loving you. I want you to be my wife. I want to your change your last name. Danielle Cooper will you marry me. I want you to be mine. I want to love you for a lifetime and even after that. Look at my shirt too," I asked? Danielle grabbed my shirt with her two fists.

"Yes, Rashad I'll marry you." I slid the ring on her finger. I pulled her in my arms for a hug. My mother grabbed Raishea' "You're sneaky Rashad how did you pull this off."

"Don't worry about it I did! The only thing that matter is you said YES."

THE END.

CONTEST ALERT

In honor of Danielle's Release! I'm bringing back the Book Bae Basket give away contest. I'm only announcing It on my personal pages inside this book! Read, Review on **Amazon** and **Goodreads**!

Tag me in your review on **Facebook** (Nikki Taylor) **Instagram** (WatchNikkiWrite) **Twitter** (Watchnikkiwrite)

NikkiNicole@Nikkinicolepresents.com. The First 55 Reviews I Get I'm Going to draw a name and ship you a basket. I do things in real time! I'm not holding it until the end of the month.

If I get 55 reviews on day 1 of this release. I'll draw a name the next day and ship the basket the following day. I'm giving away 1 basket pick your series or standalone by yours truly.

CPSIA information can be obtained
at www.ICGtesting.com
Printed in the USA
LVHW042119191219
641092LV00004B/628/P